IMPERFECT MAGIC

A DARKLY FUNNY SUPERNATURAL SUSPENSE MYSTERY - BOOK 1 OF THE IMPERFECT CATHAR

C.N. ROWAN

MAIN ROCK PUBLISHING

CONTENTS

Dedication   V

Foreword   VI

Glossary   VII

1. Toulouse, 8 March, present day   1

2. Toulouse, 8 March, present day   6

3. Toulouse, 8 March, present day   12

4. La Rochelle, 30 April, 1945   26

5. Toulouse, 8 March, present day   36

6. Toulouse, 8 March, present day   43

7. Toulouse, 8 March, present day   50

8. Toulouse, 8 March, present day   54

9. Toulouse, 8 March, present day   59

10. Foix, 10 August, 1209   65

11. Toulouse, 8 March, present day   75

12. Toulouse, 8 March, present day   84

13. Toulouse, 8 March, present day   93

14. Toulouse, 8 March, present day   103

15. Toulouse, 8 March, present day   111

16. Toulouse, 8 March, present day   123

17. Lavaur, 3 May, 1211   135

18. Toulouse, 9 March, present day   142

19. Hastingues, 9 March, present day   153

20. Lavaur, 3 May, 1211   160

21. Hastingues, 9 March, present day   170

22. Hastingues, 9 March, present day   176

23. Peyrehorade, 9 March, present day   183

24. Peyrehorade, 9 March, present day   187

25. Lavaur, 3 May, 1211   195

26. Bidache, 9 March, present day   205

27. Bidache, 9 March, present day   211

28. Bidache, 9 March, present day   216

29. Bidache, 9 March, present day   225

30. Bidache, 9 March, present day   233

31. Bidache, 9 March, present day   244

32. Bidache, 9 March, present day   252

33. Bidache, 9 March, present day   259

Toulouse, 14 March, present day   268

Afterword   277

36. Chapter 1 - Toulouse, 8 April, present day   285

About The Author   288

Also By   290

For Ayana

You burned so very brightly, little starlight dancing.
Memories light up still with your presence.

FOREWORD

Welcome to the first book in The imPerfect Cathar series!

This book contains lots of very bad language – sorry, mum – and some graphic violence.

It's also written in British English, which means it occasionally needs to take a cup of tea and talk politely about the weather, but also means words with extra U's probably are supposed to be written like that. See also S's for Z's. Which sounds like a really cool shoegaze band.

This book has been rigourously vetted by editors, proofreaders and even me. But we are all human – despite what the History Channel keeps trying to say about me – and mistakes may happen. If you do come across one, please let me know by emailing chris@cnrowan.com. I'd love to hear from you anyhow!

If you'd like a free prequel novella about what happened just before this story – involving a Nain Rouge and an inescapable locked room mystery – there's a link at the end of the book where you can get it by signing up to my newsletter. If you've already got it, there's a different free story available as well. So you've just got to survive 80,000 words of my insanity to get to the freebies. Talk about a bargain. Or flip there directly, if you want to cheat.

Now, without further ado, on with the show. Let's get into a story that could start with *once upon a time* and as that's my story that's exactly how it'll start.

Once upon a time...

GLOSSARY

Mec – Modern French slang for a male friend.

Cadorna – Ancient Languedoc insult, literal meaning old cow.

Saabi – Arabic slang for friend

Laguna – Old Occitan/Basque slang for friend

Ami – Modern French word for friend.

CHAPTER ONE

TOULOUSE, 8 MARCH, PRESENT DAY

A rancid cellar, re-evaluating some recent life decisions.

M agic is an overpriced escort, glammed up to the nines and looking for a good time.

It'll make you feel great. It'll flatter your ego, and there's plenty of times it'll blow your mind. The more you invest, both time and finances, the more it'll play the game, the more it'll feel like a genuine relationship until you think it really cares — that it honestly has your back.

Don't be fooled. It's all just business.

The thing about business deals is, sooner or later, you're going to get screwed over, however solid you think your relationship is. Not in the good sense either. Happens to the best of us.

I mean, getting tortured to death by a shit wizard wasn't on my agenda when I blew in through the front door of his house, overpowered to the nines, a magic-wielding badass ready to fuck things up. Funny how things work out, and by funny, I mean agonisingly painful, like being suspended from a set of depressingly solid, rust-stained chains currently doing interesting things to my various cracked and shattered ribs.

And by interesting, I mean if "how far out of alignment can you put parts of the human skeleton without it killing someone" is one of your topics of interest.

Incidentally, if it is, please stay the hell away from me and mine.

The only thing allowing movement is the blood slickening my skin around my ankles and wrists. The cold iron strums my forearm bones like washboards played in a skiffle band, only even more annoying. Just about. Have you ever heard a busker on a skiffle board? Every time one plays, I want to shower them in coins. Preferably heated up till they're white hot.

My breathing's transition from bubbling gurgles to maraca-like rattles doesn't require centuries of medical expertise to recognise it as probably a bad sign.

It's not just the agonising pain that makes the basement I'm in depressing. Mildew is not the décor choice of optimists. Through the sheen of grimy sweat stinging my one unswollen eye, the ethereal glow of magic sigils taunts me. The sneaky bastards. The language of the angels doesn't make for comfortable reading, at least for a mortal mind like mine. It does a damn good job of keeping me trapped in place though.

Said sigils —all intricate swirls around the sweeping curves of the Kabbalist lettering— are also light-years beyond the capabilities of the spittle-flecked shithead of a mage standing before me.

Working out he's incapable of having created the Enochian containment runes glowing on the walls isn't hard. I'm more surprised he's capable of walking without tripping over his own feet. Hell, one look at the complete fuck-up he made carving runes of persuasion into my flesh shows how rubbish he is. *Top marks for gratuitous damage. Must try harder regarding actual magical prowess.*

His efforts, displayed in inch-deep gashes across my skin, look like someone gave a spirograph set to an alcoholic deep in the DTs. They wouldn't compel me to talk even if he had the magical knowledge and artistic temperament to engrave them correctly. But even assuming he *could* master writing that level of magical script correctly without it making his brain explode, I'm still totally out of his league *talent*-wise. He's not got the *power* to force me to do anything.

As he continues to rant and rave at me, trying to get me to tell him what he wants to know, wondering why the runes of persuasion aren't working (simple answer — because he's a shit wizard), I temporarily zone out. An inner debate as to what is a worse form of torture —being physically sliced to ribbons or having to be this close to his body odour— distracts me. It's a tough call to make. The continued screaming up in my face brings me back to the situation at hand. While the rancid breath accompanying it is a painful reminder of the importance to brush after every meal, as well as being further evidence that cleanliness was an early offering on the altar in his quest for magical power.

His scraggly, food-matted facial hair underlines that.

He clearly feels a beard lends him an air of Rasputin-level dark mysticism, but I'd go more with drug-addled village idiot chic, personally. He looks like Doctor Moreau got funky with a rat, a toad, and an incel.

His failure at forcing me to answer his ridiculous questions has driven him from 'guy to avoid sitting next to in the pub' to 'Jesus, Mary, and Joseph, get the fuck away from that lunatic' in a relatively brief space of time. The erratic swaying of the gore-stained knife he keeps waving about would be disturbing enough even if it wasn't *my* gore doing the staining. I was bloody attached to that gore.

'Tell me what you are!' The vein at his temple throbs like his head is about to pop. Sadly, I doubt I'll ever get that lucky. 'You aren't human; else, you'd never have found my lair and been rendered helpless by my power.'

His power. Pah. What a load of bollocks. I'm not sure how these runes are restraining me, but one thing's certain. It's not because of his power.

The knife's drunken dancing weaves closer to my one remaining good eye. 'You don't need to see to speak, creature.' The squeaky tone, his voice cracking like an adolescent hitting the first agonies of puberty, doesn't really aid him in his attempt to be menacing.

I chuckle, sending little tributaries of blood dribbling from the corner of my mouth to join the river currently streaming down my body. 'Your lair? Sorry, your lair? Are you... are you serious? What are you, a fucking Bond villain? No, wait, don't tell me — you're an alpha lone wolf or coyote misunderstood by a society that will one day regret it ever dared reject your magnificent superiority.'

I flick my eyes up and down his spindly form. A filthy magician's robe that looks suspiciously like a hastily altered threadbare dressing gown hangs from his bony shoulders. It doesn't give him quite the aura of evil genius I suspect he was going for. 'Nah, *mec*, you don't fit as an alpha wolf. More likely a weasel or...' I take a sniff, wincing. 'Skunk, I'd say.'

I roar my agony at the low-set cement ceiling as a razor-like knife is buried several inches into my right shoulder. It being pulled back out again isn't a barrel of laughs either. I gulp down desperate mouthfuls of air as it resumes its two-step choreography in front of my iris. Panting, physically broken, I look past its vanishing point to the insane little shitspawn wielding it.

'Okay, okay — I'll tell you,' I whine, struggling to draw in enough whistling breath to make my words audible. A punctured lung will do that to the best of men. I am definitely not the best of men. 'I'm...'

He leans forward without the knife ever leaving its threatening proximity. Greed for forbidden knowledge is carved more clearly on his pock-marked grubby features than his rubbish attempts at runes are on my body. 'I'm... so... so...goddamn sexy, I wish I could have switched eyes with your mother to watch myself fuck her brains out last night, *cadorna.*'

Pithy put-down issued, I slam my head forward, embedding the blade's tip deep into my brain. Then, accompanied by the sweet, sweet lullaby of his screams of impotent rage, I die.

Again.

CHAPTER TWO

TOULOUSE, 8 MARCH, PRESENT DAY

Somewhere other than the cellar I just died in. A sentence I end up using more often than I really should.

I heave in air, filling flattened lungs that have forgotten how to inflate. They had one job to do, dammit, the lazy sods. Mind you, as they've been dead for a while, I suppose I can let them off.

My eyes snap open by force of will as I shoot bolt upright. As the lenses start getting their groove on, bringing things back into focus, the round face of a balding fellow looms above me, midway through snapping on disposable surgical gloves. He looks about as shocked and terrified as one would expect upon seeing a several-days-old corpse suddenly sitting up. I, meanwhile, continue my forward momentum, snapping my forehead to connect between his eyes with a satisfying crunch. The look of fear morphs steadily into glazed confusion before he slides to his knees.

I rub at my frown lines as nerve endings in my brand-new, second-hand body fire up. A quick pat in the appropriate places confirms I'm male again. While female incarnations do happen, they're rare. With my reacquired manhood trying to climb back up into my body because of the freezing mortuary air, I swing my legs off the table and, with only the most miniscule of momentary wobbles, regain my feet.

Let's pause here, with me cold, naked, and hardly in the most dignified of postures, and I'll tell you a story. There's not time to tell you everything, but perhaps a little background is a good idea. So I'll tell you a tale that could begin with "Once upon a time" — You know what? As it's mine to tell, I will do. I like fairy tales... even though this one doesn't end like they do in modern times. More like a Brothers Grimm original. But anyway...

Once upon a time, in the south of France, there was a religious group whose beliefs became the latest craze sweeping the Languedoc. They were called the Good Christians at the time, although nowadays the term "Cathar" is used, and they had some beliefs that the established Church thought were pretty wacky, like vegetarianism, reincarnation, and dualism (two Gods — one good, one evil. Guess which one they thought made the world?).

Then there were the beliefs we had —yes, I was part of it— that the Church considered downright dangerous. Beliefs like equality between the sexes, tolerance for other religions, and that, perhaps, priests should concentrate on living humble, morally spotless lives rather than trying to amass wealth and power. I'm pretty sure the last one was the straw that broke the camel's back.

The Church showed all its accrued Christian values by launching a crusade against us. They spent a hundred years wiping us out, along with everyone who'd ever supported us, creating the Inquisition as they went. Which is, I'm pretty sure, not entirely what Jesus Christ would have done in their shoes.

Back then, I was a Good Christian Perfect — a priest. As happens to most of us, I died, although how I died is a stranger tale than most, involving dark magic during that terrible, bloody crusade. What's even weirder is that it didn't stick. Instead, I woke up in the nearest dead body, and I did so every time I died. For over eight hundred years. Time changes a man. I might have been a Perfect once, but nowadays? Well, let's just say I don't think anyone's likely to come to me looking for moral guidance. Better off asking a magic 8 ball. Or smoking one, maybe.

As I stand up, my feet seem to stretch, my legs enlarge, and my body becomes defined by centuries of martial arts and street fighting rather than channel surfing and TV dinners. Looking in the mirrored aluminium lining the sidewall, I see my original bronze, hawklike features staring back. Deep-brown, practically pitch-black eyes quirk sardonically. My hair's short, kept cropped by preference. Thankfully, the magic seems to recognise that. My curly locks might look fabulous grown out, but they're too convenient for enemies to grab hold of. I look like I'm in my mid-thirties. I'd say that's a more accurate count of the number of lives I've lived except I burnt through thirty-odd bodies in my first couple of centuries. How many times have I died since? I lost count long ago.

My dark Mediterranean skin is a natural result of centuries of Spaniards intermingling with North African rulers and Gallic northerners venturing towards the mountains. Occitans of my era were closer, both geographically and spiritually, to our cousins on the other side of the Pyrenees, and I blend easily into the cultural mix of modern-day Toulouse. I'm assumed to be from the Maghreb or have dual heritage or else hail from Gitan travelling folk — and in a way these are all the case. More precisely, my ethnic mix predates such distinctions.

Looking at myself in the burnished metal, I see the same physical form I've worn time after time, life after life since I died. Is this really the body I have now? Well, yes and no. The magic definitely reshapes it little by little. But I don't get it all straight away. I look like myself, fully, sure. But underneath it, my physical tone remains that of an unfit late-twenties male who would struggle to walk further than the nearest takeaway. Thankfully, with my hectic, death-defying (or often, failing to death-defy) lifestyle, that will rapidly adjust. It's an accelerated process, all tied into my reincarnation magic somehow. The only difference I've noticed when I come back compared to my first life is a slight change of height to keep up with evolutionary differences over the years. As a nifty bonus, I also come back without the scarring, amateur sigils, and loss of most bodily fluids accompanying my latest death. Personally, I just accept it. Cleverer minds than mine have tried to unravel the mystery without success. For me, looking like myself makes adjusting to a new body easier to manage. I'll take that as a win, thanks very much. Maybe the magic is just responding to how I see myself in my head, reshaping my new body to fit my self-image. Call me vain if you want, although maybe not too loudly. Insulting powerful magicians who can make your eyeballs boil in your face is rarely a good survival tactic.

'Right,' I mutter to myself, well aware and long past caring that it is a sign of encroaching madness. 'Coldcocked one innocent bystander. Should keep me safely anchored.'

I don't know if it is my over-active imagination, but I feel like I can sense the comfortable weight of sin on my soul, keeping me tied to the mortal plane. You might think after eight hundred years I'd be ready to let go and give it a rest. And honestly, there were a few times in my many lives when I felt ready to call it quits. Problem is, when a Cathar Perfect stops being perfect, there's no happy afterlife waiting, no giving the wheel of Dharma another spin. The soul turns to dust on death. Gone. Obliterated. I broke my vows, sinned willingly. When I finally die once and for all, I'll cease to be. End. Finito. I'm not ready for that. Not yet. So I have to make sure to never get too close to being Perfect.

I crack and roll my shoulders, wincing as the muscles perform a Mexican wave from left to right and back again. The stretching helps settle me though. I turn my attention to the unconscious heap next to the table; my first job is to verify he's still breathing. I know I didn't hit him hard enough to do any serious damage, but his romantic entanglement with the floor could have come with additional complications, so I give him a proper once-over. He seems to have escaped relatively unscathed apart from chipped upper incisors and impact bruising to the left temple. If left untended, it'll stain the side of his head in an Impressionist seascape's vibrant greens and blues. Pretty but painful. Like a rose's thorns. Or reality TV stars trying to act.

Summoning the enamel shards to my hand with a thought, I carefully reconstruct his tooth casing. I heal his tissue damage partway — enough to be believable he fell without causing him too much pain past his initial waking up.

'Sorry, Pascal,' I say, patting his cheek. The poor sod always seems to be on duty when I die. I swear I don't check his work schedule beforehand. Maybe he's a workaholic, or my dying just syncs naturally with his roster, but I have to say, I've started finding his presence comforting. Like waking up to be greeted by a friend. Only one that you headbutt rather than say hi to.

I force muscles screaming in protest at being press-ganged into action to haul the deadweight coroner into a more comfortable position. He'll wake up, assume he slipped over, and then continue with his day, blissfully ignorant that he is one corpse down. I can always pull what Aicha, a dear friend, calls my "Jedi Mind Tricks" on mortals when needed, but there isn't any need.

The body being forgotten is an integral part of my reincarnation magic, no effort required on my part. The funeral will be closed casket, the families will ask no questions, and the 'misplaced' body becomes Paul Bonhomme, wandering the Toulousain streets once more. Pascal won't question the situation any more than to sigh and make himself another coffee or, considering the clock on the wall says we are past midday, a pastis, going light on the water. It's strange. Mind magic is normally bad news. This, though, seems like something else entirely. Just one more of the endless enigmas around my continued existence.

I want to stress again though, *reincarnating*, *not* body stealing, dammit. No matter how much Aicha enjoys pointing at me and screaming every time I turn up in a new one.

I make a slight gesture to open my etheric storage space, an invisible storage locker that follows me everywhere, if you will, and take out one of several burner phones I stashed in there. Tapping in Aicha's number from memory, I let it ring three times, hang up, ring back for four rings, hang up, then call back again. I sigh at the questioning tinny squawks vibrating out of the speaker.

'Look,' I say. 'Just get over to Purpan Hospital's morgue and pick me up. Yes, again. Yes, I know. I'm less than happy about it too, but we can save the berating for later.' I smile with all the friendliness of a mob boss discussing late repayment options. 'Priority at the moment — we've got a shit wizard we need to fuck right up.'

CHAPTER THREE

TOULOUSE, 8 MARCH, PRESENT DAY

Cursing myself for forgetting to stash sunglasses alongside my burner phone. To be remedied at a later date.

I stumble out of the main doors of Purpan Hospital, wincing into harsh streaming sunlight, my eyes still struggling to get their act together regarding basic focusing muscle movements. The warmth feels good. I've thrown together illusory clothes so as not to dish out heart attacks to the poor patients and doctors, but they're not doing anything to actually stop the goosebumps rising on my skin. A tram glides to a stop opposite, discharging a mixture of hospital employees, glum visitors, and the occasional walking wounded lucky enough not to need an ambulance but not lucky enough to have a ride to A&E. The bustling hubbub ends, the hand-off of passengers in and out of the metallic carapace complete. After a momentary blare of a siren, the hushing slide of doors brings a comparative quiet back to my world.

With the smooth disappearance of the tram, I see Aicha across the tracks, waiting against a sporty looking Alpine A110. She certainly wasn't driving that the last time I saw her. I don't know how much time has passed since then though. Time flies when you're having fun. Or when being artlessly carved up by insecure and mentally deranged mages. Potato, potahto.

Aicha regards me with the patient expression of a trained killer who knows the exact worth of every second currently wasted. The slight frown shows the chances of her demonstrating said skills on me for free are increasing equally rapidly. Tight black curls frame her sharp cheekbones and haughty features. Her eyes are two dark teardrops burned back into the shadow of the aquiline curve of her nose. A siyala tattoo divides her chin, its tree-branch growths like sprouting arrowheads, the interspersed seed dots marking her passage into womanhood. Although she isn't tall, her presence carries the weight of character and experience, making people instinctively move aside to let her pass. Excluding the terminally stupid. I never cease to be amazed at the ability of some people to ignore the silent alarm bells that her aura must set ringing in the primal part of their brain, just so they can make some sleazy or sexist comment. Comments that usually precede them needing to visit the same premises I just vacated to have their foot surgically removed from their mouth. If they're lucky.

She gives me a terse half-nod, flicking her head back, telling me to get in the car. Explanations can clearly wait.

Clambering into the backseat, I am beyond relieved to find a change of clothes. Jeans and a plain grey T-shirt, some dusk-blue Timberland Nubuck boots, and a grey-and-black Avirex jacket.

Once dressed, I scramble forwards through the middle aisle. Aicha, opening the door, pushes me towards the passenger seat, the instruction brooking no discussion.

'I detest your driving when you're fully settled in a body, *saabi.*' Her constant, coiled-spring readiness is present in her voice and her posture. 'The idea of allowing you to run amok in a new ride with a new ride —' She snorts. 'Is not my idea of advisable. For either of our health.'

'Good to see you too, *laguna*,' I reply. 'And happy to be chauffeured about. Wouldn't dream of objecting. Honestly, I'm just happy to be in one piece again. The last few day...' I stop. 'How long have I been missing?'

'Three days,' she answers. 'Three days, thinking, "Surely he's not such a dickhead, he's died again already." Three days, waiting to swing by here or Ranguil after realising that, yes, you are precisely such a dickhead. Here's an idea. Try not dying for a bit.'

She clicks her tongue at me. It is as effective a castigation as any finger-wagging lecture ever could be. She has a point too. I don't take good enough care of my borrowed forms. *At least it's distracted her from her usual reaction.*

Suddenly, her face goes slack. Her arm rises slowly level, her finger pointing at me. 'Aaaaaaahhhhhhhhhhhhhhhhhhhhhh!'

Apparently, it hasn't sufficiently distracted her. I half-slap her hand away, groaning. 'Yes, thank you, Donald Sutherland. That still feels as fresh as ever, multitudinous bodies later. I shall revoke your Netflix privileges if it continues.' I wag my finger at her. *The power of shared passwords compels you.*

She responds with a dismissive wrist-wave. Then her features lock down again, and she returns to her high-strung, uber-vigilant state, sliding out into the flow of cars.

'Where to then, Paul?' she asks. Her visual scanning rate is a marvel, the sort of thing government spooks would kill to master. She is constantly aware, analysing all the pedestrians and vehicles in our vicinity, every glint and reflected image. Hundreds of years of survival as an independent woman in societies that would rather you simper in silence than get intimate with violence has honed her to a weapon-like readiness. Only the Nazis ever got the drop on her. She's never filled me in on exactly what happened, but I'm guessing they used incredibly clever trickery combined with overwhelming force. Either way, being caught unprepared is not something she intends to allow to happen again in the next millennium.

Leaning forward, I switch on Radio Booster, one of the local stations. I know some people think radio is outdated, but hey, so am I. I can live with that. The live back and forth of young rappers thumps over boom bap beats, and I relax, enjoying the mix of wit and braggadocio.

I think if you asked most people how they'd imagine someone who was over eight hundred years old, a sage greybeard would spring to mind, every eye crinkle a trove of hidden knowledge. Alternatively, they might picture a grumbling curmudgeon, his fist waving at a world he no longer understands. Personally speaking, while there are times I feel every day of those eight hundred years weighing me down, I've never lost my passion for innovation and originality. I don't look back on the past with rose-tinted fondness. If you think modern music is lewd, you should have heard the troubadours when they did their rounds of the Pyrenees. Prudishness over coarse language and sexual imagery is a modern invention. Me? I'm glad to see open expression becoming the norm once more. Change is the one constant. Rolling with it keeps life interesting. I look to each arriving generation to reinvigorate my soul with their new outlooks and approaches.

'Over towards Arenes,' I reply, the whoosh-click of the seatbelt synching momentarily with the drumbeat. I settle back in the seat, forcing my new usage-sore muscles to relax. There is no point in them complaining. I'm not about to break the habits of a hundred lifetimes just because they are a bunch of softies. 'We've got a mystery to solve.'

'Jinkies.'

'Thanks, Daphne.'

'That's Velma, you fucking idiot.'

'Thanks, Velma.'

'No worries. You're still a fucking idiot though.'

We ease our way off the roundabout onto the Rocade, the ring road that loops round the periphery of the city like a three year old's first crude attempt at a circle.

I fill her in as we drive. The short ten-minute trip is long enough for me to update her on my misadventures in tracking down the Mighty Wizard Tim wannabe.

'You didn't even get his name?' The sharp eyebrow arching once more speaks volumes about her opinion of my poor detective work.

'I didn't really get any opportunity to ask questions outside of "Eh?" and "What the fuck?" before he started carving pretty patterns into me,' I respond, frustration creeping into my tone. 'Again, *the most powerful Enochian runes I have ever encountered*. From a cretin with such little *talent* that calling him a mage at all is like calling a duck an aquarian hell-beast. I was entirely blindsided!'

'I'm assuming you have a better plan this time than "walk in blindly and get tortured to death"?'

Aicha is a perpetual planner. She insists it's a positive character trait. I think it screams PTSD. My preference to avoid getting stabbed in the face means I keep that to myself.

"Of course," I lie, then immediately start navigating her through the packed patchwork urban sprawl, heading towards Patte D'Oie before she can call me out on it.

Brutalist grey cubes dominate the skyline, brightened only by flag-line streamers of washing drying in the sun. Resilient concrete weeds sprout amongst a bouquet of individual buildings that look thrown together from different eras and areas. A mountain-air-fresh-blue-and-red chalet on one side looks plucked out of the backdrop to *The Sound Of Music*. On the other is a bright white mini-minimalist seventies dream of two-up, two-down. Together they squeeze like over-enthusiastic bodyguards the two-story shack between them. The shit wizard's abode.

Reds and oranges paint the corrugated roof. Water stains run down the imperfect steel. Cracks emanate from each angular point of every piece of framework, and the wooden shades of windowpanes are an unhealthily swollen umber underneath the few remaining paint chips of sun-bleached green. The garden is littered with metal ephemera. Parts of rusted machine skeletons lie half swallowed by the rampant weeds and grass, nature winning out in the long run (she normally does). Broken glass shards refract anaemic rainbows from the sun's lazy descent behind the hulking neighbouring tower blocks.

I point the house out, and we position ourselves across from it, snagging an on-street parking spot with views of both the building itself and the corners of each intersection. The road lies strung between two larger residential streets. I make enough illusory changes to my face to make me unrecognisable to the schmuck, but Aicha doesn't bother. He didn't know who or what I was. The chances of him being aware of who my friends are remain minimal. I swivel my gaze back and forth. Aicha is much more naturally aware than I am, but she's not seen the guy, and his *talent* isn't strong enough to make him obvious at a distance. I keep myself on high alert.

It turns out to be unnecessary. Within a few minutes of taking up position, the door cracks open. Out comes our shit wizard, nose-first, like a rodent scenting for danger before locking up. He ducks his head, which is wrapped in a filthy old tan raincoat, and engages in a brief tug-o-war with the half-unhinged wire gate at the edge of his property. I am not sure he is going to win, in all honesty, but eventually he stumbles out onto the pavement, then dips left and heads towards the corner store.

We follow discreetly, pacing him, casually closing while never giving him cause for alarm. He's skittish though, his hands trembling violently. It looks like my suicide and the following "magically disintegrating corpse" trick is causing him more distress than the act of heinously torturing me. He turns onto a narrow footpath between two towers and finally glances backwards. We are already within arm's reach. On its own, our closeness, undetected, would have been unnerving enough, but it's not until I raise a *don't look here* barrier at each end of the alleyway that the first inkling of his predicament trickles into his expression.

Aicha catches him around the Adam's apple with one hand and pins him against the crumbling concrete of a wall. He squawks like a tonsillitis-ridden parrot. I release my illusion, and his eyes, already saucer-like, grow to the size of dinner plates. When Aicha pulls her hand back to leave him suspended against the wall, the reality of the situation is self-evident in his terrified expression as he gasps and chokes for air.

I suppose I should pity him. He's a nothing, a pathetic failure from an uncaring society who discovered another secret, wondrous, magical society underneath and then promptly failed at that too. He is a reject of rejects, and if I was in a better mood, I might feel some sympathy for his predicament. But spending three days being carved up like a turkey after the person serving guzzled half a bottle of sherry has strangely reduced my capacity for sympathy.

'So, funny thing,' I start, walking over to him casually. 'I don't know your name or what you're doing in my city, but what I do know is that' —I tap him on the forehead in time with each word— 'you... are... a... shit... wizard... Say it with me now.'

He coughs and splutters as a red flush spreads up his cheeks. Aicha eases back on the Darth Vader grip, and he sucks at the air like a kid in an ice-cream soda parlour with a blocked straw. I give him a few more taps on the forehead as a reminder.

'I'm a shit wizard,' he says, showing a capacity for learning I wasn't sure he had.

'You are. But credit where credit's due, you kept me captive. Which shouldn't have been possible, so let's have a chat about that.'

'Sure he's not capable? Doesn't look like it, but looks can be deceiving.'

It's a valid point from Aicha. I've run into people who didn't seem capable of hurting a fly but actually took great pleasure in plucking limbs off ogres for fun, like petals off a daisy. She loves me; she loves me not.

'True, but in this case, if it walks like a duck and talks like a duck...'

'You should probably lay off the class A hallucinogens?'

'Again, true. Point is... Well, let me show you.' I wave my hands, and an image of the half-cocked attempts at runes of persuasion he carved into me pop up, rotating holographically in the air.

Aicha looks at them, then does a double take like a nineties cartoon character. She slowly swivels her gaze from them, to him, to me, to the runes again. Her cheek muscles start twitching, almost in spasm, and a corner of her lips does a minute up-curl. 'Are those... are those meant to be runes of persuasion? I've seen kobolds with palsy that can draw better than that. As for thinking they would work on him...'

The shit wizard looks terrified. I guess her expression *is* closer to a grimace than anything else. Also, she's holding him dangling a metre off the floor by the neck with her *talent*, which I can understand isn't casting her in the most positive light. But to me, she looks like she's cracking up in hysterics, ripples of amusement spreading out across her expression. Micro-changes no one else will notice in her locked-down features.

I grin. It's a genuine pleasure, honour, and privilege to see her loosen that rigid composure even a tiny bit. Few people get to know the woman underneath that hardened shell of self-control.

I wave a hand in his direction. 'Plus, *look* at him. Even if he had the knowledge to draw them properly, do you think he's got the power to make these work?'

Aicha fixes him with a gaze, her eyes unfocusing slightly. I know she's looking at him in the magical spectrum, assessing how strong a Talented he really is. She looks again at the hovering hack-job runes, then pivots towards the sheet-white mage she has pinned against the wall, her features locking down, shaking her head. The small smile, precision-placed upon her features, holds no humour, no joy, and little of that treasured humanity she fights so hard to keep. This is her in her Erinyes aspect, the embodiment of furious justice.

'Not at all. Now me, I can make these work just perfectly.' She uses her finger to pull the translucent image across, overlaying it like a hectograph across the terrified creature. 'I could use this as a working guide. Tattoos are so last season. Scarification is all the rage. Tell us who you work for.'

He blubbers, weeping huge, heaving, gasping sobs. 'I can't — I would, but I can't.'

She pulls a knife from the air, its edge luminescent with arcane forces. 'Oh, I beg to differ,' she purrs, dark lightning stirring in her irises.

His collapse is instantaneous. This is not a man blessed by nature with an abundance of courage. Or *talent*. Or charm. Or indeed, very much at all. I kind of feel sorry for him, like I want to offer him a shoulder to cry on. Then I remember him driving a razor-sharp knife into said shoulder and so instead, sit back and let the good lady break the bastard.

'I'll talk, I'll talk!' Snot spumes out of his nostrils like nasal bubble gum. Incidentally, why has no one invented nasal bubble gum? Wonka missed a trick there. I mentally add sending an anonymous suggestion to the top confectionery manufacturers onto my to-do list.

He opens his mouth to spill his lily-livered guts and then stops, a single swift choke interrupting him. His tongue swells from the usual speckled white and pink to a mouth-filling mass, spoiling to sable in colour. It wiggles in a manner so unnatural, it's clearly come loose from its moorings and is now operating as an independent agent. It undulates and pulses, then slithers rearwards, disappearing from sight. His features constrict with horror as his throat engorges, a slug-like shape visible through the stretched skin, crawling down his oesophagus.

'Don't you want to do a Nostromo two-step backwards?' Aicha asks me. I look at her, blank-faced.

Forehead creasing, she stabs her eyebrows at me as if unable to understand my innate idiocy, then with a sigh, pops her eyes wide as she puts her right hand to her chest bone. With a rhythmic back and forth, she mimes said hand bursting from her sternum, snapping out towards me with a mouth made of her fingers and thumb. I am a little disappointed she doesn't mime the second set of teeth somehow, but it finally clicks.

'Ohhh — got you.' I hastily shuffle backwards, pulling my sword from the ether in case we go full chest-burster, and step into an inside stance, my blade point aimed at his upper torso.

The shit wizard's eyes roll backwards as he shakes seizure-like, the flickering of his eyelids like one of those eighteenth-century zoetropic hand spun animations, the red capillaries straining on the visible white parts of his eyes. As we prepare ourselves for the possibility of doing battle with a hoodoo equivalent of a Xenomorph from *Alien*, his ending becomes less dramatic, if no less disturbing.

Around his midsection, the spasmic movement speeds up, becoming a vibration. His stomach roils, rippling about like a lake peppered by hailstones in a sudden storm. The motion becomes increasingly wavelike, spreading up his torso and down his thighs. As we ready ourselves, the centre of the agitated mass blends together and the stains on the raincoat slide downwards as if sluiced off by a high-powered hose.

It isn't simply the stains slewing away. The raincoat itself goes too and so does the shit wizard himself. Flesh liquefies, and a rapidly expanding hole forms in his guts, the chalk-grey concrete visible through it, growing from the size of a euro to a fist. I can make out a faded graffiti tag by Spazm still left as a piece of history on the wall behind him. The trickle becomes a torrent, and the wannabe Oscar Diggs disintegrates, liquefying before our eyes.

'Well, that was anticlimactic and yet still mildly vomit inducing,' I say, peering into the puddle of brown, red, and white slush quickly evaporating into nothingness.

'An effective hex to have used on an ineffective shitstain.' Aicha clicks her tongue as she frog-bends her knees to peer at the last traces of the nameless, *talentless*, luckless wizard. 'Did you recognise the spell at all?'

I stretch my shoulders back, letting the tension dissipate, standing down from my readied state. 'There are various schools of magic that could pull off similar curses. But it looked like the Eastern Yaga school sort of work. Although... I've seen something not dissimilar worked by a pissed-off cail-lech in the Wicklow Mountains as well.' When so many of us magic users are long-lived, intermingling of magics is a natural by-product. Useful when we want to learn, less so when pinpointing origins.

We trudge back to the squat, ramshackle house — a drunken celebrant held upright by the accommodating arms of his long-suffering neighbours. The garden itself is unwarded, and the front door carries protections so fragile and poorly constructed that I went through them the first time I busted into his house without even needing to break them. This time, I slow down and *look* past the first layer of the workings cast by our Arnold Toht impersonator.

I *look* underneath the flaking emulsion, beneath the poorly shaped sigils, further and deeper in. As I concentrate, I can make out the sensation, then the visual shape of the Enochian runes that bound me, holding me powerless as soon as I entered. I'm reasonably skilled at deciphering and deactivating Enochian markings —I studied under the best, even if crafting them isn't a main part of my skill set— but these are leagues beyond my capacity. That's why they so effectively unmade my *talent* after my grand entrance, sapping both my magical and physical strength and leaving me at the mercy of the bargain-basement spell slinger I stumbled across.

These aren't just beyond the shit wizard, though. They're beyond me, beyond almost every Talented I've ever come across. There's only one person I can think of who might have done this level of Kabbalist working — Isaac, and that's because he created Kabbalah. Well, there is one other. Problem is, he's been missing for over two hundred years. I'm pretty sure he's dead, however much Isaac's never given up hope.

Have you ever had a mentor, someone who's there to help and guide you, to tolerate those moments of plain stupidity or rash foolishness, to help you become a better person? Could be a friend or a family member or a teacher. Doesn't matter. Point is, it's someone who changes your life, changes you. Someone who stays with you, guiding your steps forwards. A constant you can turn to when all else seems like shifting sands.

Then one day, something happens. A loss, a death. A pain that mentor figure can't fully conceal because it is breaking something in them. Lessens them. For you, they never cease to be the giant they've always been, but you see behind the illusion to the human hurting under the façade. Perhaps they become quieter, less active. Or withdraw, disconnecting little by little from the world around them. That's what Isaac did when he lost his brother Jakob, when his searching turned up nothing.

I look over at Aicha. 'Could you do this?' Simple question. Not that I believe she did it, but because I know she'll be brutally honest. Brutality and honesty. Two things you can rely on Aicha for.

She looks, cocks her head, considering. Then shakes it. 'No. Could undo it. Or smash it to pieces. From the outside, at least. But make it?' She shakes her head again.

As I thought. Aicha's a master of force, but this sort of finessed working isn't her forte.

I try a different tack. 'Who could work this?'

Her eyes narrow, concentration evident. 'The Sistren of Bordeaux combined, perhaps? Still, not likely. Can't think of any off the top of my head. Needs to be a top-tier Talented and Kabbalist.'

She's right, as usual. It's not just the terrifying level of power you'd need. I couldn't have come up with these sigils, and I studied under the man who invented the whole discipline. A man I love like a father. A man who's been consumed by the search for his lost brother. A brother, who is the only other Talented I can think of who could do these workings... if he isn't dead, after all.

After all, he was there at the start of Kabbalah with Isaac. He carries an angel inside him too.

Problem is, if he isn't dead, then where's he been? He can't have been held captive. The *talent* it'd take to constrain a Bene Elohim, the angel merged with him, should be beyond anyone from this plane of existence.

Problem with saying "can't" in our world, though, is only three things ever limit you. A lack of knowledge. A lack of *talent*. Or a lack of imagination. Maybe the last one is my stumbling block.

Perfect example. Knowing the deadly silent killer opposite me as I do, radiating power and potential violence, I can't imagine anyone ever getting the best of her, coming up with a way to hold her captive. Even though I know they did.

After all, I rescued her.

Chapter Four
LA ROCHELLE, 30 APRIL, 1945

I t's nerve-racking work, infiltrating an Ahnenerbe stronghold. At least, it is when you can't just kill every living creature you meet.

I don't want to be here. The Good God knows I've worked hard enough to avoid open confrontation with the occult forces on the opposing side. Thwart them? Sure, wherever I can. But this war has been one long fucking atrocity from start to finish. If that becomes open warfare between the Talented on each side as well... it might replace the First World War as the War To End All Wars by becoming the War To End The Planet.

Some things can't be left uninvestigated though. The Allied Forces are pushing back the Germans and their Axis step by step, and all of France is finally liberated. All of France, that is, apart from this one little corner. A single city, out on the western coast, complete with u-boat submarine bunkers, has been left alone, isolated and besieged by British troops. But it doesn't add up. Plane drops are getting through each week despite Allied dominance of the skies, and there's just no push to recapture La Rochelle, to free the citizens and defeat this last Nazi stronghold.

So someone had to come and have a look, and that someone ended up being me. The reason became immediately evident. The shimmer covering the entire city is visible from miles away. Of course, you'll only see it if you're Talented. The effect though? That works on everyone. A persuasive magic to say, hey, this place isn't worth it. Leave it be. Carry on. Nothing to see here. They can't cast a *don't look here* big enough to make people forget La Rochelle exists, but this is the next best thing. An impressive working. I'd appreciate it more if I wasn't terrified as to where they are garnering the energy to power it.

Luckily, there's a limit to how much you can pack into a working so diffuse, covering such an expansive area. If they want people to look away, they can't make it an impermeable barrier or a wide-scale alarm system. At least, I hope not. There's been no sign so far that I have triggered anything like that by hopping over the city walls. No one's attacked me.

Even more impressively, I've not attacked anyone else either.

Believe you me, that's not easy. The stench of the Ahnenerbe is thick in the city, both woven into the working itself and present in the dark tendrils that permeate the collective psyche. Local inhabitants huddle indoors day and night, except where forced into service by the Nazis. The effect of the dark magic the German occultists are working, whatever it is, has crept into their minds, dirtying their dreams, disturbing their days. The few faces I see look gaunt, haunted. Just living here is a form of torture. Sadly, torture is a speciality of this particular brand of Talented fuckers.

So despite my more impetuous nature, I make my way through the town without slaughtering every man I meet wearing that ridiculous grey uniform that hides a heartless killer. Perhaps on the way back, I'll indulge. First, I need to find out what the hell is going on here.

It has to be something big. Has to be. And the magical signature, that stench of dark power that pervades this place, all seems to emanate from the docks, drawing me towards it.

The huge metal door of my destination looks like it's been lifted straight from a submarine, complete with locking wheel in the centre. I can't help wondering what they've got behind there that they feel the need to keep it under such air-tight, precisely regulated conditions. It probably means I should favour caution. I've done enough of that for tonight though. There are limits to everyone's self-control.

Is it a waste of *talent* to explode the door inwards, crumpling the frame and burying it into the concrete wall opposite? Probably. Still, there's anger and grief aplenty inside me from all we've found out about what these Nazi shitheels have been up to these last few years. I'll burn some of that for a while.

And then, two doors later, I don't need to burn any of my stored-up emotions anymore. There's plenty to fuel my rage, right here.

It's a lab, of sorts, that bastard hybrid the Ahnenerbe love to make. Rows of gleaming metal, test-tubes, scientific equipment. Esoteric symbols, glowing cursed artefacts, runes of power. The mixture of science and magic that seems to sing to their twisted little souls. And then there's the experiments.

There's a particular horror to finding a dead friend. It's worse to find them dismembered, labelled up in their respective parts, floating in formaldehyde. Even more so when it's more than one. Chonobis, Farlon. Sweet Symatae. People who welcomed me into their homes with rites of hospitality that spanned back almost longer than their extended lives. Sure, they weren't human, but considering what's been done to them by my species, I'm not sure that's exactly a negative to hold against them.

Jentilaks and kobolds. Gnomes and nains. The Good God knows I'm tempted to get a message to Summer or Winter, to let King Oberon and Queen Maeve know what's been done to their denizens in our world of late, even if some of them have been so long absent from the land of the fae as to hardly count as subjects to either anymore. Except, then their ire might get raised, and they might decide to do something about it. Which would probably be worse even than the fucking Nazis. It'd be a close call.

Some are just dissected torsos or heads, bobbing about in the preserving fluid. Those are the lucky ones. There are others whose suffering isn't over. Not by a long shot. Male loup-garous (werewolves) have their skin stripped back to reveal their distinct musculature, their flesh rippling through a forced change back and forth, rictus agonised grins exposed by the bottom half of their faces being nought but gleaming bone. A dryad bleeds sap into a funnel, where it's whipped away into a machine. Maybe they're analysing it, seeking to replicate her ability to stimulate crops. Or maybe they just like making her bleed.

Then I find the children. Two centaurs, a boy and a girl, age hard to tell because of their suffering but not yet teenagers, close enough in features to be siblings at least, perhaps even twins. They've been halved, separated off into their two parts. The horse limbs kick weakly. Their faces stream with tears, their innocence and childhood stripped away from them just as completely as their lower bodies. I can't tell what's keeping them alive — they're surrounded by technology I don't understand and aglow with magic I don't want to. Tearing through the invasive wiring and the unholy wards, I *pull* their bodies back together. It does nothing. The minute the stasis is broken, they're gone. I've no regrets. There's no way I'd have left them suffering like that a moment longer. Actually, that's a lie. I've lots of regrets. Regrets I didn't find out about this and get here sooner, early enough to save them. That I regret.

If I didn't just have to kill two kids, didn't just see their suffering slowly fade away in relief along with the light in their eyes, the next thing might have been the worst thing I've ever seen. Stories are emerging of exactly what horrors the Nazis have perpetrated against their fellow humans for the flimsiest of reasons. The truth of that's already been clearly demonstrated by what I've seen. But humanity has always been good at convincing themselves that anyone who isn't categorically human —or even categorically the same kind of human as us— doesn't deserve equal treatment. What I'm seeing now? They can't use those sorts of excuses.

Have you ever had a friend who's been simple in both their manners and perhaps a little in their mind but who could not be lovelier? That lack of layers, of pretence, that purity of being exactly who they are at all times only makes time spent with them a delight.

Gregory Noble is such a friend to me. He lies on the lowest rungs of the Talented ladder, little more than a hedge mage who delights in using his little power to help bring bumper crops to his neighbours and perform minor miracles for his village without them ever knowing. He's a nobody in the circles of *talent,* but his door has always been as open as his heart, his fireside warm, and a meal and a bed ever available.

There's not much left of that man now. They've sawed the top of his skull off, exposing his brain, and have shoved electrodes deep into the grey matter. His hand is outstretched, flicking constantly, producing a tiny flame each time the electricity fires into that part of his cortex. The muscles around his eyes spasm, flickering in time with the appearance and disappearance. His eyes themselves hold nothing but pain, a pain that's consumed the simple, homely man I call friend. Shutting off the machine stops that pain, but it doesn't bring back Gregory. He's gone. All that's left is to close those eyes for him as he drifts away at last.

I've lost so many friends over the centuries. Failed them, watched them die. Often because of me. Their faces haunt me every single night. Gregory's going to join them. He'll be in good company. The best. All dead because of me.

To say I'm angry now is an understatement. I'm a maelstrom, composed of purified rage, and I am ready to tear the roof off this accursed place. The next door crumples before my fury, the metal liquefying and then fleeing from my path, dissolving before my white-hot temper. It's fair to say I'm ready to vent.

And here's my chance. In front of me stands a Talented. I hardly have to even *look* because he's clearly the creator of the shielding covering the city. Strands of dark energy pour out, then back in through him, twisting together, forming circuits through which the pollution streams out across the near sky. He's a scrawny character, his face sunken and grizzled, with pepper grey hair that might be from age or might be from the shit he's seen and done. His SS uniform looks at least a size too big for him. Maybe it's from losing weight. Maybe they're running low on supplies. I don't give a damn. He's not going to need it for much longer.

He's saying something, barking syllables at me, first in German, then in French. I speak German fine, but I can't understand what he's saying. Can't really hear it. All I can hear is the sound of my blood pumping in my ears, my heart hammering in time to the throb of my pain. He tries to throw up a shield, but he's powering a major working right now that's draining his energy. I'm not interested in finesse. Just in results. I throw a condensed ball of *talent* straight through his shield and into his chest, then trigger it, shredding him, exploding his viscera outwards to paint the walls, floor, and ceiling.

Seeing that red liberally spread across the whole chamber allows me to calm down from the red I was seeing previously. With the goose-stepping fucker dead, the barrier will slowly come down. La Rochelle will probably fall in the next few days. Good. When it does, this place will no longer exist. I'm going to raze it from existence. First, I need to see if I can find anyone else alive in here. To save them if they're prisoners. To wipe them off the face of the earth if they're jailers.

Eventually, I find a secured bunker. It's twice as thick in terms of the poured concrete as any of the other rooms, and the heft of the locked door puts all the rest of the steelwork and security to shame. There's a placard, a reference number on the door, and a set of notes on the desk. Sadly, no one to set on fire. It looks like the Nazi scumball I blew up was the last man standing in this base. The rest have all fled on U-boats for the Americas based on the first set of notes I pick up. Our man wanted to finish up the tests he was running before grabbing a submarine due to dock in a couple of days. I cannot tell you how glad I am that he'll never make it to the shores of Argentina.

Part of me wants to just tear the door off again. But there's some mighty powerful Talented out there —people and creatures— and some of them don't like humans even when they haven't been captured and experimented on. Whoever and whatever is in here might not take too kindly to me when I come through the door. I need to know what I'm about to find. There's a reason why, in a facility designed for experimenting on Talented, this room's built to an even higher specification. It suggests whoever is inside is the living equivalent of a Highball bouncing bomb. Knowing who or what I'm walking in on might make the difference as to whether I walk back out again.

I leaf through the files, and the name rings a bell. Aicha Kandicha. A name I've encountered in travels through the Middle East. A demon, the boogeywoman of Morocco, an evil djinn who brings death and misfortune to all. Except...

Except according to their notes, that's not the case at all. According to this, she was a Moroccan noble from Al-Jadida. Born in the ninth century, she left her area after she used her femininity to seduce some raiding Portuguese pirates, leading them straight into a trap. The Arab world might have been considerably more enlightened than Europe at that point but not enough to save her from her reputation being ruined. Faced with scandalised murmurs and evil eye gestures thrown up behind her back, Aicha Kandicha headed east.

The next set of documents are the bits the Nazis have pieced together about her once she left Morocco. As far as I can see, she ended up in what's now Lebanon, and fell in with the Druze, an offspring of Islam still alive today, although considered heretical by many Muslims. Surprising amounts of similarities with the beliefs of my fellow Good People from my first life. Dualism. Equality between men and women. Reincarnation. Interesting...

The next sheet sets out their primary target, the reason they took her prisoner. Apparently, once accepted into the Druze's inner circle, she ended up the Guardian of the Aab-al-Hayaat. The Water of Life. So that's how she's still around over a thousand years later. The notes are pretty dry but horrific nonetheless, listing all the ways they've tortured her, trying to get information out of her as to the location of the source of eternal life.

There are some universal truths that can be held as objective in our world — water is wet, fire is hot, any sentence prefaced with, "I don't mean to be rude but..." definitely will be, and everyone breaks under torture. Except she didn't. Nothing they've done to her has made her crack. And they've done a lot. Fuck me, they've done a lot.

Apparently, she heals instantly from any injury. Something they've put categorically to the test. They sliced her to pieces until she resembled a pile of pulled pork; they super-heated her skull until her brain boiled within; they hooked her up like Loki himself and poured steady drips of acid into her eyeballs, set to drop in just as they regrew. For three months solid. Nothing could get the information from her. Eventually, they decided she'd magically sealed her tongue and moved on to other, equally horrific experiments: trying to grow clones from her by slicing her down to minuscule pieces (all of them died except the one that regrew), timing how fast she would regenerate after the incinerator she'd been dropped into got switched off, and other such charming examples of just how twisted human ingenuity can be when we really set our mind to it.

By this point, I've read enough. More than enough. I *pull* the door and half the concrete surrounding it backwards. I don't want to risk hurting her. She's been hurt more than enough.

Inside the room, once more lit by harsh artificial lighting and covered in machines to monitor and inflict agony on the inhabitant, stands a man, holding a head. Turns out the Talented arsehole I painted the walls with wasn't the last Nazi alive in here. This one's no magic user —he doesn't glow when I *look*— but he's a monster nonetheless. His white robes might be intended to mark him as a man of science. I just see a creature of pure darkness.

He's polishing the base of a severed head with a rag. Based on the noxious smell emanating from it, I guess it's some form of acid. Perhaps he's trying to inhibit the woman's ability to regrow, to allow them to package her up for a cruise under the Atlantic to the shores of South America. Perhaps it's just another sick experiment.

I don't really care either way. I flick a ball of *talent* through his forehead, dropping him like a stone. Him, I couldn't care less about, but I leap forward to catch the tumbling head. There's no way I'm letting her hit the ground. She's been through quite enough.

Turning the head to look at me, I see her eyes are open. They're hard to look at. Their dark depths are marked by what they've lived through. For the last five years, according to the charts. Yet, despite that, there's a fierceness there, a power and a fury that her strong curved nose can't hide in shadow. She looks every inch the Moroccan princess and every inch a warrior despite the indignities that have been visited on her.

Her expression blazes, burning a question she can't vocalise. It's damn hard to do that without lungs and vocal cords. It's clear though. I know the answer she needs to hear.

'They're dead. *He's* dead. The Nazis are losing. The war'll be over soon. We're leaving.'

Her eyes close, deliberately slowly, then reopen. An acknowledgement. A thank you. A single tear rolls down her left cheek. She doesn't need to say more.

I turn my back on the dead body and the horror chamber where they've kept her for so long. As we walk away, I toss a ball made of all my remaining *talent* backwards over my shoulder. I can practically hear it humming. It'll stay like that for a few minutes while we clear the facility. Then this place is getting razed. No one is ever going to find that research, ever.

Without a backwards glance, I carry Aicha Kandicha out of this hellhole, away from all the horrors the Ahnenerbe wrought on her. Time for her to see the light of day once more.

Time for the Druze Queen to be free.

CHAPTER FIVE

TOULOUSE, 8 MARCH, PRESENT DAY

Really don't want to call in help, but time is of the essence. Not least because the entire building looks like it could fall down if a wind blows on it too strongly.

Our choices are limited. However much I don't want to, there's only one thing I can do. So I do it. I call Isaac and ask him to come join us.

As we wait, I pace back and forth across the garden. Aicha's clearly picked up on how stressed out the situation's making me. That's why she's being so considerate, letting me wear a furrow into the overgrown lawn instead of pinning my feet in place with a couple of the multitude of daggers stashed about her person.

'You think it's Jakob?' Her voice is calm, monotone for such a momentous question. She's always been better than me at keeping her cool regardless of the pressure though. And the Good God knows I'm feeling the pressure right now, worrying for Isaac.

I stop, swivel, raise a finger. 'No.' Pause, lower the digit. 'Yes. Maybe?'

I sigh and wave a hand, *pushing* a selection of glass shards and tetanus-covered springs out of the way so I can sit down without needing to go pick up another new body. 'Look, you know Isaac, right? Mr Nice Guy, clean as the driven snow, struggles to say naughty words, turns red at the slightest double entendre?'

'Obviously, dickhead.' Aicha's known Isaac as long as she's known me — almost. He's been a pillar of strength for her too. I know how much she loves him, how much she respects him.

'Jakob *was even more so.* Like, the nicest dude you ever met. Heart as big as a whale. Clever as fuck, but a bit...' I search for the word. 'Look at it this way. He made Isaac look worldly wise, okay? Jak always wanted to believe the best of everybody in every single situation. He was the kind of guy who'd get attacked by wolves and then end up persuading them all to turn vegetarian and start running a hospital for poor injured woodland critters.'

'Hundreds of years ago.'

Ouch. It's a harsh point but a fair one.

'Yep, you're right. But if he's gone over to the Dark Side, then something's gone terribly, terribly wrong. Plus, he's still soul bonded to a Bene Elohim. The angels might be aloof fuckers, but I can't see them endorsing the kind of curse that hit the shit wizard.'

'So you don't think it's Jakob?'

I look at her plaintively. 'I'm hoping it's not. All I'm really thinking about right now is what Isaac's going to think.'

Because that's what really matters to me. Down in the depths of my selfish heart, I know there's one person who's never shown me anything but open-handed, honest love. I don't want to see him suffer.

Before Jakob disappeared, the two brothers shared everything. They changed our understanding of reality, of magic itself. They performed the impossible, opening up a portal to a higher dimension. Then they topped *that* by bonding with an angel each, tying their souls to them. And they loved each other deeply and dearly.

Getting Isaac to give up his search for Jakob, the search that tore him apart little by little, took me decades. I helped him, of course. We travelled the length and breadth of the known world, seeking the tiniest bread-crumb, the smallest hint as to what happened to him. Being an angel-bear-er, Jakob should have been untouchable, impervious to anything and everything our world could throw at him. Instead, he just disappeared. No trace. No trail. Just gone.

But in his heart, Isaac's never accepted that, never really believed Jak dead like I do. Or did. And I'm starting to regret quitting the hunt myself. Because now, after all this time, magic only he could have pulled off, aided by Nanael, his soul-bound angel, appears in my city? Colour me suspicious, but I find it all just a teeny bit too coincidental.

None of which addresses my most pressing concern. I get back up, start pacing again. 'How do I tell him, *laguna*?'

'I'd...' She stops and turns her head sharply. 'I don't think you'll have to. He's going to find out for himself.'

An eggshell-beige, antediluvian vehicle smokes and splutters its way around the corner closest to us, a familiar form hunched up over the wheel.

'Long past time you traded that rust bucket in for a newer model, Isaac,' I call out, trying to inject a breeziness to my tone I don't even vaguely feel.

Isaac can only get out of the car by reaching through the half-dropped window to the outside handle of the Citroen 2CV he insists is a 'classic'. He smiles haphazardly as he straightens, his gangly form projecting a scholarly air that suggests all the accompanying stereotypes of forgetfulness and flights of fancy. It also underlines his razor-sharp intellect and magical brilliance. His styling in both clothing and mannerism presents him like a college professor, right down to the tweed jacket and crumpled shirt.

Although he only looks a few years older, when we met, he had already been alive for a lifetime. Sage, teacher, confidante, and healer — the only constant for me during my second existence, as I became part of a magical world I'd never known existed.

Looks-wise, behind the bookish persona, he's a handsome man with a smile as warm and as open as any home he's ever kept. While we are often mistaken for half-brothers or cousins, his natural kindliness colours every encounter and sets him apart from my more jaded nature (yes, I know, hard to believe). Ladies (and, indeed, many men) fall head over heels for his antiquated mannerisms. He remains entirely oblivious, his only devotion to his bonded angel. Nithael.

There are advantages to not being limited by the labels we apply to things. Depth. Height. Dimensions. These are of little interest to something as mind-bogglingly powerful as a Bene Elohim. Nithael shouldn't be able to fit into the Citroen. But then, he shouldn't be able to fit into our reality either. Only the tether Isaac made of his own soul keeps him here. The best comparison I can give is the internet. Data is whizzing around our heads constantly, so many gigatons of information that it shouldn't be possible to breathe. But it doesn't impinge physically on our reality even though it's an integral part of it now.

Once Isaac's out of the vehicle, if I *look*, Nithael will be making a beacon of him. He's like an angelic aura, an electric-blue illumination towering over us, over the buildings themselves, neon-like wings stretching out across the road until the pinions seem ready to strum the taut electric wires strung across the pylons on either side of the road like a Fender Stratocaster. Except Nithael doesn't interact with our world. Not unless it's to protect Isaac.

Of course, I don't *look* at them. As there's nothing, theoretically, in our dimension as powerful as an angel, they've little to fear in displaying their power. I don't look because staring at Nithael for too long is a good way to start crying blood or babbling in tongues. Our brains just aren't made to handle beings from the higher dimensions. Or the lower ones, at that. Their very presence is likely to break us. That's why no one's ever been able to replicate the work Isaac and Jakob performed — welcoming the Bene Elohim here and joining with them. *That* and the fact that anyone who's tried has found themselves spread too thin. Across a sixteen-kilometre radius. There's only ever been two angels who have come down to our world. One of them in the man facing me. One missing, presumed dead, along with Jakob.

I try to keep that thought from my face as I step forward to give him a hug. He pats my shoulder absent-mindedly as he breaks the clasp, then turns towards Aicha, his warm smile entirely genuine. Isaac has never pried into her back story, but from day one after I rescued her, he made himself present. He bumbled about next to her in companionable silence, reading some obscure and doubtless priceless tome at an ink-stained desk positioned next to her favourite seat for watching TV. His calm quiet was a source of inspiration for her to learn to live with herself again. I think he, more than I, helped Aicha to teach herself how to be at ease again with another being. He was the serious calm. I was just the comic relief.

Aicha's smile back is as much a joy to behold as her amusement was earlier. There is nothing controlled or contrived. The gesture spreads outwards from her lips, easing the weight from her brow as it goes; the minuscule muscle relaxation is the spiritual equivalent of Atlas hurling the heavy weight of the world from his shoulders. Good God, it does me good to see. Only makes the next part even more difficult.

Isaac is, of course, burning with curiosity. He is that most dangerous of individuals — an academic. Give him a mystery and he'll not rest until he's solved it. And me calling him out to Patte D'Oie without explanation is enough to make his brain itchy.

'Right, what's going on, lad?' The tone's friendly, but firm. He knows me too well. Doesn't mean I'm not going to try stalling, at least a little.

'Good to see you too, 'Zac. What's new?' I smile, aiming for warm, probably arriving at 'vaguely tepid'.

Isaac frowns, seeing my expression, and looks over at Aicha. 'What's going on? What bloody idiocy is he pulling us in on now?'

She shrugs, then mimes zipping her lips, pointing at me. The message is clear. She's not getting involved; sort it out with said idiot. Wise move.

The long-suffering expression, patience and frustration intermingling as can only happen when those we love drive us to distraction, turns my way once more. 'Paul? Can you please enlighten me, what on earth is happening and why you told me to drop everything to come here straight away?'

I scuff at the overgrown grass, only one evolutionary step away from a throttling weed, and search for the words. What I want to do is find the ones that'll ease him into what's happening and what I've found without hurting him. "Zac, I found something. Well, rather, something found me. Trapped me for the last three days.'

'The vagaries are wearing a trifle thin, lad. Spit it out, will you?' He's still smiling, joking with me. That only makes it worse.

I look over at Aicha, who shrugs. The meaning's clear: your call. Fuck. Maybe it's better just to get it said, get it all out in the open.

'Enochian runes that kicked my ass.'

Isaac's naturally playful expression freezes. 'You couldn't break them?' There's a forcefulness in his phrasing.

'Way out of my league. Both theoretical and *talent*-wise.'

He swings towards the lean-to structure and moves forward now with a completely different rhythm. His purposeful gait carries him through the front door, which blows in like a gale before his forceful presence. I follow, watching him anxiously as he halts in front of the basement door, its time-warped frame the main thing keeping it hanging in place.

It's been a long time since I've felt such intense focus from Isaac. I'm clenching my fists so hard I can feel my nails piercing the skin. It's so hard, so damnably hard to bring him here, knowing where it might take him back to. Deep down into that pain again, the same one I can always see, just at the edge of his eyes, never fully hidden by that ready smile.

Seconds pass, crawling away from us like shrapnel-ridden soldiers across a grave-stained battlefield. I can feel the energy crackling along the peeling wallpaper and half-snapped banister. Then suddenly Isaac sits backwards hard, plumping down on his backside with neither thought nor care about the stains he's putting on his trousers or the bruises on his arse from the rock-hard flooring.

I rush to his side, terrified it's some sort of ingenious trap triggered by his presence. A feedback loop when the angel met the Enochian runes.

Seeing his face, I breathe easier again. His dazed expression is reminiscent of trench shell-shock. His elbows rest on his knees as he rubs his hands across his face, as though trying to ensure he isn't dreaming or to force himself awake if he is. After a few moments, he raises his eyes to mine and pins me with a look that mingles astonishment with hope.

'Those runes, Paul,' he murmurs, his gaze locked on to mine. 'Those runes *are* Jakob's. He's still alive.'

CHAPTER SIX

TOULOUSE, 8 MARCH, PRESENT DAY

This still doesn't seem possible. Coming back from the dead is usually my party trick.

A s I clasp his forearm and half-support, half-swing him back to his feet, I don't really know how to feel. He's so full of the possibility that his brother might still be alive, he's not thinking about any of the rest of it yet.

'Isaac, are you sure?' I ask gently.

Isaac grips the bridge of his nose between his fingers, crease lines radiating spiral-like out from the pinch point as he presses his eyes closed. 'Paul, you know Kabbalah is all about the power of words and especially names. Mastering the Enochian script, the language of the angels themselves. For me, this entire building is simply one enormous signature saying, "Jakob and Nanael woz 'ere".'

I can see the moment Isaac remembers how I said I came across these runes, his excitement fading slightly, and it breaks my heart. That boyish joy slides away, concern deep in his eyes as he massages his knuckles.

'How did you say you found these, lad?' He's worrying at his lip with his top teeth without even realising it, obviously replaying what I said, hoping he heard it wrong.

'I've been a prisoner here for the last three days, 'Zac.' Good God, I don't know how to say it without hurting him. 'There was a wizard — not Jak and Nan, a shit one, totally incapable of pulling this off. He... tortured me till I managed to kill myself.'

'Then where is this wizard?' I can hear the slightly manic tone to Isaac's voice, the way he's looking wildly around, as if I've got a shit wizard hidden under the stairs, just waiting for the right dramatic moment to bring him out with a flourish.

So I tell him. I tell him about us trailing him, the little information we got, the terrible curse he unleashed on himself when he tried to talk. By the time I get to the end, Isaac's shaking his head back and forth.

'No,' he says, though I'm not sure if he's talking to himself or to me at this point. 'No, it can't be them. Jak and Nan would never do that.'

'I agree.' I'm trying really hard to keep my voice calm, to not let an edge of pleading penetrate. He needs to work through this all for himself. 'So who did it?'

'The curse? That could be anyone, but the wards?' He looks at the doorway again. 'It must be them?' I can hear the question there. I wonder if he can. He steeples his fingers, presses them to his chin.

'Could it be forged? Could someone have made it look like an angelic working?'

'No.' He fixes Aicha and me with a stare so intense it makes my eyes water. 'This is definitely the work of a Bene Elohim. Even assuming some-one could replicate the theoretical work Jak and I did to create these sorts of Enochian runes, you couldn't power them without an angel. Perhaps if someone *could* enslave Nanael and drain every bit of knowledge from

Jakob before destroying him, then they might plausibly have been able to forge such an effect, but frankly —' He releases the fingertip pressure and looks at me plainly. 'If that were the case, Occam's razor suggests that we'd be facing a malevolent being of such unlimited power that we'd all already be enslaved or dead. Jakob wove this magic or else something is simply toying with us, and our doom and complete destruction undoubtedly awaits.'

It's fair to say Isaac isn't being as upbeat as usual. Sadly, I can't disagree with him. Isaac told me what he and Jak had gone through to get Nith and Nan to share souls with them. Runes carved onto themselves, making golems out of their own flesh. Others tried to replicate it, students. No one succeeded. Or survived it to make a second attempt. It seems to have been some freak alignment of their own exceptional levels of *talent* and their unsurpassable academic genius. Along with the purity of their intent and souls, I suspect. After the first few deaths, they destroyed their research, determined not to be responsible for any more. The likelihood of anyone else replicating that is infinitely small.

'Well then, let's go with Option One as the working assumption, shall we?' I shift uneasily under his relentless gaze. With his bookish delight for curios and arcana, the tendency is to associate all the power in the relationship to Nithael. It is only in these rare moments, where his dander is forced to rise, that the weight of his drive and mental strength become plain as a chief force behind the pairing. 'What can we do?'

'I can study these runic entanglements and patiently work out how to deactivate them without...' He pauses, and I can see the mental calculations expanding into multiple digits behind his expression. 'Destroying most of Toulouse to the West of the Garonne. You' —he jabs his index at me— 'can go fetch me some pizza while I do all the grunt work yet again, lad.' His attention peels away from me and slaps itself like an aggrieved Band-Aid onto the enchanted enigma.

I sigh in relief at the dismissal, unable to shake the sensation of being pinned butterfly-like by his Victorian lepidopterist glare. I remember that craze well. People who decide the best way to celebrate natural beauty is by driving a fucking pin through its spine are not my idea of a good time. They still give me the creeps.

Aicha and I trot over to Pizza Felix by Arènes and order a varied selection of vegan pizzas before heading back. I've remained vegetarian as far as possible over the course of my drawn-out lifetime. Sometimes it was a choice between starving or getting my meat on. In those situations, I just accepted it as a necessary sin and avoided eye contact with the relative flocks or herds for a guilty few weeks after. Veganism is a more modern arrival in the West, particularly to the land of dried meats and duck parts that is the southwest of France, but I enjoy flirtations with it whenever I encounter it outside of Europe, and I take advantage of the option when presented.

I array two cartons where Isaac can reach them, cardboard tops flipped open, as he continues to focus on the etheric fabric with laser-like attention. Aicha and I position ourselves outside the front, and after a small cantrip to persuade passers-by to pay us no mind, conjure up some comfortable seating by hardening the air.

This serves two purposes. First, it gives our legs a well-earned break. My muscles are still trying to get over the shock of not actually being dead anymore and are expressing their confusion in no uncertain terms. Second, it protects us from the seriously high chances of catching tetanus from the various rusted implements secreted throughout the long grass.

'Could it really be Jakob, *saabi*?' Aicha amuses herself, stacking various discarded pieces of metal into an impressive Gundam knock-off with her *talent*. Torn beer can shards form wings, nails forming studding on the armour. The scrap drags itself into the shape of the gigantic mechs, although the rust rather undermines their credentials as fighting space robots. I can't imagine they'd be very aerodynamic.

I hum and haw. 'I'd tell you it was impossible if that wasn't a sure-fire, guaranteed way of making sure Sod's Law throws Super-Powered Evil Jakob into our lives faster than you can say, "Stop tempting fate, you massive dickhead".'

The tin-can Gundam picks up a hubcap as a shield and strikes some suitably manga-style poses with it. 'Wasn't Jakob the guy who was so nice, he made Isaac look like a blue meanie?'

I nod. 'He really was. Always looked on the bright side, always tried to find reasons and justifications for the errors or evils of others. He believed most people were just misguided and needed help, a guiding hand, a second chance.'

Aicha makes the robot pick up a discarded shard of glass and uses it to lay waste to the forest of overgrown grass in a series of blistering ninja-like moves. 'Doesn't really match with making someone choke on their own tongue, then dissolve into a puddle of goo, does it?'

'Not really, but none of us are the people we were centuries ago.'

'Speak for yourself, dickhead.'

Living for centuries, you learn change is the only constant. That and the instinctive prejudgement of our fellow humans. It is amazing how many people still wear that as a badge of pride rather than as something to be challenged. I enjoy challenging it. Preferably with a big stick.

Does the idea of Jakob going full on murderous evil psychopath seem impossible to me? If I'm honest, no. Highly implausible, yes. But hundreds of years of people letting me down —and an equal amount of time of me letting other people down, myself most of all— shows me it's not outside the realms of plausibility. I'm certainly no Perfect anymore.

'Do you really not feel you've changed who you are over the years, *laguna*?'

Maybe now's not the best time for these questions, but honestly? I'm feeling more than a touch lost. The possibility that Jakob's still alive is beyond huge. The possibility he's gone evil? It throws everything out of whack. I don't know how I'll get Isaac through it if it's true. Hell, I don't even know how it's possible if you're hosting an angel. Then again, they've always been above us —or at least believed themselves to be— as far as I can tell. Perhaps our petty limitations of morals aren't as important to them as I thought. Or perhaps they changed too after closing in on a millennium stuck on our plane of existence.

'Nope.' Bored with making her tinpot robot run a training gauntlet, Aicha turns her *talent* to constructing a secondary Gundam ready to battle. Multi-tasking show-off.

'Not even...' I don't want to say it, but I don't need to either. Aicha knows what I'm talking about. *When* I'm talking about.

'Nope. People have always been shit. First life — saved my town, got condemned as a demonic harlot for it. You don't save people cos they're good. That'll only ever lead to disappointment.' She looks up at me sharply, that intense burning gaze fixing on me. 'Save people because you're good. Even if you're a twat too.'

Her eyes flick back down to the temporary battle arena she's made in front of her. The original robot swings his glass shard sword in an elegant sweeping arc, decapitating the newcomer, who collapses into discarded rubble. Aicha wants me to look at that, the battlefield destruction she's wrought. She doesn't want me to look at her own clenched jaw muscles. I don't miss it though. Her own unpleasant history involving a certain group of goose-stepping shitbags is coming to the fore.

I try to distract her. 'Did you know that was the only time I'm aware of that Isaac and Nithael fell out? During the Second World War?'

She looks over at me, surprised, her robot gladiators forgotten. 'You never told me.'

'Yeah. Isaac wanted to go on the offensive, especially once word reached us about Auschwitz and the other camps. Nithael refused. Even in a situation like that, he was only prepared to go on the defensive.'

Isaac's a Power, capital P, in his own right. But like I said, "theory" is where his *talent* lies. Without Nithael on board? He knew he couldn't go storming in and win the war. Not against all the arrayed occult forces on the Axis side. And Nith...

'Hold on, Aich. Nith wouldn't even kill a bunch of fucking genocidal wankers even as they swept across Europe.'

'So if Nithael wouldn't go all out on fucking up the Nazis...' she says.

I nod again. 'Then I can't really see Nanael getting on board with melting shit wizards, can you?'

As I finish speaking, a hum builds like the swell of a colony of bees swarming from a gale-fallen hive. An accompanying pressure prickles across my senses like the promise of rains capable of washing away the world. Then the hum breaks, and a relieved, calm silence pours through after it — the equivalent of fresh breezes heralding cooler nights after a heatwave. Aicha and I exchange glances, then hurry back into the house.

Chapter Seven

TOULOUSE, 8 MARCH, PRESENT DAY

Heading back down into the shit wizard's "lair". The pretentious fuck-nugget.

The pizza boxes remain where I placed them, tops folded back, content rapidly sliding down the scale from lukewarm to ambient. Wouldn't stop me from eating them, but Isaac doesn't even spare them a glance. His attention is entirely focused on the doorway. Guess the possibility of finding Jakob has blunted his appetite. I suspect what we'll find below isn't likely to bring it roaring back, so I close the boxes, then take point.

The stairway is narrow, those peculiar steps seemingly having been poured specifically to be of the precise depth and breadth that will send you tumbling down into the darkness on the tiniest slip. I conclude that one, it is a dirty architectural kink concerning cellars, and two, I go creeping into murky basements far more regularly than anyone should.

As we descend, the stale air grows danker with the olfactory jumble of visceral suffering and the shit wizard's specialised brand of body odour. The rumbling of a plane passing overhead will have been a full-throated roar out on the street, but the clay-packed depths filter out the raw power of the engine.

We step into the chamber below. My presence remains literally and liberally painted across the four walls. Although my old corpse has dissipated, cracking down into its component atoms, losing far more than twenty-one grams when my soul departed, the body parts and vital fluids separated from it prior to death still linger. The place looks like a study in monochrome, the nicotine beige doused in reds of varying depths, the darkest garnet of the first few investigational drops the shit wizard took from me submerged in the wide-ranging impressionist brushstrokes that were painted floor to ceiling when he carved me like an apprentice butcher, *oohing* and *ahhing* at each new choice cut he revealed.

In a corner, the first eye he plucked out of my head with needle-nose pliers sits dejected, slumped in a leaking pool of vitreous humour. *Aww, sad eyeball.*

Hurled strips of flesh of varying thicknesses, ranging from thinly sliced chorizo to whole pink gammon steak, slid down the walls, leaving burgundy snail trails to the floor. To smell separated parts of yourself that have started to rot is a unique experience not recommended for the faint of heart or stomach. Aicha stands in the doorway for a second, every muscle tense. Fuck. She looks up, and for a moment I see a flash of pain there in her expression. Then she locks it back down, face smoothing over, and gives me a nod. By the Good God, she's impressive. Even trauma, no matter how justified, won't constrain her. She refuses to bow, mastering it instead.

Isaac strides into the room, his eyes scanning everywhere, cataloguing, *searching.* I see disappointment cloud his expression. Perhaps he hoped he'd find his brother standing here, under a gaudy banner, blowing a party streamer. It's funny the tricks hope can play on our minds, making the ridiculous seem possible even if only for a moment. Sadly, the decorations aren't really geared towards a celebration, being as how they're made of my discarded flesh. I see the moment he clocks that, when it penetrates past that scientific curiosity. His skin pales, greening, and the huffs he takes are smaller, tighter breaths through the mouth, trying to keep his equilibrium. A little shimmer of *talent* flickers under his nostrils, and his breathing eases slightly. At a guess, Nith has just filtered the air, reducing the smell. As much as the angels might be abstract in their attitude towards humanity as a whole, there's no doubt that Nithael cares for Isaac, hates to see him suffering.

I address them decisively, my expression fixed. 'This...' I wave my hand. 'This is not me. Whatever it is, it is not me. This...' This time, the gesture is an expansive head to toe movement. 'This is me. I am here, not there. The rest is just spoiled meat. We find what there is to find, we get out, and we cleanse this place with napalm if need be, but we need to know how these wards got here.'

My words aren't gentle, but my compatriots aren't wilting daisies. One doesn't approach a millennium without being mentally tough. It has the effect I wanted. Aicha didn't even need the words — she was already moving, *pushing* slabs of fat and fibrous muscle aside, searching. Isaac gives me a nod, straightening his back. He may not have regained his normal colour, but the green tinge is gone, and he's back in analytic mode, examining the esoteric markings covering the surfaces, albeit more gingerly than Aicha in how he steps past the sticky puddles staining the floor.

Anything of worth will be inside this room. This was the shit wizard's hidden sanctum and the only place carrying wards, whether his own or, inconceivably, Jakob's. We find the odd "spell book", but most are meaningless junk, low grade and obfuscated. How he learned anything is a credit to his persistence in the face of overwhelming crap. Missing are any texts on Enochian runes, Kabbalah's secret names, or anything that holds any sign of Jakob — where he is, whether he was here, or even if it really is him.

We regroup in the middle, dejected and dispirited from our poking and prodding in this entirely awful place.

'There's nothing here, Paul.' Isaac fiddles with a ring on his finger, unable to meet my eyes. He looks as close to broken as I've seen him in half a century. To have these last embers of hope fanned into a furnace, only to have them royally pissed on is enough to cause his heart to crack almost audibly. We trudge back up the cold rutted stairs. Isaac pulls me aside as Aicha storms ahead.

'How is she holding up?' His brow furrows in concern. Bless him, the man is dealing with the sudden possible re-appearance of his long-lost brother, including him having maybe gone to the Dark Side, and he still has the mental energy to worry about Aicha's well-being.

I look up the stairway to make sure she is far enough ahead not to hear us. 'I think... I think she's dealing as well as we can hope.'

Her irate voice echoes back down off the concrete walls from above us. 'Less male bonding in icky torture chambers. More getting the fuck out of Dodge, please.'

We take the hint and get moving again. As we make to leave the stairwell behind us, Aicha pulls to a sudden halt, her head half-cocked, her features radiating concentration. She turns slowly, a semi-spin on her heel, and stalks back towards the rickety staircase.

'What is it, Aich? Did you hear something?' I ask, about to reach through the ether to pull my sword.

She waves my hand back down as she looks at me. 'Vzzzzzt, vzzzzzt,' she replies, mimicking the buzz of a phone, and starts the ascent to the floor above.

Fucking great. Why couldn't the shit wizard have taken it with him to the fresh air outside? I glance longingly at the path to sanitation, then sigh and turn back for the stairs.

CHAPTER EIGHT

TOULOUSE, 8 MARCH, PRESENT DAY

Wishing the shit wizard didn't dissolve into a disgusting bubbling flesh pool just so I can give him a piece of my mind about the importance of cleanliness and hygiene.

The technical term for the room we enter next is "bathroom", but the idea anyone could imagine they would get clean in it is absurd. Dust has settled on long-ignored dirt that clings tenuously to grime so profound it seems cultivated. Rampant mould clusters in corners and peeks from between shattered tiles, having long since evicted any grout that was in residence. It is the filth equivalent of a West Side Story turf dance-off.

I can almost understand his poor personal hygiene; the concept of standing naked in this rampant petri dish is frankly terrifying. Pink-flecked droplets from a half-hearted, post-torture clean-up form spatter patterns across the splashback and the vivid orange floor. Tiling fights to be visible underneath cast-off clothing and troubling stains. The discarded brown towel hanging over the side of the sink (a sensible choice of colour, one suspects) was obviously used as a flannel to clean away the worst of the marks before the shit wizard left for the shops. Aicha turns to me, her lips puckered like she's stuck lemon slices to her palette with a vinegar and gooseberry paste.

'Sword,' she practically spits, her hand held out.

'Sorry, what?' I reply, distracted, wondering why I'm fighting harder with my gag reflex in here than in a room coated liberally with my rotting insides.

She thrusts her hand dagger-like, stabbing through the air towards the fuzzy, scum-stained towel. 'Sword,' she repeats.

'Oh god, really? I'm going to need to coat it in litres of hand sanitiser to bear touching it ever again. I'll feel bad using it on even the worst of people, knowing it's touched that. It'll taint everything it ever touches. Don't you want to find an old broom handle or something?' I plead with her, giving her the full-on puppy dog eyes.

'Less moaning. More sword-giving,' she responds, her outstretched hand the God of the Old Testament demanding Abraham's sacrifice but without the possibility of reprieve.

Distaste clear, I pull my sword and pass it to her. She gingerly lifts the be-fouled fabric and dumps it unceremoniously onto the floor. Underneath is an older generation iPhone, a small screen crack meaning it's a miracle it still works at all. It displays a Bouygues network connection and has the symbol for one received message on the locked screen. I check and breathe a sigh of relief when I realise it's sufficiently recent to allow fingerprint locking.

There's only one way to get access to the information stored inside it. I slow my breathing, calming myself as I close my eyes and enter my mind palace to relive my recent torture in slow motion. Not my preferred leisure activity for a Tuesday afternoon.

It is impossible to live for eight hundred years and hold on to all your memories. The first time you realise you've lost something precious, that some inane fact booted the face of your first love or the smell of your mother's kitchen out of your brain or that the memory just disintegrated under the weight of time, it's a blade to the heart. The loci method has been around in various forms since Grecian times, and you learn little in the world of Western magic without studying Greek and Roman texts. While I mainly use my mind palace to store my most treasured memories, I also tie it to recent memories, allowing me to hack my short-term storage. I transformed the room in question into a cinema room —there's little more comfortable or stylish than a home theatre setup— so I sit back in the faux-leather recliner I included in its furnishing and replay my recent unwilling tenancy in the basement on the big screen.

My host was nothing if not animated, insanity having driven him to ever higher extremes. I watch as he waves his hands in my direction, waiting for the right moment. When it aligns, I mentally pause and study the concentric designs of his fingerprint, rubbing and kneading my thumb as I do so. I feel the tip becoming plasticised, then like putty as I invest my *talent*, reshaping it and modelling a new print in the physical world.

Normally, when I am inside someone else's wards, using my own *talent* would be exhausting. I'd need a good long lie down, a hearty meal, and a couple of cold pints to get myself back in the game. But the wards covering this house are shit and outside of them is Toulouse.

Talent isn't evenly distributed, and study only gets you so far. The three of us are top tier — the magical equivalents of the Duracell Bunny. The shit wizard was more like half a mouldy lemon with an electrode stuck in it. But right now, it's like I'm not running off of my stored power. I'm hooked up to the mains. Toulouse is mine, and inside my territory, I can pull off stuff like this all day long. Long story short? Don't fuck with me inside the city boundaries. I mean, if you value your life expectancy, avoid fucking with me as a rule of thumb — otherwise, I'm likely to snap yours off and shove it up your nostril — but that goes doubly so in Toulouse itself.

My eyes open, and I put my thumb on the phone's scanner. The screen lights into existence, and I'm free to search out its secrets.

It is a sparse and barren trove. The internet icon is either unused or cleaned out, and the only other applications are the phone's text and telephone icons. Someone has scrubbed everything else. There is one recent number that was called, and it is the same one that sent the only text, which reads:

Have you found the Vernicle yet? My patience wears thin.

I show it to the others. Isaac rubs at his stubble, which is more inattention than fashion. 'The Vernicle? In Toulouse?' He hums doubtfully, unaware of the mounting frustration from Aicha and I.

Aicha does a rolling motion with her hand. 'Which is...' she prompts, incredulous that it is necessary.

Isaac coughs bashfully. 'Sorry, I forget memorising relics isn't everybody's idea of a wild Saturday night, lass. The Vernicle was the veil used by Saint Veronica to wipe Jesus' face as he walked to the cross. Attributed with many miraculous capabilities: healing the sick, instant absolution, restoring lost senses. It was even believed to raise the dead! Stored in the Vatican for the longest time but lost in one of those seasonal ransackings that were all the rage around the fifteenth century. I think they have a copy still, but even they acknowledge it isn't the original nowadays. There are a couple of other imitations around, one in Vienna and one in Spain, that are believed to have properties in their own right, but most believe the original got burnt during the looting of the Vatican.'

'So we now know, at least, how a dickhead like the Incredible Melting Mage got such a runic upgrade with a kick-ass curse thrown in to sweeten the deal; he was a minion shitticus, otherwise known as the common or garden lackey. No doubt someone fed him enough knowledge to gain a little actual power, which would have been all that was required to get him to sign his soul away.' I look again at the number we have on the phone. 'The question now is, do we ring his immediate superior and demand to speak to the manager?'

'The service was pretty awful, Paul.' Aicha gives me that lip-twisting, fleeting grin that makes me pity the fool who messes with her. 'I don't think a poor Trip Advisor score is going to cut the mustard, to be honest.'

I suck in a breath, pause, then hit redial.

CHAPTER NINE

TOULOUSE, 8 MARCH, PRESENT DAY

Ready to have serious words with a very naughty boy or girl. I'm like a souped-up, pissed-off Santa.

The ring tone is the Morse code dash, standard for a French call, so at least we're dealing with someone in the same country. On the fourth elongated *burr*, the call connects. The moment of silence seems to be pregnant with possibilities before a cracked tremolo quaver speaks at last.

'Did you find it then, boy?' I can tell I am on the line with a man of advanced years, but the voice's distortion is solely caused by passing time. There is nothing comical nor kindly about it, just coldness in the timbre, an arctic blast of intonation. This is not someone talking to a friend or even an appreciated employee. The shit wizard wasn't an apprentice but a despised flunky, a necessity, a means to an end and nothing more.

'If he did, it got eaten up as part of his ice-cube-in-an-oven impression,' I answer casually.

Silence stretches thinly across the airwaves. When the speaker returns, his distaste amplifies immeasurably. 'Do you think I will not protect the valuables I seek in crafting my own curse? We are not all such fools, Monsieur Bonhomme.'

The three of us exchange glances, unspoken questions passing between us.

'You appear to have me at a disadvantage, Monsieur...' I fish speculatively with little expectation of success.

'And I intend to keep you at one. Again, I am not a fool, and my patience for being treated as such is incredibly limited. I assume by your inventive description that the house's previous occupant is no longer living?' I am not surprised at the lack of sadness or regret in his speech. It is a completed business transaction, and he has already turned the ledger to the next page. 'An annoyance but not unpredicted, your potential involvement. It leaves you in my debt, Paul.'

'I'm not sure I agree with you. Although I can't imagine the average shit wizard carries much of a market value these days anyhow.'

A rapid heaving whistling echoes through the tinny speaker. It takes me a minute to realise it is his geriatric attempt at laughter.

'He was... he was a shit wizard, wasn't he? Eh heh, I see that the trademark Bonhomme humour was not overstated. Your turn of phrase again does you credit.' The breathing pattern slows. He inhales a moment, then clears the building gargle at the back of his throat with a wet cough. 'Regardless of whether you consider the debt to exist, the fact remains that I still have something you want very much, I suspect. Or certainly, that those whom you value do. Is Nithael's mule with you today, Paul?'

Shock slaps my solar plexus, the sharp exhalation that escapes my lips outside of my control. Aicha moves to steady Isaac with a calming hand on the shoulder; he looks ready to collapse again.

'Whether or not he is, I know he won't be far from you, eh? Such a pity, really — all that time he wasted searching, all those many heavy years so distant, so frustrated. Could just have waited in his little lab, poking and prodding at the universe instead of searching for his long-lost brother. What wonders might he have discovered by now?' A half-hack, half-cough carries its high moisture content to my ears. 'Or he might well have destroyed us all with his meddling. Maybe I've done us all a favour, eh, boy?'

The surprise is wearing off, and anger is angling to replace it. 'I think I've a few years on you, *boy*,' I hiss back.

There is a reflective silence. 'Perhaps, Paul.' For the first time in this lopsided conversation, I feel as though I've exposed a chink. My response has given him pause, at least. Sadly, it's not telling me the stuff I need to know. Which boils down to who is this man, and what is he after? 'Maybe we will have time to have an antiquated dick measuring contest about our longevity before this is through, hmm? In the meantime, my requirements don't vary. I would like very much to receive a present of apology for the inconvenience caused by the murder of my associate —'

'His death is on your hands, not mine, asshole.' My top lip peels back, anger manifesting in my tone.

'I never specified who murdered him, did I, Paul?' A long-suffering sigh echoes across to me, filled with tried patience and eternal disappointment. 'To have lived so long, yet to still be servant to our emotional responses is a saddening sight indeed. Again, I require recompense. A certain lady's face covering would be sufficient. Then perhaps we can set up a happy ending for your friend, eh? Family reunions are always such touching scenes.'

I bite down on my response like a battlefield tongue depressor. The Good God be damned if I'll give him the satisfaction of rising to his bait. Instead, I measure my response, cutting it to the fit of the conversation. 'Where would we find such a gift? And how would we deliver it to you if we did?'

The satisfaction in his voice edges towards gloating as he replies, 'I'm sure a man of your capabilities will succeed in locating it where the, eh, shit wizard failed so miserably, no? As for the delivery, let's organise that once you have it wrapped up in a bow, shall we? You have my number now — or rather, a number I allow you to have. I think you are some way from having my number, *cadorna*.'

The line cuts, the absence of the almost undetectable background static the only sign of the man's departure. I look at my companions. Aicha has passed beyond her normal state of anger-fuelled readiness. Her rage is now so ice-cold it comes close to absolute zero. Isaac has recovered from his second significant shock in so many hours, and his features are an open book for those who know him — the skin tight with concern and stress, his fear clearly displayed.

Not only is his brother apparently being held by the eminently danger-ous individual we just spoke to, but we're going to have to tangle with someone capable of restraining and controlling a creature from a dimen-sion well beyond our own in terms of *talent* and power.

Pressure wraps itself around us, huddling us instinctively closer together as it beats at us from the flickering shadows cast by the ceiling's epileptic neon tube. I chuckle with a need to ease the pressure, shoving the phone and my hands into my jacket pockets, forcing my shoulders to relax, to portray an ease I am a long way from feeling.

'So... anyone else feel that he was more Palpatine than Old Ben?' I en-quire casually.

The oppressive tension lessens a notch, just enough to allow space to breathe more easily. Aicha half-rolls her eyes at my *Star Wars* reference, but she knows what I did and why and appreciates my efforts. Isaac nods his thanks, but the worry doesn't move from his expression.

'I don't doubt that you are correct, lad, but who on earth is this creature? Enslavement has never been a concern for me with Nithael around. I've never met a force that could perform such a task — hell, never heard of one in all my travels or time researching. Now we find not only has someone succeeded in something I'd have said was impossible, but knows all about us and is press-ganging us into service? This can't end well, Paul, not any way I look at it.' He unconsciously rubs at his temples with bent knuckles, though whether he is kneading away tension or trying to get his brain to work harder, I don't know.

Now it is my turn to sigh. 'I don't doubt it, *ami*, but it doesn't change the facts of the situation. Right now, he has us over a barrel. You and I have gone gambling enough times to know there's only one thing to do when someone holds all the cards.'

'Yes, I know — you cheat, and normally drag me into some unfortunate altercation because of it. So how do we "cheat" in this situation?' Isaac looks doubtfully at me, curving his eyebrow.

I sigh again. 'I have no idea. We're going to have to wing it, try to get some ideas together as we go. Find out who or what we're dealing with and what they truly want whilst keeping them happy by searching for this bloody veil that they've insisted we get. That's as refined a plan of action as possible for now.'

'Which is to say about as developed as your self-preservation instinct,' Aicha inserts, catching me off guard. That dry deadpan style is a killer of a delivery, and I can't help but crack a genuine smile. I nod my thanks. She more than repaid my own efforts.

'So, accepting that we really need to refine the game plan as soon as possible, what's our first play?'

Isaac tugs absent-mindedly at his shirt sleeve, taking his time to think as he worries at a loose thread that has danced out of a buttonhole like a charmed cotton snake. 'I think I would be best suited playing to my forte. I'd suggest I head back to crack on with researching what magic might be capable of dominating an Elohim and find rumours of who could even conceivably wield that power. I'll dig in the books and reach out to anyone I can think of that might aid us in terms of information.'

Aicha looks grim and speaks with great reluctance. 'I don't see that we have much choice, *saabi*. We need to speak to the same person who pointed you towards this hovel in the first place. We need to have a talk with Franc.'

Chapter Ten
FOIX, 10 AUGUST, 1209

The sun is incessant, demanding. It strikes us about the exposed face, where my black cowl cannot provide sufficient shade, and burns us where it can catch our skin.

Our walk from Toulouse has been a matter of judging when we might make the best progress and when a tactical retreat to either a leafy overhang or a friendly home is the best plan. My robes, marking me out as a Perfect of the Good People, still gain me respect and hospitality for the moment, but the northern lords and the Pope's servants are seeking to change that. Already troops are massing, and the Languedoc prepares itself for invasion. Hope for talk is failing. We've been marked as heretics, and there's no room for that in the new vision of Christianity.

We're nearing our destination now. The mountains rise steeper and stronger with each passing day even as our food bags empty. The river is a blessing though. Without the Ariege to keep us company, the distance would be impossible on foot in this heat.

'Drink, Paul, for the Good God's sake!' There's a gentle chiding to Benedict's tone. I have to stifle a chuckle. Sometimes I think he believes I'll waste away, forgetting to eat or sleep if he weren't here to prompt my memory. It's all from the best of sources —a good and caring heart— but I'm no fragile flower, liable to shatter if breathed on too hard. My life before the robes was similar to his. Perhaps a little less hard, with a little more love but not much of a difference. My abstinence from earthly matters —my attempt to live up to the role of Perfect— might mean I won't raise a fist in my defence now, but I brawled aplenty when I was a lost young man.

Still, that's his role. Until he takes up his own robes, he's my strong right hand and guardian. For me to sin would mean the loss of my soul, disintegrating into nothingness upon my death. A price I paid for my consolamentum, the ceremony that raised me to the position of Perfect, priest of the Good Christians. Of course, it also means as long as I don't sin I'll finally escape this mortal plane when I die. For Ben, until he does his own ceremony, sin carries no weight other than a likely longer time reincarnating before escaping from this material prison and joining the Good God outside of the bonds of the physical world. Not that he sins much. Unless you count his frustrated cajoling of me as a sin.

Of course, I hope he'll see his own aims through and join me in wearing the robes once he's ready. If he becomes a Perfect, this will be his last life too. Like me, he'll break free from the fetters the Evil God dressed us in, chaining us to this physical world. His heart is there — full of love and hope. He just needs to shed the last few restraints of his upbringing, and he'll be ready to wear the black.

'Drink, Paul, you stubborn bastard!' His insistence grows and shatters my reverie. I sigh. He's right, of course. I take the gourd he's offering and drink, then smile my thanks. It's weak and thin, much as I feel myself. Not from lack of eating. No. It's the weight of the burden we carry. Until it's safely in the vaults of Foix, I'll not rest easy. The Pope would love to get his hands on it. I don't doubt he's not the only one.

My eyes aren't really on where I'm going, and my foot catches in one of the dust-concealed holes in the well-trodden path. With an effort, I check my stumble, stopping myself from sprawling across the road, but Ben's there immediately. His arm steadies me, his fingers strong but with a tenderness to his grip, supporting me, keeping me from falling. Always there to keep me upright, steadfast. A staunch friend.

He looks at me hard, his eyes tracing my features, no doubt noting the lines the journey's wearing into my face, the bags like bruises under my eyes. His gaze lingers on those. 'We rest. Now.' There's an insistent growl, the result of having to deal with my somewhat contrary resistance to his attempts at looking after me. He's right, of course. As usual.

He gives me an arm to lean on. I'm not that old —only just gone thirty— but it's true the responsibility of our charge has meant I've not taken care of myself as well as I should in this blazing heat. I can feel the strength return-ing to my limbs when we get under the cover of the boughs overhanging the bank of the river. The gurgle of rushing water is a beautiful melody, and I take a moment to breathe it all in. These moments are precious, and it's so easy to rush from duty to demand and never appreciate them fully.

'My apologies, Ben.' I turn another strengthened smile his way and see the delight light up his features. 'You were right as ever, my friend.'

'You've no need to apologise ever to me.' He slaps me lightly on the arm. I think he's still afraid I might keel over if he claps me too hard. His hand rests gently on my shoulder. 'Just be less bloody pig-headed and let me take care of you, for goodness' sake!'

It's fair. 'You're here to keep that banditry away. Not to be my nurse-maid.'

'Then stop acting like you need one, you daft sod.' His returned grin softens the word, takes any sting away. He's only worried about me, and I know it really.

A cough behind us breaks the moment of camaraderie. The sight of the person coughing? Sends shivers down my spine for reasons I can't explain.

A young knight, broad-shouldered, armoured, and with a full red beard, stands up on the roadside some metres away, where we descended the bank. His face is amiable, but his sword is drawn, and there's... *something*. Something in the way he stands, in his passive expression. In his eyes, where for a moment I think I see something flash far more claret than his hair. In that instant, there seems to be an elongation to his face, more muzzle than mouth. The next, it's back to normal, nought but a ruddy visage, but the disquiet remains.

Looking over at Ben, I see his hand is wrapped around his sword's pommel, the unease in his expression a reflection of that in the pit of my stomach. He steps forward, drawing the attention to him, the Good God bless him.

'Greetings, stranger,' he calls it out loud and clear, broadcasting his confidence, his lack of fear. 'Do you hail us? How may we help you?'

The man smiles, and for a second I think I see incisors longer than a carving knife's blade. Again, it disappears, so fast I wonder if the heat is affecting me worse than I imagined.

'Well, a fine sight, a fine, fine sight,' he shouts back and starts to slowly advance down the slope. Ben's sword clicks free. Not drawn yet but ready to be liberated at a moment's notice.

'Again, sir.' Ben's tone is polite but insistent, readied. 'I must ask what your business is with us?'

'A Good Man, a Perfect no less, out on the roads in these troubled times? With, and by no means do I intend offence, only one such as you to guard him?' He spreads his hands, a peaceful gesture undermined by the presence of three feet of steel in the right one. 'Why, to offer my aid in ensuring your safe conduct to Foix.'

He's getting closer, slowly, and every step he takes towards us, my dread increases. Whoever this man is, my instincts are screaming at me to not trust him, to flee him if we can. The Good God gave me them for a reason. I think I'll do well to pay them full mind.

Before I can refuse, Ben raises an excellent point. 'And what's in it for you?'

'Why, nothing much. Perhaps to alleviate your load a little. Whatever you carry in that battered old knapsack will do.' He points with his sword straight at our treasure.

My blood chills to ice. How does he know? The greatest prize of the Good People, the treasure given to us long ago by Mary Magdelene herself. How can he be aware? Have we been betrayed?

The brigand —for brigand he is, by my accounting— sees the question on my face and laughs. 'You've no need to worry about treachery, Good Man. The content of that bag shines like the heavenly sun for those of us who can *see.*' There's a weird emphasis on that last word, which makes it clear that we aren't included in that number.

Ben's sword is free in a moment, and he takes another step forward. 'You'll take it from us over my dead body.'

'As you wish, my good man.' The brigand steps forward again, and it seems to me as if he expands, growing, his muscles lengthening, his face becoming more animalistic, losing some of its human traits. Terror pours through my system. There is something terribly, devilishly wrong with this man.

'What goes on here, then?' Another unfamiliar voice rises from the road, and I look up, wondering who it is, whether someone is riding to our rescue.

Not by all appearances. The man wears a simple brown tunic, his hair clipped short, a Star of David hanging on a pendant. He has a warm face, handsome, with a scholarly air. A rabbi, by all accounts, come to act as a good Samaritan in our hour of need.

The man's face fades back to fully human. I expect him to laugh at the stranger, another holy man unlikely to offer a villain such as him any obstacle. Instead, he turns a sneer, as bestial as his face looked a moment previous, on the newcomer.

'What want have you of knowing my business, Jew?' His words are angry, full of promised violence.

The rabbi doesn't blink. 'Only to see all is well for another seeker of truth. I hope you are not bothering them, *valf?*'

The man snarls, fully snarls, like a caged beast brimming with rage, and steps towards the interloper. My fear rising, I'm about to prompt Ben to intercede, to act and save our would-be do-gooder. But the rabbi simply raises a peaceful hand and says one word to the devilish bandit.

'*Look.*'

Again, there's that same strange pronunciation, the emphasis on the word as when the other said *see*. Whatever it is, the thief stop for a moment. I get the impression he is inspecting the rabbi, though in a way different from how I would. It's impossible to explain how or how I know, but I feel sure of it.

Whatever he sees changes everything. The brigand shrinks in on himself, and a whimper, low and long, comes from him, like a keen of a wild beast over a dead mate. He backs up, his head lowered.

'Time to be on your way, wouldn't you think?' The rabbi's voice is calm, placid, but there's a force behind it. A force the man responds to. Not with words. No, the villain turns, angles himself for the road, and flees, racing to escape the presence of the quiet, scholarly-looking holy man who stands above us.

Incredible. I've no idea what I just witnessed, not really, but my instincts tell me it was something quite extraordinary, that more went on than my eyes could see. 'My thanks!' I call out and step forward to go greet our benefactor, but Ben's arm grips mine, pulling me back.

'Careful, Paul!' he hisses through clenched teeth. It strikes me he looks more afeared now than he did when an armed man was closing in on us. 'He's an accursed Israelite. There's dark sorcery at work here.'

I turn to him and let him see the sadness in my gaze. It is a terrible thing to be so marked, to have such terrible prejudices so deeply ingrained. 'My friend. So was Jesus of Nazareth who carved us this gift. So was Mary Magdelene who brought it to us. He's a fellow holy man. What happened was a miracle, a religious working. Not dark magics. You do him a disservice, as well as yourself. And me.'

I can't fully keep the stern tone from my voice, but he needs to hear it. The words penetrate, and I see him hang his head, although I notice his eyes still smoulder slightly at the rebuke. This isn't the first time we've had this conversation, whether about Jews or Moors or even our own Good Women. Sadly, I don't think it'll be the last. Some things take a long time to unlearn. Still, that's my role as his mentor and friend. To help him pass over such ideas, to grow beyond his own background. We'll get there in the end.

I clap him on the shoulder this time, to break the built tension. Hopefully that's enough to stop him from stewing too much on his guilt and bad feelings while I go speak to our benefactor.

'Well met!' There's truth in that, though the rabbi's tone carries no sense of pride or of us owing a debt. It's genuine, warm, welcoming. He offers his hand to help me up the last part of the sloping bank, and I accept it gratefully. His clasp is firm, and it's a matter of seconds to scramble the last part. Not my most dignified of movements, but I'll leave those sorts of pretensions to the Catholic priests. I know my own clumsiness. And the value of an offered helping hand.

'That was quite something, Rabbi...' I pause. Though I've encountered the Jews plenty of times —for there's nowhere else in Christendom they're more accepted and welcomed by my reckoning— here in the Languedoc, it is the first time I've crossed paths with one of their holy men.

'Isaac.' He smiles easily and pulls out his gourd, then plumps himself down on the top of the bank. The mountains on the other side rise heavenwards, as though we could climb them and escape this plane then in a single bound. Only the view of Ben, kicking stones at the water's edge, mars the view slightly. I sigh and let that one go, sitting myself next to this Rabbi Isaac. There'll be time for soothing his temper later on.

'Well, Rabbi Isaac, that was some strange occurrences. Upon my troth, I'd say you came at just the right moment.' I let my gratitude fill my voice, let him know how much I appreciate his involvement.

'Ah, a pleasure, Good Man.' So he recognises my own robes. No surprise. Despite what the local priests might believe, we Perfects are still the main holy order in this region. At least in terms of who the common men and women turn to and trust in.

I lower my voice. 'What was that, sir? It seemed to me, for a moment, as though he... changed. And why did he fear you so? Whilst I don't doubt your capacity to take care of yourself, I cannot understand the danger he saw in you which he saw not in myself and Benedict. Not least, considering we, or Ben at least, are armed, and you are not.'

Isaac looks across at me, studying me carefully. 'So you saw that, did you...' He pauses. 'Do you know, Good Man, I do not know your name either?'

'Paul.' I offer my hand once more, and we shake again. He merits it.

'Well, Paul. There are stranger things in this world than even those of us who serve God's people might at first believe. Some are gifted — or cursed according to others, with the ability to *see*.' Again, that strange emphasis. 'For those who can, what you carry draws both the eye and the desire.'

My alarm rises. Is Ben right? Is this strange rabbi after our treasure? Isaac sees my reaction and chuckles, spreading his hands open and empty, waving me to calm. 'Relax, Paul the Perfect. I'm not after your artefact, whatever it is. I'm simply warning you it might leave you open to risk. Have you much farther to go?'

I shake my head. 'Only to the keep at Foix. Once we're there, it'll be a simple matter of passing it off to Lord Raymond. He's a loyal friend to the Good People. His sister, Esclarmonde, is a Perfect, after all.'

I see doubt in Isaac's eyes. 'Forgive me, but I am not sure any mortal can provide true security for such as you carry.'

My wariness is back. 'Still, so have I been charged and so shall I do.'

He shrugs, spreading his hands again. 'You must do as you feel right.' His eyes narrow, a thought clearly striking him. 'Tell me something, Good Man. How important is it to you, protecting your charge?'

My indignance rises. 'Why it's on my honour. I will happily trade my life for its safety.'

Isaac plucks a grass blade and rubs it between thumb and forefinger, back and forth. 'Will you be staying to guard it?'

'For as long as my duties allow, aye. There's trouble brewing, storm clouds on the horizon. Eventually, I'll need to return to my people.'

'If I could give you a gift, to allow you better to identify potential threats, would that interest you?'

Now it is intrigue that rises up. 'What sort of gift? And why do I feel like there's a hidden addendum to this offer?'

He grins and chuckles, slightly abashed. 'You're a good read of man, my friend. The gift I can give will make it easier to spot those like you just encountered. Stranger people or beings who might be interested in your prize. The other side to the coin is that it'll also make you more visible to them. Once you leave your post at Foix, the likelihood of you encountering the strange and supernal will increase.'

'We are all flawed creatures.' I return his amiable smile. 'And the Good God knows curiosity is one of my worst. I'll take your gift, rabbi. If it will let me stand better in my duties, have at it.'

The rabbi places his hand on my forehead and closes his eyes. He mutters something, words with strange syllables, harsher and more guttural than I'm used to. A warmth spreads from our contact, passing through my body, and for a moment he seems radiant, surrounded by a white illumination, as when a sunbeam strikes through a cloud, lighting up the edges.

Then it passes. 'It is done, Good Man. You will sleep well tonight. All I've done is unlock the natural abilities already present in you. *Seeing* those like our friend who fled or like me myself will become easier over time.' He looks pensive, chewing his lip. Perhaps he is not wholly convinced he has done the right thing. 'If these troubles now facing your people should ease, then I think further guidance may be needed. In that case, come to Montpellier. Seek me out among the Hachmei Province, the elder counsel of the Jewish community. I'll be there to aid you should you need.'

I smile, nod, and offer my thanks. It seems rude to denigrate his offer, to point out I have no expectation of our troubles easing. Not while either the Pope or any of the Good People of the Languedoc draw breath. We exchange a few last pleasantries, then he stands, dusting the pollen off his robe, and bids us farewell.

We too set off once more, heading for the chateau at Foix and the hopes of safety. Ben is quiet along the route, perhaps ruminating on his own conduct, perhaps mortified by mine. My mind is elsewhere.

I cannot help but wonder how long anywhere, even the mountainous bastions such as Foix, will be safe for those like me who wear the black robes of the Good People.

CHAPTER ELEVEN

TOULOUSE, 8 MARCH, PRESENT DAY

Still reeling and not relishing our next course of action in the slightest.

It is a terse parting as Isaac climbs into his Citroen and, after persuasive coaxing involving everything short of beating it with a fallen tree branch to get it moving, pulls away. I dump my jacket in Aicha's Alpine, then shut the door as I stand beside it. The cooler March morning that greeted me as I staggered from the morgue like a Friday-night drunk-tank candidate is giving way, the breeching sunlight growing in confidence. Warmth radiating from the buildings and pavement only augments the effect.

We're a good distance out from the centre of the city, where we need to go. There are metro stations little more than a stone's throw away, but I'm not looking to get there quickly. Hell, I don't want to get there at all, but when I see Franc, I want to be ready. And if that's going to be the case, I need to move.

Movement is essential and not just in the "if you don't, your joints will rust up and you probably won't be able to get out of bed anymore, especially if you eat that third helping of Crème Brulé" sense. It ties us to our surroundings, anchors us in the here and now. We become more part of our world when we are walking through it, experiencing it directly. There's magic in that.

We enter the measured twirl of the unconscious dance of the street and its occupants. Our confidence makes partners out of the strangers we encounter, our side-steps a do-si-do. We pass over a train track and wend from the smaller roads up into the Avenue Etienne Billières, just east of Patte D'Oie. From there we cross Saint-Cyprien, the market bustling, the bars serving coffees to some, spirits to others, and head for the Pont Neuf to cross into the city proper, looking for Franc.

Beings of *power* —at least, those who don't get themselves killed by pitchfork-wielding locals or greedy rivals— live for considerable spans of time. We solidify our holdings by claiming territory. Cities become the purview of one dominant individual, with other magical entities only allowed in by their gracious permission. Usually.

There are exceptions to the rule. Typically, my situation is one of those exceptions.

I'll never forget when Franc and I first met. Returning to Toulouse in the nineteenth century after a long and painful time away, I was in a pitiable state, wounded in spirit and desperate for familiarity and stability. Instead, I felt Franc's magics like an oil slick polluting the dark waters of my home. Pulling my sword and firing it with my *talent*, a blazing green fire dancing its edges, I charged nihilistically towards the source, not even caring normal people might see me, ready to do battle with this invader polluting my home.

But the strange creature didn't come looking for a showdown. Instead, he waved a flag of parley as I approached, a bedsheet stained with dark bodily fluids he'd stashed in a crumbling hole in a wall by the riverbank. He wheedled and parleyed, insisting we could co-exist.

His offer was simple — if I allowed him to stay, he would become my eyes and ears, detecting powers when they entered the city and hearing the unguarded discussions of potential threats, alerting me to risks to my home. All he wanted in exchange was for me to leave him in peace to gather his "lovely lads and lasses", as he called them. He wasn't evil, he insisted. Yes, he fed on the misery of humans, but his was a trade, always a trade. No one would die. In fact, he'd be doing them all a favour. And was he such a monster if he dulled their pain even a little and kept them alive? They'd not get such a kind offer from any of the other options. The gutter. The workhouse. The forced labour of prison. The hangman's noose.

Only the truly desperate get drawn to Franc. When they are, if they swear fealty, he takes care of them. Sort of. He doesn't make their lives easy, doesn't take away their suffering. Doing that would undo the very reason he wanted them in the first place.

When the cold bites like piranha teeth, it will still feel like the flesh is stripping from their bones. When their heroin is cut with too much rat poison or, more ironically, is too pure compared to their usual supply, it'll still feel like a raging fire consuming their veins, boiling them from the inside out. But they won't die from hypothermia or overdosing. They'll always scrounge up enough food to survive, though it might differ from the things they once were prepared to put into their belly. They'll learn to live with that constant companion of a hollow emptiness that is kept just a notch above terminal. And Franc? Franc feeds off that misery. It's sustenance for him. That's the trade.

He's no friend to his people, but he is clear, categorically clear, before they enter his services. They meet him in their dreams, their feet leading them to kneel at the water's edge. He'll tell them the implacable truths of what he offers and not one thing more. Those who hold on to hope are allowed to go, forgetting him in the mists of morning — but they are few and far between.

I don't like him or trust him. But we struck a deal, and I'll not be the one to break it, not without good justification. So ours is an uneasy truce, leaving us sharing the city sprawl. Shared meaning we don't try to kill each other. Although honestly, it's still my first inclination every time I see him. Or think of him. Or remember he exists. Be in awe of my willpower and self-restraint.

Nonetheless, we're both still standing, as is Toulouse, so that is a win, all things considered. Who'd emerge victorious if we tried to kill each other is far from certain, so I've accepted uneasy cohabitation as the best option.

When we pass onto the downslope towards Esquirol and Toulouse proper, I start *looking* out more actively for Franc's people. Walking the streets of Toulouse like this —attuning to the city's pitch and key, then marking it as mine like the filthy old dog I am— is a necessity to protect it and its people, a sigil marked in long-shank strides. It also brings me into sync with the undercurrents of the city, both light and dark. I'll be able to find Franc by using myself as a dowsing rod. Of course, that means I need to sink into it, submerge myself into that syncopated heartbeat of the city just under the surface, made of footfalls and market-cries, of pigeon chitters and the swelling murmurs of individuals subsumed in the crowd. I'm *looking*, but I'm also *being*, joining with the city so it draws my attention into the loop of Toulouse. In theory, it makes me vulnerable. While my attention is all *there*, very little of it is *here*, where I am, this physical body walking the streets. My attention's too diffuse, my state almost trance-like. Of course, I'm not in the least bit concerned. Anyone attacking me will commit suicide-by-Aicha. Messy way to go.

A couple of potential candidates stand on the southern corner of the bridge, half-pints in plastic cups from Le Filochard bar. They could well be his. She's young, only just out of her teens, if she is even that old. One side of her head is shaved. Lime green filaments of her mohawk she didn't take time to style drape over the stubble. Parts are still rigid from a previous fix up with soap; other parts lounge across her head. Screamo and metal band fabric patches dot her leather jacket. I'm willing to bet she's not listened to most of them. Her style mixes punk and emo — holes torn in stockings under frayed jean shorts, her stomping boots Doc Marten knock-offs. Still, the closer I get, the more I realise she isn't Franc's. Not yet anyway.

There is too much artfulness in the combination. Too much precision and attention in the looping black lines of mascara tracing out from her eyes, the vestiges of hair stiffener more likely shop-bought product than coarse soap. She's not desperate, not yet. She's only recently stepped outside of the world most exist in, outside warm houses and second chances. Given time, odds are good she'll go to him. Once the itching need kicks in, once the doss houses give way to cold alleyways, then she might go seeking his blessing. For now, she remains an outsider.

Her companion looks a more likely bet. By my reckoning, he appears older, perhaps as much as a decade, but the wear and tear of life on the streets means it could be half of that. There's no posturing to him. Brown nicotine stains paint his lopsided grin and trace the swirls of his fingertips as he pulls on a prison-thin roll-up.

His lived-in face matches an outfit that has likely come from the thrift shops off Capitole, selling clothes by the kilo. Life has torn through the knees of his jeans, not the fashion-seeking scissors of a trend's demands. The dirt marks on his Dead Kennedys T-shirt are a map, calling cards of squats he's visited for shelter or a safe space to get high. His hair is cropped short, lank brown strands hacked off by scissors wielded without sufficient skill or attention. The couple top up their goblets from a can pulled from the faded khaki army bag at his feet. The longer I *look*, the surer I am that he is Franc's.

To find Franc, I need to talk to him through one of his people. He doesn't trust me any more than I trust him. Wise monster.

But the girl isn't claimed by him. Not yet. Perhaps her rebellious phase will pass. She can still choose another life path. If I expose her to Franc, I'll be making that choice for her. There'll be no turning back.

There's plenty of Franc's people in the city. No need to take the risk. I dismiss them and continue to let my feet lead me down towards Esquirol.

Our dance partners increase in number as the bustle builds by the cross-point of the metro station. Southwards lies Carmes, a collection of street-food locales pitching themselves shamelessly as clientele flows past towards the bars and restaurants surrounding the parking lot. To the north, the central ditch of the cobbles is an arrow pointing upwards towards the Capitole. A mixture of known brands, independent boutiques, and shop-based hustlers adorn both flanks and the adjacent side roads. As the shop windows enlarge, displaying haute couture offerings, I turn north towards the Place Saint Georges. The middle-class kids, protected by money's influence, swing off the wooden rib cage of the dragon-shaped playground without a care in the world.

Approaching the roundabout surrounding the Jardin Pierre Goudouli, I see another of Franc's chosen. A man, only just more than a boy, sits huddled in a corner, crushing his hunched-up body back into the elegant brickwork he's leaning on. He's almost naked, his dirty grey boxers the only thing providing him any decency. His body vibrates as he shivers, his eyes on a discarded coffee cup sitting at his feet. He stares at it, zoned out, acknowledging no one and nothing except his own misery.

I approach the beggar and drop a euro into the cup. As I do, I push a small tendril of *talent* into him, letting it tap against the magic that binds him to Franc, like knocking on the door. When the boy's head shoots up, his eyes are white eggshells in an utterly vacant face.

'Back again, my little lordling? 'Tis an honouring, so soon and suddenry, upon my oath.' The voice has the cold-cracked pitch of the youth in front of me, but the cadence, the structuring? All Franc's. One detail of the deal he strikes with his people. They serve him. Always. If he needs to see from their eyes, to speak from their mouth? There's no choice for them in the matter.

I don't even try to keep the distaste out of my voice. 'Franc, I've neither time nor patience for pleasantries. We need to speak in person. Now.' I don't feel the need to sugar my words. Dealing with Franc is a necessary evil, not a pleasure. It brings me down to earth *hard,* and I have neither the energy nor the inclination to engage in banter.

'Ah, my boyo, then you'll be needings to come to me, will it not now be? The little fishy walkers get themselves all edgied up if I climb out by their busy spaces. Not good for the peace, my little lord, is it? Not good for our dealerys and agreementings all finery-signed and filigreed.' The smile that splits the boy's face looks neither genuine nor entirely human.

I suppress a shudder. 'Where can I find you then, Franc?'

'Wend your feet pattering up towards the twinny bridge, clone-stepping with your delectable shade-sword next to 'ee. Clamber the handholds down to my river-side promenaderings and under the eaves amidst the droppings. I'll be with you in a jiffied shimmy, good manling.'

The head shakes, an unnaturally rapid side-to-side movement, covering multiple back and forths inside a single second, blurring the features. Then the young street kid is back, dropping his gaze downwards to fixate once more on his feet as the shivering starts up again.

Dropping a ten euro note into his cup before leaving, there's pity and anger mixing up inside. I saw the track marks on his inner arm. I know where that money will go. Some people justify not giving money to street-folk by stating how they'll only spend it on drugs or booze. That displays only their own poorly absent humanity rather than that of the likes of the poor sod in front of me.

I spent a year inside an opium den at the turn of the eighteenth century when misery had made a mess of me again. Lost in the loving embrace of the poppy until the den owner slit my wretched throat without a thought or care. Dirty deeds done dirt cheap.

Being murdered saved me. I skipped the misery of physical addiction. Even so, the mental suffering was intense and only stressed the grief responsible for me being there in the first place. Still, I could escape to a new body, to money stowed and property accrued, to rebuild myself and reclaim my place. For most people, once the streets take you, whether you are Franc's or not, they sever you from society's connections. You become isolated, hopeless, and helpless. I can understand the need to escape, to blank out that destitute monotony of suffering defining your every waking moment. I don't think it requires much empathy nor the need to endure the excesses of addiction to sympathise with those in that situation and realise our choices might not look very different in similar circumstances.

Aicha looks at me. Her eyes are ablaze over the sight of the kid being ridden like a loa by Franc. She's made her opinions about his presence in Toulouse very clear. I think she probably saw elements of her own suffering in that of the poor wretch too. I only really know the bare bones of her story, but there are some things she cannot stand. The exploitation of the vulnerable —as she sees it— is not to be tolerated.

It was a long time after our return to Toulouse from La Rochelle before I told her about Franc. We then had many long heated discussions, followed by solemn promises extracted before I allowed her to come with me to meet him. I've always held on to the bigger picture of the damage a clash between us would cause and the lives of those unaware of our world, undeserving of being caught in our battles. Aicha is more of the "if the shoe fits, use it to kick him in the nuts" school of thinking. She maintains that wrong is wrong. And beyond any doubt, beyond any possible question, Franc is most definitely wrong.

CHAPTER TWELVE

TOULOUSE, 8 MARCH, PRESENT DAY

Already regretting this before even having properly started. I suspect this may be a metaphor for how Life herself must have felt when we crawled out of the oceans.

We cut back across Capitole and down the Rue Léon Gambetta towards the Quai de La Dorade. We keep to elevated pathways; university students fill the green spaces of the dry dock below, alongside others of similar ages, socialising over cans of beer and cider bought from the corner grocery store. The boozy order of the day is cheap and strong, like prom date aftershave. I spot the couple from Pont Neuf earlier. They are now entrenched in a conveniently isolated corner with some similarly dressed individuals, with a bastard mongrel dog belonging to their new friends frolicking around their feet.

As we walk along the raised quay heading towards the Place Saint Pierre, my gaze meets the boyfriend's. His eyes flash white, a grin distending unnaturally as he blows me a kiss, then clicks back to normal. His girlfriend, noticing the gesture (if not the transmutation) looks over her shoulder, searching for who he saw. Her eyes settle on Aicha, and she scowls, her body language closing inwards in a way painfully reminiscent of the beggar boy we spoke to Franc through. The jealousy is clear, but she isn't about to challenge him on who the stunning North African woman is. She isn't prepared to open that can of worms, her desperate need for his approval painfully clear. Insecurity is a bitch.

I pull my gaze away and turn back to the Garonne. Sadly, I suspect I'll be seeing more of her on the Toulousain streets in the future. Maybe with eyes that flash freaky white to match her boyfriend's. The couple that gets possessed together nests together. Or something along those lines.

Approaching the Pont Jumeaux, my stride falters. My walking becomes more stilted, less rhythmic — jerking, scratching steps that make me wrap my arms around myself, hugging my T-shirt to my chest. My head drops, and my shoulders hunch. In my mind, I am back in the opiate haze —or back for the first time after in a new body— but with my same old fucked-up mind screaming for the poppy's release all over again. The need for escape, for temporary oblivion, the need to flee the here and now. I shudder, and the motion becomes a feedback loop, amplifying itself as we walk until my teeth are chattering so hard in my head it feels like someone has wired my jaw to a jackhammer.

Aicha studies me throughout. She knows when I reach my most pitiable state and lays her hand on my shoulder. 'We're here, *saabi*. You can come back now.'

I drop the city-sigil magic I've been laying out since we set out from the shit wizard's old abode. Sympathetic magic woven through the streets to bring me to Franc means working myself into the same state as one of his people. The memories are still plenty fresh of how that feels. Lucky me.

Looks like it's turned out to be unnecessary because Franc's been honest with us as to where he is. Doesn't mean I trust the slimy fishfucker. I'm still far from sure he hasn't betrayed me, setting me up by directing my attention towards that petri dish of a house. I'll trust my magic over his word every day of the week.

The curving height of the wall creates the illusion of being right next to the swirling waters. A look over the edge gives the lie to that. Rungs lead downwards like giant staples buried into the concrete. I swing a leg over and clamber down to the real bank of the river. A small abandoned path overgrown with brambles and strewn with glass shards from long-dropped bottles keeps its more modern, more commonly used walkway companion up above company.

Light streams overhead, hitting the Pont Jumeaux's metal frame. It forms a shadow-bridge, extending from the opposite bank almost to our feet, a pathway for dark business and night-time dealings that translocate into early morning. Where it touches our side of the bank, a large pale hand covered in tight black curling hair reaches up out of the water towards us. Another appears, perpendicular to the water's edge, along with an arm as thick as my leg. A black coat swaddles it, an elbow the same translucent white as the hand poking through the frayed fabric. Then Franc heaves himself out of the water to stand before us.

Franc is powerful in all senses of the word. He's also ugly as sin, inside and out. He towers over me, well over two metres tall and equally broad. His black Cordovan hat is battered, its brim only allowing a peek of the thin white band circling its cake-like crown. Knot-tangled locks stream out wildly underneath. His coat billows, a badly patched tent of black reaching to knees the size of hydrant bonnets. Just as worn out are his trousers. Black boots poke from the ragged hems, nondescript except for their bulk, which seems to demand they are a custom job. He is easily a size twenty if I had to take part in some weird "guess the size of the monster's feet" competition.

His face is swollen and bulbous, his nose a stained wreck cratered with acne scars. His ruined proboscis and bushy eyebrows seem to have come to some sort of arrangement, teaming up to hide his eyes, at least partially. The rest of his skin would reduce the most confident of dermatologists to a quivering wreck, and his grin reveals a dentistry emergency. Broken rotten teeth line skinny lips so leached of colour they have turned a diseased mint-green sheen.

There is something of that shade to his colour generally — the same one fish gain by living far below depths frequented by man, where the sun's touch dies away and pigmentation is an unnecessary eccentricity. I often feel like he is kin to those creatures — ancient, and with no love for those who live in the light. He is of the shadows and the hidden depths.

Then there is his power. For those who are *talented*, looking at Franc even without *looking* will reveal snatches of the creature behind the veil, a momentary view of a nightmare manufactured in the corner of their eye by an overactive imagination. Briefly, the broken teeth will sharpen to points, the back of hairy hands will become more like furred scales, and vague webbing will snatch at one's attention as he gestures.

The cloak's wafting movements aren't in sync with the air currents, seemingly suspended, floating around him. His hair moves similarly, and those knots in the tangled mass appear, for an instant, more like air sacs embedded in waving kelp strands than unkempt hair.

The eggshell eyes are the same ones that pop into the faces of those he possesses, but he isn't blind. He just thinks things like ambient light and pupils are unnecessary luxuries, I guess.

Aicha and I have discussed Franc's origins many times. General consensus is he must be the offspring of a troll and a naiad. Contemplating the logistics of such a coupling makes me want to hit myself repeatedly in the eyes with a clawhammer; I wonder how much of a role love — or even consent played in that particular coupling. Little would be my guess, based on his personality and preferences.

Isaac believes Franc to be a naiad that is a relative of the Mourioche —
or the kelpie, as they're known throughout the Gaelic world. I've not seen
him in equine shape or in any guise other than the one standing in front
of me. I don't believe he has revealed even half his secrets during the time
I've known him, so anything is possible. It isn't like we head to the pub to
sink a few pints together. We only meet up when I have no other choice.

Franc leers down at us, his broken teeth nauseatingly stained columns
standing out against the blackness of his gullet.

'Well met, prettyman. The swordling too. Though I think I sense mis-
tastings of my aroma, yes? Did the midge winged sting harder than your
mightiness was expecting then, lordling?'

I swear there's a gleam in his eye, but Franc has his own particular (and
very annoying) turn of phrases. There isn't enough there for me to be
sure he's betrayed me. Aicha clearly doesn't feel the same way. In a swift
movement, she pulls her longest knife and, within an eye blink, has it
pressed against the creature's throat. I draw my sword an instant later,
crackling green *talent* edging wrapping round the razor-sharp blade.

Franc expands — trickles of power cracking through his disguise before
threatening to flood out, a hammer-blow of an aura all around him as a
huge cutlass springs to his hand. It is rust-stained, as though it has slept
at the bottom of the sea in a sunken pirate ship for eons untold. The
monster underneath peeks through properly, a creature that will send most
screaming and weeping to the asylum, their minds shredded by the sight.

'Is it today then, my beloveds, is it? The day when we're trialling and
testing, the breakery of compact expanding, eh? Will we make our blades
to sing their carols, little endless one, and see what tra-la-la-laaing they can
bring? Honourless, it makes you, but I'll stand true-form and open-paged
if this is the moment in which we slip ourselves into, eh? What insult is

your doings to honesty-me, ill-wounded by such active disgustings. Poor I, poor I, is it not?'

Aicha doesn't blink throughout this, action-readied, but my eyes are on the blade. It radiates power like a suddenly uncloaked lantern in the pitch black of a starless night. I feel I understand some of Franc's phrasing, for it seems to sing a song of misery and death and a desire to drink deep of both. Aicha will not move, will not hesitate, but I fear what effect that weapon might have even against one such as her. All forces have an equal opposite, and the Water of Life she drank to gain her immortality so many centuries ago might yet not succeed against a sword soaked in liquid baptised death.

'Did you set me up, Franc?' I ask, direct and to the point.

There is a slight widening of those full-moon globes. Not much but enough for me to know. It wasn't him. 'Set you up, manling? No, no. Here is my shimmery metal presence, my waterlogged siren-singer. If I comes for you, hop-hop-hopper or your fine febrile thrown-up matter-bricker, so quick to re be, you'll know that the night is a-calling and ready for the midnight jiggery. Meantimings' —his blade vanishes, and he shrinks back down to his normal form— 'I'm this shelled shaping that greets you with a hungriness to be knowing the mismoving that led to such assumptivities.'

I move forward to rest my hand on Aicha's shoulder till she steps back, the knife vanishing sheath-wards. Her hands are empty but no less ready.

I contemplate what to say, how much to give this untrustworthy ally, formed of necessity. 'The mage you pointed me towards had angelic runes light years beyond his capacity coating his workspace. He was working for someone else, someone many leagues more powerful, but it was only this poor fool who caught your attention?'

Franc goes dead-still, motionless. I know that much of how he presents himself is part of his method for disarming us. He plays the fool for the court, using his japery to seem less than he is even when raised to anger.

Now there is no playing. He is an apex predator, and he is unhappy with something, calculating and dissecting the information I shared.

'Monitored that homely hole for moons and suns with mine-own, I did.' He growls softly. 'My knowings that I give gifts of always are true. Knew he wasn't much but still my little back-head me was so insisting "yes yes" that I did keep the watchings through shadow and eye-blind. No indictery in the to-fros, no. Just tinier than tiny little sadness flesh-wearer that I served up as easy devourings for your fine lordlings. Don't like to be missing these bobs, brittle bits, motes of import, no. Some chattery and word shovelling will be the next step-two-three that I'll be whirly gigging through my boys.'

'So you've no idea who he was working for or why then?' I demand, pushing further. I am mostly convinced, but I have zero confidence in Franc to give me a straight answer, and I want to know if there is anything he is keeping from me.

'Nothingness,' he hisses through clenched teeth. 'No whispering winds into the earlugs of my congregate nor lighting of the beacons by such weavings of *talent* rubbing their backs as they caper. Hidden — from my knowing!'

The frustration turns to anger, and I don't want to be those of his flock who were on observational duty of the shit wizard in the run up to our encounter.

'No hurting them though, Franc,' I warn the looming mass, my sword feeling like a mouse showing its claws as it weaves around an owl's talons. 'The deal remains in force; the strictures are unchanged.'

Franc smiles — skin-splitting, ear-wide, and overly full. 'Hurt my little charges, my brightling knight-lord? No, never. As we did agree, all promiseries and pactings long past.'

'You kick them when they're down, and strangle them with the lead you put around their neck. I don't doubt you do the same to their mongrel dogs. Probably eat them too.' Aicha's visceral distaste hangs in the air, an unspoken insult, the unwanted guest at the party who can't keep from the centre of attention.

Franc's eyes narrow to craggy, encrusted slits, and he leans forward with his entire presence, bearing down on the woman in front, who does not bend or yield. 'I like... dogs,' he hisses venomously, his manner mirroring hers but with the weight of his incomparable size and power packed behind it. 'Never eat a dog, little dusk born and walking. Like them more than the sun drinkers, more than the endless skip and jumper you strolls in comrade arms along with.'

Then he leans back, the smile becoming somehow transformed, the threat dissipating. A genuine jollity forms in his creased features. 'You, though, brave as butterflies on the maiden meadow flit, ey? Not fear-lacking, no, not the stupid, empty headery of the wanton heroic, eh? Knows your fears, don't you? Sleeps with their embrace and walk arm-in-arm even more closer than your long-living adjacentry. Still, don't be shrinking back from old Franc even when the happy-friendly goes to the drink and the horror comes a-calling. Real plucky. Pluck-plucking the strings, ready to start our singsong duetting, isn't you? You —' His smile splits wider still, his jaw seeming to dislocate like a giant serpent ready to swallow his traumatised prey whole. 'You, I likes, little danger-blade. I'd dance the notes we struck and see their tremoring reflecting ripple-mirror in the earth's back and forthery.'

He tears his attention away from the somewhat stunned warrior next to me and, sweeping his hat from his head, offers an elegant deep bow towards me. 'I will bid my leavings, the best to be bettered then. The peekings in cavities inside pretty hair mops. With only my wordings,' he adds hastily, seeing my expression change. 'Maybe a little look-see-hear with my powerings but no pain, no marks of comings and goings. My word, Cathar-once, my word and my power upon it.'

He straightens himself, placing his hat on his unkempt, tangled mane and tugging it tight to the rear, then taps the front brim in acknowledgement. Turning, he heads in lumbering, half-dragging steps back towards the bridge. A drainage tunnel taller than a man but still forcing him to bend almost double is his destination. An echoing tuneless whistle of 'Tant m'abelis', a song of my childhood, rebounds back as he disappears, fading away as he merges into the darkness.

I put away my blade, releasing the *talent* I powered it with, a relieved lessening of the tension I've been carrying, knot-points in my shoulders slowly unclenching. I turn to Aicha. 'I think you've made a friend.'

She is still trying to look as stoic as ever, but in her eyes there's just the tiniest flicker of panic. 'What was that last part all about?' she demands.

'A good question. He either wants to fight you or fuck you, would be my read. Either way, he reckons it'll make the earth shake. Nice to have options, I guess.' The panic sparks light bigger. I defuse it before it blows, slapping her on the shoulder. 'Don't worry about it. You'll never fight him alone, and I'll gut him before I let him insult your honour in any other way — if you don't do it first!'

CHAPTER THIRTEEN

TOULOUSE, 8 MARCH, PRESENT DAY

The frustration is mounting. Mysterious forces threatening me in my own city, Franc knowing nothing... I really hope Isaac's got some answers for us.

We pull off the Route De Levignac onto the branch-sheltered dirt track running the edge of the Forest of Bouconne that leads up to Isaac's home. Isaac and Nithael prefer to keep their own company in their ancient farmhouse, surrounded by their libraries of priceless manuscripts and magical tomes. Considering how fucking irritating most people are, I can't fault that decision even though I prefer to remain in the hustle and bustle of the city itself.

Nineteenth-century palatial stylings define the outside of their home, once all the rage among the landed community of the southwest. When they built it, Isaac and Nithael mixed the Maison-Toulou-saine-style fine-pink bricks with features pinched from nearby chateaus. The bright-blue wooden shutters are gaieties, bringing some relief to the pompous grandeur elsewhere. Actual crenellations run along the rooftop, and its tower seems purpose-built for defending archers. I suspect Isaac uses it for stargazing. With a quick knock to be polite, I open the door, knowing that the only locks he needs will always recognise and welcome us in.

I walk into the outdated but welcoming farm-style kitchen — all light woods and individually painted flowered tiles. The space is untidy, a natural bachelor pad but not dirty. Isaac won't abide by it, not with so many precious documents and last remnants of near-extinct teachings contained within. Through the door at the back, I can see the main library — not to be confused with the secondary library, the research space (which contains more books than most University facilities) or, in fact, any available surface or shelf that can be stocked with grimoires, texts, and treatises. The kitchen table, a light beech marked by the wear of time, is covered in strange multi-coloured stains not caused by cooking, except in the Walter White alchemical sense.

Hubert, a short-toed eagle and regular visitor, rustles his feathers on a rafter above the countertop. His curving beak sits under yellow eyes that show a constantly snickering smile. His white underbelly peeks through the pleated brown of his folded wings. Isaac leaves a high round window ajar when it's not too cold for Hubert to come and go as he wishes. He peers haughtily down at me, disapprovingly. As I hold his gaze, I wonder, not for the first time, if the short-toed eagle can *see*. He seems to take great delight in making diving runs through the space above Isaac at Nithael even though the angel isn't visible to those without *sight*. The ballsiness of the eagle wanting to rumble with an angel always makes me want to applaud him each time he tries.

Striding into the cosy attached to the kitchen, we find Isaac sprawled in a high-backed armchair, a book of cryptic crosswords in hand, a pen balanced precariously across his right forefinger, which is gripped round his coffee cup. He starts guiltily before gazing plaintively up at me.

I feel like I've already done more than my daily quota of sighing at this point. 'Laser-like focus, Isaac,' I huff.

'Of course, lad, of course. Nothing but. Just felt like I'd started turning cognitive circles, couldn't get out of the mental feedback loop. Needed a momentary discharge before firing back at it. Fighting fit.' He beams up at me. I find it impossible to stay mad at him however much I occasionally want to clap him round the back of the head.

'So how did it go with the aquatic toerag, my boy?' Isaac offers an apologetic grin to go with the obvious subject change.

Wincing, I ease myself into a matching chair opposite him as Aicha browses the jumbled and over-stacked bookshelf behind us. This body is still adjusting to the high demands that both I and my *talent* put on it. 'Well, he wasn't in on it and knew nothing. That's all I've got. Oh, and he seems to have a crush on our erstwhile colleague over there.'

Aicha quits browsing and fixes me with a *look* that, while not magical, certainly hits just as hard. My wide-eyed innocent expression lasts about ten seconds before both Isaac and I dissolve into cackling fits. She dismisses us like a worn-down parent of unruly, hyperactive spawn and returns to the better quality of conversation found in book spines.

As we compose ourselves, I ask Isaac what progress he's made. His humour evaporates, frustration taking its place. 'None of any note, lad, sorry to say. The problem is that we're off into realms of the theoretical, where we can imagine an equation, but we miss too many of the elements to reach a conclusion. There are two parts upon which it hinges — first, we need a spell sufficiently powerful enough to capture Nanael or separate him from Jakob. Nithael and I believe our bond powers Nithael's force in this dimension, so if something pulled Nanael and Jakob apart, then perhaps it would have weakened Nanael sufficiently enough to force them to be pliant. But that's only supposition. Second, you need a person or persons capable of wielding the spell or with innate natural abilities that make the task possible. Of the second group, there are a few known plausible options. The Sistren of Bordeaux, if they work as a unified unit, might manage it were the magical groundwork already laid.'

The Sistren. My nearest neighbours, both in terms of geography and *talent*. Run by the Mother, they verge on a religious order, structured around a very definite matriarchy. Not a group I want to tangle with if I can avoid it.

'But I don't believe they would have the finesse for the spell work needed to accompany the brute force,' he continues. 'Particularly because I think you'll need a powerful Kabbalah wielder to be involved, considering you'll need to rupture an integral part of Jakob and Nanael's co-existence.'

'Could someone be trying to replicate your experiments?' I don't want to say it, but my thoughts turn to the possibility of another angel-bearer. Just because the two we've met have been righteous —albeit a bit extreme in their 'hands-off' policy— doesn't mean all those of the higher dimensions are the same. The directions up and down the dimensional ladder are just vibrational differences. While it's hard to believe anyone who made the transition to pure thought and energy, necessary to house an angel, could be petty or vindictive, it's not impossible.

'What if it's an enemy of Nith or Nan? Come down here looking for them?' Aicha's clearly following the same train of thought.

Isaac tuts. 'Not that, lass. They assure me the other Bene Elohim aren't interested in what goes on down here in the slightest as long as it doesn't affect them. Nor anyone who wishes them harm. As for replicating our work, I didn't hear any explosions loud enough to rival Hiroshima, did you? Believe you me, even when we tried, before we used our own bodies, everything we put the Enochian runes onto went boom bloody quickly.'

Aicha arches an eyebrow. 'So tattooing yourself and making yourself the potential explode-y vessel was the next logical step, was it?'

'Don't be ridiculous, lass!' Isaac's indignant look crumbles into a sheepish grin. 'I couldn't tattoo myself. That would have been entirely implausible. I did Jak's ink, and he did mine.'

Aicha snorts. 'Big difference.'

I decide it's worth qualifying his answer, not least because it will turn his currently pinkish blush into a far more satisfyingly deep shade. 'What he isn't mentioning is the people who tried to imitate them. Three of his students did Human Torch impressions when they tried to combine scarification with the names of the Malakhim —'

'Two, lad! Only two.'

'Sorry, *only* two powerful Kabbalists self-immolated. My bad. Then there was the fella who thought he'd try to hold Yahweh himself...'

Isaac's glum expression deepens. 'Blew up his entire house. Several neighbouring houses too. Left a crater six metres deep and ten across after tattooing the first letter of God's secret name. Bloody arrogant fool.'

'And then there was the guy who dabbled with the Dark Side and wrote the name of a shedim on his forehead. Ended up eating his own arm up to the elbow before embedding the resultant bone shards into his own brain.'

'Yes, look, I think she gets the idea, lad. We got very lucky.'

I shake my head. 'It wasn't just luck, although that played a major part. The two of you are just another weight class of *talent* compared to everyone else. Considering you and Jakob invented Kabbalah, it's not that surprising.'

Isaac nods, then looks over at Aicha. 'Maybe I deserved the title of Isaac the Blind. A lot of people paid for trying to replicate our studies. Anyway, the Hachmei Provence —and we were the leading Jewish authority at the time — made it officially haram to try any such experiment ever again. We destroyed our research, and the punishments for attempting to replicate it have always been bloody severe.'

Musing over the magical tradition and what I've learned about it under his tutelage, my thoughts turn to the legendary Golem of Prague. That was the last time we heard sight or sound of Jakob — him aiding the Rabbi Leow with his creation designed to protect the Jewish ghettoes of Prague. Thinking about that, about how the Kabbalist magic was used to power their creation, causes an idea to crystalise, something that's been scratching away at the back of my mind. The Golem was powered by the magic word written on its forehead, making it both its strength and its weakness. The Kabbalah inscription of Truth (which gives it life) becomes Death if you erase one letter. Doing so would stop the living automaton in its tracks. *What if someone did that on Jakob?*

'Isaac,' I ask slowly, trying to map out the possibilities. 'Could they somehow have erased the inscription on Jakob? Or altered the lettering? Tattooed a prison over it?'

'Impossible. The tattoos are only the primary guidance to mark the path for the Elohim to join us. Once they remained, we became entangled. Those letters now are meaningless, as is the name contained within them. Our duality is now another being altogether. To efface or write over them will have no effect.'

It's strange to hear it that way. I always think of them as two separate entities, with Nith being a hitchhiker Isaac picked up along life's highway. That makes them sound more like one new being, integrally combined. It makes me uncomfortable for reasons I can't explain.

'Okay, so what have we got? We know we're dealing with a person or people of power, including an Enochian expert who has potentially managed to split Nanael and Jakob.' I come back to my original question. 'Could they have bonded with an angel of their own?'

Isaac gives it due consideration but looks doubtful. 'Nithael has always insisted that should any other Elohim descend to our plane, they will know instantly. However, if someone *has* obscured themselves from their sight and we have another force at large arrayed against us, then we're dealing with potentially world-breaking events.'

Silence reigns, a bleak, heavy, foreboding moment as Isaac and I look at each other, the weight of that weighing down on us heavily.

'So... he, she, or they are Thanos, and we're the Avengers. Got it,' Aicha says with a bored tone from behind us. The Good God bless her, it breaks the tension perfectly.

'Does that make you Black Widow?' I ask her, my grin mirrored on Isaac's face.

She answers me in the same tone, not bothering to turn around. 'Do I look fucking useless, dickhead? The answer you're looking for, if you don't fancy a ventriloquist gargle around your testicles when I've lodged them in the back of your throat, is, "No, Aicha, you certainly don't."'

I mouth, 'Ooooooooh!' at Isaac, and she gives me a double middle finger salute over her shoulders.

I consider our options, my chin resting on spread hands. 'What about the saint's hankie, Isaac?' The whole situation makes zero sense. Trying to understand where the artefact the Phone Dick wants might be seems our only way into the mystery.

'The Vernicle, as you well know, lad. As I said, it disappeared from the Vatican during one of the intermittent evictions of the Pope by the populace, lost in the Sack of Rome in 1527. I've reached out to my contacts in the modern Catholic Church, and they believe Spanish soldiers took it across the Alps, heading home presumably to dedicate the relic to one of their own cathedrals. They certainly made the crossing into France, and I've traced reports of their passing through Marseille, where they rested on their way towards the Languedoc to cross the Pyrenees.' He exhales heavily, his eyebrows twitching. 'Then I lost the trail. Our unknown enemy is not entirely foolish to look for it here though. There's something else we need to discuss, Paul.'

I can see his nervousness. In any other man, I'd call it fear, but Isaac isn't scared. He is justifiably worried. Prickles form on my skin, those little goosebumps when your body starts responding to hormones, almost before you know they're there. Whatever he's about to say, it's making my fight-or-flight system fire up. This can't be good.

'It's believed the Vernicle can raise the dead. If this caster is so inclined, can you imagine the hell he could wreak with an army of undead and the power of an angel? With Nanael's wings shielding them, I wouldn't rely overmuch on a nuclear strike defeating them. I wasn't exaggerating when I said this could be world-ending.'

I nod grimly. 'We can't possibly hand over anything that might contain that kind of power. Simultaneously, we can't just ignore it. He may have others searching for it as we speak. I doubt the shit wizard was his only pawn in play.'

'Agreed. He knows plenty about us, down to details he shouldn't have unless he truly has control of Nan. So he'll be expecting our double-cross at the first opportunity and planning against it.'

I notice he refers to Nanael each time and never to his lost brother. The agony of even the tiniest possibility of reuniting must be terrible — especially knowing neither Jakob nor Nanael would ever serve someone like Phone Dick willingly.

He taps his crossword puzzle. 'And thus why I found myself turning in circles and getting overloaded and why I took a break. So now that we're at the same point and all caught up on each other's actions and escapades, what now, lad?'

Posing my head back on my hands, I gaze at the peeling line of wallpaper poking out from behind the shelves. Some time passes in this meditative position before we both flinch at a cough from Aicha.

'Maybe the river letch knows something about where the veil went? Could it have come through Toulouse?'

I shake my head. 'I was here from the end of the sixteenth century, most of the seventeenth on and off, and part of the eighteenth. He wasn't here before the nineteenth century, else he'd have shown up on my radar long before.'

'Right, but maybe he saw this group of knights or heard something about them prior to moving here. Where was he before Toulouse?'

I look at Isaac, who shoots the same blank regard back. 'I... have no idea,' I stammer.

The disbelieving glare that meets me is as well merited as it is painful. 'You're telling me you've been preparing for the possibility of an all-out war with an insanely powerful being since the 1800s, and you never thought to research where he came from?'

My second response is as debonair as my first. 'Um, no?'

Isaac rides in heroically to pour petrol on my burning building. 'How on earth would we manage that? Ask him?'

'Yes!' Aicha slaps her forehead. 'Jeez, how did either of you even wipe your fucking arses before I turned up?' We sit there, our gazes down-turned, mumbling half-excuses and apologies. I can fully under-stand why her fellow countrymen saw her as an angry djinn; her wrathful scorn is hard to bear.

'So neither of you two muppets ever thought to just ask him? Isn't part of your agreement that he has to share information that allows you to protect Toulouse? Ask him where he was before. At the same time ask if he was in the area when those knights were passing through and if he knows where they went or, even better, what fucking happened to them. If he knows, he's got to tell you. Terms of the agreement.'

I look over at Isaac, who's scratching the back of his neck, which has gone a delightful shade of pink. I'd love to tease him for it... if I didn't suspect my own face was a similar colour right now.

'That... makes sense?' I can't help the question in my tone. Aicha can though.

'Of course it does. I said it. Dickhead.' At this moment, I can't really argue with that.

Isaac shrugs, then he nods, looking distinctly chastened. 'You're quite right, lass. We're both dunderheads, and you're far smarter than both of us.'

'Obviously. Duh.' I can hear the eye-roll, but there's a warmth to her voice too. Even Aicha appreciates praise from Isaac.

'Right. You two go deal with that. I'll carry on researching, see what I can dig up.'

I nod my head at the crossword book and pencil. 'Researching?'

He frowns back and waves an expansive hand at the piles of books and papers surrounding him. 'Research, lad. Research.'

I give him a fleeting grin, but I'm less than pleased even though we have a direction to move forwards in. And it's not because Aicha's out-thought us. Not just that, anyhow. Nope, it's that niggling, building frustration because now we have to head back to Toulouse and track down Franc all over again. It's like forgetting your house-keys and having to go pick them up off your flat-mate.

Only where the flat-mate is a giant emotion-eating river monster who you'd rather poke yourself in the eye repeatedly than talk to, ever.

Fun times ahead.

CHAPTER FOURTEEN

TOULOUSE, 8 MARCH, PRESENT DAY

More inclined to pull out my own incisors with needle-nose pliers than decipher Franc's bullshit twice in one day.

We park the Alpine and cut southward down the Avenue Honoré Serres towards Place Arnaud Bernard. The square is bustling, a last bastion against gentrification as it pushes the poor and paperless further out into the banlieues. A group of four Algerians, balanced on that tipping point of late-middle age before the scales pulls downward, drink Turkish coffee on the terrace of a small café-cum-kebab shop and argue about the weekend's football game.

The area still throngs with a lively community of immigrants and independent businesses, veined with stalwarts who love the vibrant quarter and refuse to ever leave. It extends only a couple of winding blocks in any direction and quickly cedes southward to the gentle encroachment of bourgeoise wine bars and haute cuisine burgers. The place still stands as a living monument to inner-city inclusion. It isn't the safest part of Toulouse for many, but for the sort I'm seeking, they'll feel more protected resting here than almost anywhere else; all the unwanted and unloved are still welcome here.

Balancing on the edge of the low wall surrounding the underground car park entrance dominating the open space is a man with trembling digits struggling with a cigarette paper. His bedraggled facial hair is more the colour of coffee crema than its original white, stained by nicotine and a lifetime in doorways. Each tucked line of skin forming the origami of his face is indented by a moment of suffering, carving him like a withered pumpkin. Grime accrued from a life beyond hard has muted his clothes, once nondescript frippery, the riotous clash of colours obscured by dirt and stains.

I draw in a little *talent*, ready to contact Franc, but he beats me to the draw. The old man's eyes snap up, their radiant albumen the first time they've likely brightened in a long time. Franc's unearthly grimace bullies aside the weighty folds of the man's wrinkles.

'A swifting of your moments if it does you please, my little lordling. I'd be wanting to partakery in the wagging of chins, to summarise our understandings under the skies that darken over, eh? And of course, all tideries and trillings to you, lady of the blade.'

He taps his brow at Aicha, who deliberately turns her head aside and spits. Doesn't seem to bother the bastard, but she's making herself clear. The old man is lower than me, so I crouch, positioning myself at the same height as the skin Franc's currently wearing.

'Great minds clearly think alike, Franc. I was just looking for you.'

The smile that spreads across the old man's face could hang around in dream bars, scaring the shit out of nightmares. Still, there is something else there too. Another emotion in his expression. If I didn't know better, I'd say I could see fear in Franc's pupil-less eyes. 'Greatly indeed, little one —

more of likenesses and mirrorings than many might glean in that glimmer glimmer, is there not?'

My face sets into a granite block, distaste carved in by a master sculptor. 'We are at peace, but we are not the same, Franc. Not by any stretch of the imagination.'

'Oh indeed, carrion-wearer, is that the truth the crow does caw into the one-eyed ear? Certitudes so strongly in-and-outed, weavings not wavering, ey, though dead and deadly every time? No mattering. Let your truth be your mohair wearing plaything that sees you through your own darkling schemings. No, no kinry claimed, no insult offered by the ghastly brute do-derring in his sporting of another's flesh. Rest eased in our divisive and dividedness, my good man.'

My patience is wearing out quicker than cheap shoes on a forced march. 'Enough pleasantries, Franc. What have you found out?'

The joviality and banter disappear, and the furious anger tinged with whatever it is I saw in him earlier comes to the surface. The monster peers from that face directly into mine.

'Some conferencing have I done — demanded they perform the coran-to quick-step, one-two one-two, to meet with old Franc for my as-sessery of their states and statementing.' It is his turn to display distaste, bug-mouthed and puckered. 'There was woven filthy grimmery glamour upon their hides a-hiding, all luminescent and inscribed with the tracery of the hallowed and haloed. Nauseous, it made poor I with its stenches. To hide the truth from the eyes of my own brought out such feelings as would make the up-puffed dovey croak when I did munch upon his holy bones.'

Franc's tenses are a mess at the best of times. I scratch my head. 'Are you saying you caught the one who did it? And ate him?'

Franc guffaws, a reverberating belly laugh that echoes round the square, bringing looks, although our natural glamours keep our uncanny natures concealed.

He paws at the face he wears lovingly while he speaks, his gaze almost ecstatic. It turns my stomach. 'Oh, my little lordling, so honouring in your confidence in I, to think that after such confrontery, you find me in my reposings all la-di-dah and thank 'ee kindly. No, find his radiancy I could not, only his sickening traces upon my pretty boys and girls I'd sent a-looking and a-seeing. Killed them, he did. Unmaking them with magicry and murderings. He left them, just outside your precious bounderings, all protections promised sliced and severed without my knowing!'

My stomach feels hollow, gripped with dread. Franc connects himself to his people. It shouldn't have been possible to hurt them without him realising.

He carries on, 'Notes was left, all scritchered and scratchings onto their poor hidery, skin-cut letterings. 'Twas a payment for my observings of his little wizardling and for my words given back to you.'

I don't need more details. Cutting threatening notes into the murdered corpses of young men and women matches perfectly with the impression I've gathered of the sick bastard so far. 'I'm on it, Franc. I'm going to find him and make him pay for what he's done.'

He sneers, a lip corner lifting unnaturally on the decrepit face, pulling the whole right side up almost to below the eye. His self-control is slipping, and he is manifesting more fully. 'All pretty wordlings. As pretty as the bright one's feathers, no doubt. No help, though, to my lovelies, is it? No safety or succourings to them as they tiptoe through darkened streets, upon my oath. So 'tis the last conversery we'll be makings until you does your duties and duelings, a-stopping the brightling bastard quick-sharp in his steps.'

I narrow my eyes at him. 'You're pulling back? Not prepared to help me any further? That was never part of the deal, Franc. Our agreement has always been information in exchange for peace.'

He hisses at me like a cornered snake coiled and ready to strike. I wonder for a moment if he is about to lunge at me. 'Our deal was protectering of me and mine own for my trutheries told! All my lovely lads and lasses do count in that bargaining struck long back, and that puffery dove or the jesses-holding falconer has been amongst my flockings like sharp-teethed wolves, and 'tis me and mine own does pay the pricings, is it not?'

Feeling him pulling back, about to leave, I step forward, urgency in my voice. 'Wait, Franc! I have a potential lead, but I'll need some information out of you to make anything of it. Where were you before Toulouse, Franc?'

He stays, which is something, though the hobo's borrowed eyes narrow sharply. 'Well now, my boyo, such a seekings you have never been before after. Makes my scales all prickery with sussings it does that quizzing questionary with ne'er a why wherefore.'

I harden my stance. 'Look, Franc, someone is threatening both our people and killing yours. This might give us the chance to keep them all safe. I'm telling you the information is relevant. Or is my oath of lesser worth than yours, Franc?'

He spreads his hands, a placating gesture undermined by his expression. 'No effrontery I offer against your goodly form, little lordling, no, no. Our bond is a tethering I honour all moments and manners aside. Up I came, first having come down, then followed current pulls towards the tastiness spread out upon the banqueting pick-crunch of many and all.'

'No time for riddles. Up and down and currents — you followed the Garonne? From the mountains or from Bordeaux?'

He hisses at the mention of Bordeaux. 'Never the seaward sides, goodling man, no. The sistren clink their cauldrons there, and no love have they for my vessels, no stormy port for the likes of I. No, up was where I came from, once down from companies among the eyrie neighbours. Followed the trickling torrentings 'til they became all the mightier, joining one to another. Long I was simply taking my opportunities willy-nilly at their juncture 'til your sufficient partings made entry under the weavings long-left by your comings a possibility, for tastings of the buffet of buffoonery such gatherings did give in our fine residence of now-and-then.'

I pull out my phone and study maps of the Garonne's path. Rivers and tributaries combine at various points, but the first major one after the descent out of the Pyrenees is at Montrejeau, where the Neste joins it. 'When did you come down from the mountains?'

'Immemoriality in momentaries, my fine one. Long before, early enough that I was witness to the bounties of the culling of the pesky stroll-abouts by the pestilent when the leech and bone saw wielders' buildings was packed sawdust to ceiling. I filled my gullet with its miserable delights for many a day, did I not?'

I think about this. The biggest outbreak of the plague was at the start of the sixteenth century, finishing before the soldiers passed through Occitanie. The question now is their final destination. If they were aiming for Barcelona or Girona or any of the southern coast, then they would've probably passed either by Foix or else Narbonne and Perpignan, far from Franc's observations. If they headed to Bilbao or Zaragoza or even Madrid, with a bit of luck, they might have crossed his path. Whether he noticed or cared is a different matter entirely.

'After the plague, did you notice a group of Spanish soldiers heading towards the route back to Spain?'

'Did I notice swordlings during the plague-gone days, li

When food-stuffs untended went to blight and ruin and ɩ

emptied excepting ringings of metal for the treasure laden aɴu giaɯ ɔɴɯɯ

ing tools reused by those who balanced on the rung-slip to my domain-
ry and services? Like noticing the clouds when the forked light does its
soil-tastery all around you. Harder the oblivious to be, no?'

I click my tongue in frustration. His answer is as justified as it is unhelp-
ful. 'These particular soldiers might have had a few German speakers in
their ranks. They carried a relic believed to cure illnesses, amongst other
powers.'

Franc begins what sounds like a gulping cluck. It makes me think of
a serpent choking back a rodent down its dark gullet. It takes me some
time to realise it is Franc's version of genuine, uncontrolled chuckling, the
freaky bastard.

'Oh, my lucky little one, chancy are your askings today. Lady-blessed
your questionings are in their twistings, oh yes. I have giftings to give
of them that are your wantery, my little doubtling, all answering and
revealings that might yet give you pointeries and directions. Those plated
fishes came a-dipping through my lakes and rivers, all broad of boastings,
all prancing horseback. They'd been pocket-lining with their magicry all
through their traipsings, all healed up healthy-like. Peacock struttery was
their ways of bobbing down the paths, but no gifts for my sparse under-
lings when hands was outstretching suppliants, upon my oath.

'So I sent them giftings unasked with a bitter biting sting. Sweet meats of
musings did my little ones drip-drop into their lugholes. Hidden treasures
of Castilian origins long lost, awaiting the clamouring claimings of such
noble lordlings as themselves below the barrow walls underhill.'

I parse his words through the Franc filter I've developed over a couple
hundred years. Eventually, the penny drops. I groan when I work out

here he sent them, and why no one has heard from them since. No one ever comes back from hunting in the tunnels under that village. 'You sent them off to Hastingues, didn't you? You sent them to Lou.'

Impossibly, the vividly disturbing, lip-spread smile vivisecting the old man's head seems to widen further. 'I did, my little lordling. I did indeed, did I not?'

CHAPTER FIFTEEN

TOULOUSE, 8 MARCH, PRESENT DAY

Distinctly fed up with the whole thing and in desperate need of a drink.

To say I'm feeling bleak after the conversation is like suggesting Wednesday Addams might have a penchant for the colour black. I need wiser heads than mine on the matter at hand. Phoning Isaac, I give him a rapid recap, and we agree to meet at L'Astronef for a drink.

We arrive a few minutes before Isaac is due. The roads diminish in size and activity as we leave the Peripherique for the relatively bustling Avenue de Rangueil before turning right into leafier, greener residential areas. Shared bushes and hedges force the typically unique houses to conform. It dresses them in a uniform identity, a verdant blazer worn to blend them with ash trees lining the road like an honour guard, guiding up towards the roundabout where L'Astronef stands in pride of place.

To live as long as I have can lead to a sense of disconnect from our origins, a loss of humanity if one is not careful — L'Astronef brings back that sense of association with my species and a pride in the best that we can be when we work as a unified force.

Intermingled trees and bushes screen L'Astronef, surrounding its entrance on two triangular sides. These lead to the entrance, the natural arrowing speaking of both its humble nature and integral connection to the community. Far more than a bar/restaurant, this locale is a pivotal point for the area's needy. It's all about connection and solidarity — the heart of modern French identity at its best, where the oft-uttered motto of Liberty, Equality, and Fraternity carries some weight and meaning. As well as providing upper-floor space for non-profit organisations tackling issues like housing and education, they run a library where mothers and children in difficult circumstances (whether financial or emotional) can read and enjoy a moment of peace in safety. During the day, they run workshops on art or yoga or social opportunities alongside a restaurant, and in the evening the bar is alive with a program of events. Their regular open mic covers a musical spectrum, running from traditional accordion players and classical violinists to rappers and heavy blues guitarists, all underpinned with jazz as the bass line. The profits made from the bar and restaurant all support the other associations or else supply free meals to those unable to pay to feed themselves for the plethora of reasons plaguing our modern world. If I'm going to get a drink, it's good to feel it's helping other people. And not just in the sense of reducing the likelihood I'm going to tear random strangers' heads off because I *really* need a beer.

When we arrive, I grab a pint with an accompanying homemade caramel rum shooter while Aicha settles for pineapple juice. We sit outside to enjoy the milder weather's benevolence, even as darkening skies give way to night's ascendency. This is the calm before the storm for us. There's a long trip ahead in the morning. A drive that might lead to us finding the knights or, at the very least, their trail. There's only one thing standing in our way, not counting Phone Dick.

Unfortunately, that one thing is Lou Carcoilh.

Isaac plonks himself into the nearest seat with his own pint. He taps the bottom of his glass against the metallic tabletop, rolling it round to hear the ring it creates. It's an unusually nervous gesture from a man I associate with always keeping cool, no matter the crisis. Mind you, the stakes are so much more personal this time.

He cuts straight to the chase. 'How solid a lead do you think this is from Franc? Could he be playing with us or trying to lead us astray?'

Aicha shakes her head, a small but certain movement. 'I despise that creature more than most, but I believe he was telling the truth.'

I shift in my seat. 'We'll not get anything more out of him now. He's in the wind till this is resolved, I reckon. We can't count on him watching our backs.'

Isaac steeples his fingers. 'Then I'll keep watch from here. If I can get Nith to supercharge the city's barriers, anything with Elohim origins should make them sing like a canary for us. If our Mystery Man tries to do something sneaky while you're away, we should know about it.' He leans forward. 'So the question then is...'

'What do we do with the Vernicle once we find it, and who in all of fuckery are we facing off with?'

'As ever succinct, if lacking in linguistic artistry, Paul. I don't feel at ease passing such a potentially powerful magical item over to someone who makes his minions choke on their own animated tongues. Doesn't scream of "impeccable and trustworthy character" as far as actions go.'

Aicha shrugs. 'So let's leave the thing where it is. If the prick behind all this sends people up against Lou, it means fewer people going up against us later on. Let's concentrate on finding the shithead. I'm sick of dancing along to his tune. I bet he's got shit taste in music, probably doing a version of 'Cotton Eyed Joe' on the fucking harp or something.' She pauses, considering. 'A techno remix of 'Cotton Eyed Joe' on the harp. The fiend.'

She sits back, satisfied with the strength of the imagery. I wish I could do the same. Sadly, there is a massive elephant in the room, and it really needs to be addressed.

'Isaac, I know this is your brother we're talking about, and I remember Jakob and Nanael both, but I think we should entertain the possibility that he isn't being held against his will.'

Isaac glances sharply upward, but any rebuke dies on his tongue as his gaze drops back to meet mine. There is no judgement in them. He sighs heavily. 'I cannot reconcile it with the man I was closer to than any other being ever, even Nith, but it has been a very, very long time and we are all capable of change. Many arrive at a state of Grace to fall under intentions well-shaped. In some ways, it would be the best possible solution.'

Aicha looks askance. 'In what way?'

'If Jakob and Nanael are behind this, that makes us evenly matched. If matters haven't changed dramatically over the intervening ages, I would even favour myself having the upper hand. Additionally, I can't believe Nanael would go along willingly, so if they've debased themselves, it would most likely affect their power. Mine and Nithael's willing and solid partnership would seem likely to have the advantage.

'In the alternative scenario, our adversary has proven capable of subjugating them and seems unconcerned by our awareness of the same. That seems to warrant their confidence in their abilities. Did the man seem foolhardy or arrogant to you, Paul?'

I pick up my drink and take a long, much needed slug. 'Dangerous, efficient, yes, but arrogant? More self-assured and with good reason, is my read.'

'I agree,' Isaac says grim-faced. 'If he works for Jakob, then my brother is utterly lost to us. If he's captured the pair, he is a force beyond reckoning. I see no good solution to this Gordian knot.'

Aicha slams down her glass, the effect only slightly undermined by the spray of sticky juice instead of liquor. 'If the problem is Gordian, then we treat it exactly the same way.'

'Slice it in half?' I reply doubtfully.

'Come at it directly and, if needs be, with a bit of the old ultra-violence. Sitting on our arses doing nothing isn't a choice, right? So we go along for now and look for the opportunity to feed him his own liver served on a bed of his intestines and seasoned with a reduction of his own stomach juices.'

'You missed your calling as a chef, *laguna*. A cannibal chef but a chef nonetheless.'

'Did I miss it? I've lived a long time, *saabi*. Fitted a lot into all those lifetimes. Anyhow, am I right or what?'

I nod reluctantly. There is as much sense in what she is saying as anything I can contribute, and we've exhausted all the other options, at least for the time being.

'So we ride out tomorrow for Hastingues and persuade Lou by hook or by crook to give up the veil if he has it. Then we pull a bait and switch on Phone Dick that gets us up in his grill without him getting his hands on the Vernicle. Isaac, once you've strengthened the wards, will you join us?'

Isaac rubs his knuckles pensively. 'There's still a few avenues I'd like to explore regarding seeking potential information on both the Veil and this...' He presses his lips together. 'Phone Dick — my goodness boy, you're not getting any more eloquent with age, are you? I haven't exhausted my resources, but I am scraping the barrel somewhat. My old friend I mentioned in the Vatican is searching for any further scripture about the powers, real or rumoured, of the relic. I'd feel much happier having that information before we find it. I assume you'll be heading off first thing?'

Aicha nods when I look back over at her. 'It's a fair old drive, and I want to make sure we get there while there's still morning to spare. It's been a long time since I was last over that way, and I'd rather get in and out that day if possible.'

'Plus,' I add, 'it's far too close for comfort to Lourdes. *Nobody* wants to stay that close to Lourdes for longer than they absolutely have to.'

A heavy silence settles over us like an oppressive weight. Lourdes —and its Lady— are the stuff of Talented nightmares, the thing that scares the creatures that go bump in the night.

Isaac breaks the pressure with a cough, bringing us back to the moment, although it doesn't shake the strange, uneasy feeling that's started building in my stomach. Then he raises his glass in our direction. 'I shall join you there once I've secured the wards and completed all my enquiries around mid-morning. I should be only a few hours behind you. Assuming success in finding our lost marvel, we can decide how best to approach its delivery or otherwise to the aforementioned Phone Penis.'

I lean forward and whisper conspiratorially to Isaac. 'Saying, "Dick" won't hurt you Isaac; the Dick holds no power over you. Be free from its evil influence.'

'How have you lived for over eight hundred years, and yet still have the mental age of a six year old, Paul?'

Before either of us can respond, I realise why I've been feeling so uneasy. The wards around the city have been crossed. We're close enough to the edge of Toulouse that me realising happens simultaneously with three cars screeching to a halt, pulling up onto the pavement on the other side of the hedges. I can feel the creatures who are in the car, and I don't know whether to laugh or just blow them all up instantly.

Werewolves aren't welcome in Toulouse —too much aggressive alpha posturing and macho bullshit for my likes— and they know it. I should have felt them the moment they came over the boundary lines. To stay undetected for the few minutes it took them to arrive? They must have had help. And I'm willing to bet I can guess who from.

Fourteen lycanthropes spill out of the three vehicles, about the maximum size a pack can be without them being so utterly annoying that they start killing each other. A man-mountain steps forward, clearly their leader. He has the air of a steroid-abusing gym head who has swapped his dick for man boobs. I'd lay money he thinks the long black bushy sideburns give him a Wolverine air, but combined with his excessive body hair, they just make him look like an Elvis-impersonating Sasquatch. The rest of his crew all share a similar body morphology; the shift back and forth between man and wolf is the best workout any gym-head influencer could ever imagine.

The crew still manages to look cowed. I don't doubt for a minute that their chief is an alpha-hole — it comes with the territory of being a pack leader. He looks thrilled to live up to every stereotype of "over-compensating wanker". I bet he has an All-Lives-Matter tattoo somewhere too.

'Are you Paul Bonhomme?' His attempt to intimidate me —pushing his shoulders back, his lip curling up to reveal a hint of a fang, his muscles bunching and popping out all over the place— might have been impressive if he wasn't a fucking werewolf. These guys are the cockroaches of the magical world. It's easy enough to squash them, but there are just so many of them.

I look around as if confused as Aicha throws up a *don't look here* spell around the whole area, making sure anyone inside the bar stays there and anyone passing by keeps right on going. 'Are you talkin' to me? You talkin' to me? I don't see anyone else here. You must be talkin' to me.'

This is clearly too many consecutive syllables for the oaf. His brow furrows, and his lips move as he if he's thinking back over what I said. The confusion doesn't stop when his lips do. I watch him count, then re-count to verify he's not made a mistake.

'I make there to be three of you here? I don't think she's Paul Bonhomme though.'

This is the wrong thing to say. Aicha freezes, then swivels her regard towards the Captain Caveman wannabe. 'I might be. To assume makes an ass out of you and me. Well, only out of you when I boot your kneecaps up into your pecs.'

The mutt leers at her, showing that his self-preservation instinct lost the battle with his need to be a dominant chauvinist ballbag a long time ago. 'I'd like to see you try, little la—'

The *crack*, followed swiftly by a second *crack*, makes every member of the pack wince and step back. It is a wise decision. Violence is a language even this arsehole understands. Words and actual language? Not so much.

Aicha turns towards the rest of the wolves. 'Right, so who's next?'

A less aggro version of the alpha currently rolling around howling on the floor, who is clutching his suddenly much floppier legs, raises a very hesitant hand. 'Um, I'm second-in-command?'

I hold my hand out to Aicha before she can take that as an invitation to kneecap him as well. We need to find out what is going on first.

'Have you lost your fucking tiny minds?' I shake my head disbelievingly. The whole "sprouting claws and howling at the moon" might seem cool, but it puts them a long way down the ladder in terms of power. The idea of a group of werewolves attacking us is certifiably insane.

The beta (and man, I bet that gets right up his testosterone-swollen nose as a title) looks very uncomfortable. That he still has his hand in the air doesn't help, so I wave at him to put it down. I then make a rolling gesture to tell him to get on with it.

'Look, it's not really our choice. Simeon was supposed to give you the phone.' He gestures towards their leader, who's calming down as his healing capabilities kick in, although I can't imagine the articulation snapping back into place is a barrel of laughs.

Aicha snorts. 'That's really his name? Simeon the simian wolf? Brilliant.' She goes over to the prone leader to get the aforementioned phone and passes it to me.

The screen is unlocked and already has a video playing. A group of men and women are encircled by a cord of *talent* corralling them in place. They look in sorry shape — visible cuts and bruises, their eyes swollen shut, and bloodstains on their clothing.

'Hello again, Paul and associates.' The tremulous voice is as instantly recognisable as it is cold and emotionless. 'It occurred to me that as a group, you might not feel your debts to me are worth paying. You might decide to try hunting me instead of what I asked for.'

My instinct is to rile him up, insult him, and try to knock him off balance, but I have a grim feeling that will end badly for the people in the video. 'We're already doing what you asked. What is the point of this?' I keep my cool, but it takes a lot of work.

'Lovely words, Bonhomme, but it would shock me if you were being honest. I don't doubt you're putting far more energy into trying to catch me than finding my Vernicle. So I want to make the point very clear. I think a demonstration can be so much more effective than words. Where is Simeon?'

I swivel the phone to point at the alpha on the floor. 'He's feeling a bit overwhelmed by it all.'

A disappointed tutting carries through the phone's speaker. 'That is as unsurprising as it is unacceptable. So here's what's going to happen...'

A gunshot rings out, and a young man flops forward like a rag doll, slumping against the invisible wall made by woven *talent*. There is a momentary silence and then what just happened clicks with the group on the screen and the screaming starts. It only lasts for a moment before the volume cuts off, undoubtedly because of a mute option included in the magic surrounding them, but it is clear from their shell-shocked expressions and agape mouths that they are still wailing, terrified.

'That was Simeon's partner. Not the first time he's had to pay for his lover's arrogance. Though, at least, it will be the last.'

The howl from our feet is unearthly, and the level of pain contained within is many, many times worse than it was when Aicha physically broke his knees.

'So here are the rules. You will fight my press-ganged wolves, and you will do so without using your *talent*. If you use any magic at all —and Nithael, that includes you, just to be clear— then I will shoot one of these fine people each time you do. And should I run out of their partners, I will move on to their children.'

The video clicks off, and the phone is just a dead black brick in my hand. I put it in my pocket for the time being and look at the number two. He seems almost embarrassed. I reckon he thinks that, without our magic, this is going to be an easy battle for them.

'Sorry about this, wizard. It's really nothing personal.' The next words become progressively less clear as his mouth becomes more and more of a muzzle, hair and teeth sprouting as it elongates. 'He promised he'd set them free if we killed you or died trying. No hard feelings.'

He's reaching for his own weapons by changing form, so my hand instinctively heads for my sword. Then I stop. Because it's in my etheric storage. Accessing it might count as magic.

He's got no such limitations. Fingernails stretch, turning to claws, teeth mirroring them in their change to fangs. Fur springs up along flesh that bulges outwards, distorting and twisting, writhing as it enlarges. Bones snap and splinter, changing shape. The sound of them re-knitting is even more eerie and unsettling because it's so unnatural. Of course, there's nothing natural about werewolves.

At least seven feet tall, he towers over us, and the animal cunning gleaming in his yellow eyes looks far greater than his limited human intelligence. That twelve other hulking biped beasts flank him probably helps with his confidence. Grief might have distracted the alpha initially, but the mass change of his pack has pulled him along with it, and he's now the largest wolf I have ever seen. He snarls and snaps, nothing in his eyes but primal rage. Any humanity is lost, submerged beneath misery and beast.

I don't want to kill them. Don't get me wrong, under different circumstances I'd have sent them packing with their tails between their legs. Or running off on their legs with their tail wrapped in packaging after I'd chopped it off. But they didn't choose this. They don't want to be here. As the beta said, it's nothing personal. They're just doing what they have to do to save their loved ones.

So we've got to make a decision. Kill them, save the people they love. Let them live, kill their partners. Except, despite all the evidence to the contrary sometimes, I do pay attention. Phone Dick told us what comes next: if the adults he has hostage die, he'll move on to their kids.

Way I see it, there are two types of adults: those prepared to die willingly to save a child and those who deserve to die because they chose themselves over a youngling. So that makes my decision for me. I reckon these wolves are the former, ready to lose their lives to protect their kids. And even if they weren't, I'd kill them to save the youngsters. The ringing of blade on sheath tells me Aicha's reached the same conclusion.

Of course this is going to be easier for her, seeing as how she's actually armed to the teeth.

I'm going to be fighting the fourteen killing machines with no magic and no sword.

Brilliant.

Chapter Sixteen
TOULOUSE, 8 MARCH, PRESENT DAY

If you collect all their shed hair and make it into wool, then knit it into a jacket, would a werewolf wear wolf? These are the questions that keep me up at night.

Aicha doesn't wait. She springs forward, katana and wakizashi, two Japanese swords so sharp they look like they're cutting ribbons out of the moonlight shining on them. I'm never quite sure how much of her martial arts is magic and how much is centuries of training. One thing's certain. Her two-sword ensemble is far more deadly than the six-inch claws dangling off each of the wolfmen's fingers. One wolf flanking the beta bounds towards her but only for a couple of steps. It's hard to bound when you're missing your legs from the knees down. Chopping off limbs with swords is hard. Unless they're razor sharp, magically imbued, and you're a blade master. That's three out of three for Aicha and her weapons then.

Leaving the squealing lycan lying behind her, she rolls under a claw that's being swung with enough force to take her head clean off her shoulders. Instead, she separates the hand from the wrist with a perfectly timed cut. The claws ring out as they bounce off the table's metal legs.

It might sound like she's playing with them, but this is Aicha at her kindest. Werewolves have impressive regenerative skills, and by amputating limbs, she's taking them out of the battle without having to kill them. Plus, she's using normal steel, so reattaching their limbs is possible. That is incredibly generous, considering I don't doubt that she has at least one silver-tipped weapon on her.

Dropping, she twirls and lops off another two pairs of feet at the ankles. Just as I think the battle will be over before it even starts, a hulking black shape barrels into her, tearing out her left bicep with its slavering jaws. They roll together, but I lose sight of them at this point as one of the other wolfmen steps forward to engage me.

I take up a defensive stance. By letting them come to me, I can use their own force against them. Another of the wolfmen swings his base-ball-glove-sized paw at my head. I glide sideward, letting it flow past me. Jabbing at him with my fingers, I strike at the pressure points on his side as his momentum carries him past. His arm drops limp, immobilised. The first wolfman closes in. Launching myself through his legs, I hit each ankle as I slide through. He crashes down like a ton of bricks into one of his comrades, who just tried to seize my foot in his jaw.

Standing, I wince at the sharp pain in my side. Even though they didn't make contact with me, I have that salty taste in my mouth that says I'm close to vomiting from overexertion. Breathing is rapid and shallow, my muscles aching from the strain and tightening painfully into a cramp. I already need a break.

When I get one, I wish I didn't.

The tinny, broadcasted noise of a shot rings out, and everybody freezes. I pull the phone that I took off Simple Simeon out of my pocket and look down. Another of the crowded bodies has dropped to the floor as the others push themselves backwards, away from their dead friend.

'What are you doing, you evil bastard? We didn't use any magic!' I yell despite the pain in my side.

The voice sounds bored, entirely disinterested. 'You may not have, but one of you did. I warned you specifically, Nithael.'

I look over my shoulder to see what's happened. One of the pack must have sidled around the action and launched himself at Isaac. He's now held, suspended in mid-air by angelic hands, whimpering at the burning brightness of the otherworldly light. White-faced, Isaac shakes his head, though whether in denial or disbelief, I can't say.

'He had me bang to rights, lad. Nithael won't let me die. I'm so sorry.'

Another of the pack raises his head and howls, and suddenly the air fills with a chorus, venting their grief and misery. I feel desperately sorry for them all — not something I had ever expected to feel for a bunch of werewolves, but this is a no-win situation for them. That they are here at all means they value the lives of their loved ones more than their own. They came to an unwinnable battle. Wolves versus mages is always going to be like bringing a knife to a gunfight, and even without our magic, anyone versus Aicha is shitty odds.

This whole scenario is unjust, and there is only one way out of it. Clearly, Aicha has come to the same conclusion, the wolf in mid-air suddenly sprouting a blade tip from his right eye, the knife having entered through the back of his head.

Within moments, thirteen of them are dead, knives secreted around her person having flown through the air, burying themselves into critical points —eyes, ears, hearts— for instant kills. Most of the wolves didn't even have time to react. Only Simeon is quick enough. He launches forward, huge shaggy head twisting at the right moment for the blade to whip past his ear and drive itself into his shoulder instead. It doesn't even slow him. He's gone feral, lost to a pain well beyond the physical.

Aicha sheathed her swords to throw knives now gone, so she reaches across her body, going for the shorter stabbing impact of the wakizashi. Before she can draw it, Simeon's closed the last of the distance and buries his muzzle into her chest, tearing all the flesh surrounding her left ribs off, getting underneath them, cracking them as he goes.

I want to leap forward, to help, but it's unnecessary, of course. Aicha draws the short blade with her left hand despite all the damage done on that side, and slides it under his snout, inside her own chest. I can't see clearly what happens, but there's a sad squeal, like a kicked puppy. Then Simeon collapses, huffs of steam coming from his nostrils. By the time he hits the ground, Aicha's already almost fully healed, the last white gleam of bone visible for a moment before the flesh covers it once more.

'Ana asef,' she murmurs in his ear as she slits his throat. *I'm sorry*. Aren't we all.

Shoving her face into the phone as I hold it, she snarls, 'They're all dead. Release the prisoners. Show some slight honour.'

The fucking bastard dares to give us a slow clap to accompany his rasping, dry-throated chuckle. 'Well done. I knew you had it in you to be callous in your killing. And it only cost you two innocent lives.'

The fucking heartless wanker. Two? It's a start. Sure, two completely innocent people, but I make it sixteen. These fourteen wolves might have been arseholes, but their deaths are no fault of their own. As far as I'm concerned, all the fault lies on the shoulders of the shitstain on the other end of the phone. I can feel my lip curling, my own snarl forming. Good God, I want to get my hands on that fucker. Let him taste my blade.

But Aicha doesn't blink. 'I can be endlessly callous in my killing. And inventive. And for you, I'll include exceptionally sadistic for free as well. Come meet me. I'd love to show you.'

His humour evaporates. I doubt he likes anyone else stealing his thunder. 'I don't think I shall, Ms Kandicha, if it's all the same to you. Now then, I am a man of my word despite what you may think. However, there's one more thing I require you to do first. Well, not you. I think it will be far more amusing if the Hebrew does it.'

I look at Isaac, whose face is still white with shock. He'll be struggling with the guilt of the trade-off Nithael made —his life for the hostage's— for a while to come. Living beyond a normal human lifespan sometimes feels designed solely to provide ever more nightmare fuel. I wonder if any Talented sleep well, or if we all wake up screaming in cold sweats more often than we get our recommended eight hours. No wonder we're cranky as a rule. I suspect Phone Dick's problem is more than just a terrible night's sleep though. I am also certain that none of us are going to like what he wants next.

'It's a simple requirement. You broke the rules, Isaac, and that poor, poor man' —his voice drips with sarcasm— 'paid the price for your selfishness. You cost him his life by inaction. Your god is ever quick with justified retribution, isn't he? An eye for an eye, and all that. So it's simple. If you want me to let all these people and their children go, kill Paul.'

'What?' I didn't think it was possible, but Isaac turns an even whiter shade of pale. Like Procol Harum eat your heart out pale. This is totally not in his wheelhouse. Aicha wouldn't have hesitated. She gets it. This body is just a shell. Crack it open, and I'll fly off and find another one. But Isaac? I might not be a blood relation, but I'm the closest thing to a son he's ever had and the only thing resembling family since Jakob's disappearance.

Phone Dick's derision broadcasts itself loud and clear. 'Come along, Isaac. This time you get to play the role of the father Abraham. A sacrifice made to save their lives. Aicha, would you be so kind as to lend a blade?'

Slowly, Aicha draws another of her wickedly sharp knives and carefully hands it to Isaac. She makes sure to catch his eye as she does. 'It's okay, *saabi*. Paul's coming straight back. We're gonna do much worse to that piece of shit when we get our hands on him. For now, concentrate on what needs to be done.'

'Bravo, Ms Kandicha, a rousing speech.' The slow handclap starts up again. Good God damn. I've had enough of him sneeringly taking the piss out of us. 'Now get on with it, Isaac. There's a good fellow.'

The blade quivers, its sides glinting as they catch reflections from the bare lightbulbs swaying from the awning above us. Shakily, he advances towards me. I desperately don't want this to traumatise him. Wrapping his hand with mine, I help him get the trembling under control.

"Zac, listen to me.' I speak quietly but firmly as I raise the tip up to my breast. It isn't easy stabbing someone in the heart — almost as if ribs are there to protect it just from that. But luckily, I've been stabbed so many times, the phantom pain of a blade sliding in is a reliable guide. Good to find the silver lining to being brutally killed over and over. 'It's like the mess we found in the shit wizard's basement. It isn't me. It's just flesh and bones. He just wants to fuck with you, to see you hurting. I'll be right back. Get it done. Get them free if we can. Anything after that? It's on him, not us. Not you. Got it?'

Isaac bites his lip and nods. His hand steadies, and I release it. We can't have the shitbag saying I killed myself, that I guided the knife in. Isaac has to do this on his own.

I nod, not letting eye contact with him drop. 'Do it, man.' For a moment, I think he'll refuse, but then he pushes sharply forward. The pain washes over me, an electric overload in all my nerve endings as this body's motor seizes up. Then I am gone.

I snap my eyes open. I'm lying in an upright position, which is unnerving. It isn't something I am used to; people don't leave dead bodies propped upright unless some psychopath ruler has called for the taxidermist because they need a new hatrack.

Terror strikes me. I'm trapped again. Bound like I was in that fucking basement. I can't move. Can't raise my hand, can't seem to do anything but blink. And Pascal is here. The mortuary assistant is right in front of me, the same face I saw when I came back to life after escaping the shit wizard's clutches.

Only this time he doesn't faint away in terror at the corpse he's working on coming back to life. Instead, a confused expression crosses his face, like trying to solve a particularly tricky crossword puzzle over Sunday breakfast. Then horror spreads across it. *My horror.*

I watch the features melt into mine, and I realise why I've been strapped to a table vertically. I'm facing the mirrored wall. Pascal isn't standing in front of me.

The body I've woken up in is Pascal.

Looking down, I see straps holding my arms and legs in place. They're necessary; otherwise the cadaver would have collapsed to the floor before I took it over, no doubt ruining the surprise. No prizes for guessing who set it up.

With some careful wiggling, rubbing my wrist raw against the leather restraint, I free one hand from the straps. Then it's a simple matter to undo the others and stumble off the table. I'm trembling, shaking, but I don't think it's from the cold this time. A pocket on my new loose-fitting canvas trousers vibrates, and I fumble out a phone showing an incoming video call.

I take a moment, biting back my shaken fury to regain my self-control, then accept the call. The same video scene pops up again. The terrified, traumatised prisoners are all still scooting away from the two dead bodies stuck inside the magic circle with them.

'We did what you asked, you bastard. Let them go.' My voice is steady by will alone. I deserve an Oscar for not tearing strips off him for his complete lack of humanity.

'I will, Paul, don't worry. Your other friends are watching on the other phone, but I've muted their call. I wanted a moment to speak to you first. Then I'll let them go.'

It's hard to keep my hand steady, but I manage it through force of will. I don't know if I believe him, if he'll really follow through and release them or if he has some other sick, twisted game in mind first. 'What do you want to talk to me about privately?'

'I just wanted you to know that this is how it will go if you try to resist my orders. It's not like you have many friends, but any you have —any you've ever had— I'll track them down. I'll make them suffer so much that even you, with a million painful deaths under your belt, could not imagine it. I'll send them all to their end as slowly and horribly as anyone could dream of. Then I'll move on to the likes of Pascal here. People you've just met. Momentary crossings where they've drawn your sympathy. The girl who catches your eye and brings a smile to your lips. The man who gets a nod of thanks for stopping his car to let you cross. More of those poor wretches that serve your watery friend who can't stop his fishy lips from flapping. I. Will. Kill. Them. All.'

There isn't a threat to what he says. It is a statement of fact, an absolute promise. An unquestionable, terrible certainty. I stand stunned to silence by the casualness of his preparedness for mass murder as he carries on. 'If you deviate —if you allow your friends to deviate— from concentrating on finding the veil and bringing it to me, other people will pay the price over and over for your failings. All those innocent deaths on your shoulders. Do you think you can bear it? More weight to add on to all those centuries of errors you have to carry already? Oh, and one last thing…'

The off-hand words don't match with the loaded intent, and honestly? It terrifies me. This isn't Columbo. The "one last thing" isn't going to break open the case. I am more worried it might be something to break my heart.

'Do remember, I know all about you. All of you. Isaac and you are pretty little conundrums, probably too much work to be worth the effort. But Aicha? I know the Aab Al Hayat. Intimately. In the end, it's just another elixir, a positive poison, if you like. And every poison has an antidote. So don't dawdle. There's a good fellow.'

For a moment, I think my heart stops beating. The silence of the morgue grows, amplifies, and seems to resound in my chest, an absence of noise echoing around the empty cavity. Without the Aab Al Hayaat, Aicha will be mortal. That attack by the werewolf leader wouldn't have inconvenienced her. It would have killed her stone dead. If the bastard is telling the truth, he's just raised the stakes dramatically. Terror floods my system, every inch of my body vibrating at the thought of losing her.

It's only when I hear fumbling and then another line connecting before Isaac's voice carries through that I feel my pulse again, sure my heart is beating after all. 'Paul? Paul? Are you there, man?'

'I'm here, 'Zac. Everything's fine. Relax.' I keep my tone calm. Spooking the others as badly as I am won't help matters. 'Let them go. Now.'

On the screen, the magic holding the assembled people vanishes. We can hear doors slamming open. From the left of the screen, natural sunlight streams in, illuminating an old, abandoned warehouse. A gaggle of scared kids run in, their faces marked with tears and terror. The adults, traumatised in their own right, quickly shepherd them outside. Away from the two bodies left conspicuously behind. Two more scores I need to settle with this phone dick piece of shit.

'There,' he says kindly, like a grandfather fussing over a child's grazed knee. 'All done and dusted.' The tone goes flat, cold again. 'I let them go because I can find them again any time. I don't need them. Their death or life serves me no purpose for now. If you stay motivated.'

'Listen...' I start, but he cuts me off.

'No, you listen, Good Man. I will not be dictated to nor distracted, and you will do as I say. If I believe for a moment you are deviating from my instructions, that you are searching for me instead of the prize I've demanded, you will pay. The price will be innocent lives, and I will find more and more innovative ways to make you kill them. Each death will rest upon your shoulders. So make your choices, all of you. Are you hard-hearted enough to hunt me down? Or are you going to do as you're told like the good man you are? Don't doubt for one minute that I'll be watching.'

The screen blanks, and somehow, I can sense it is final. I don't know if he's fried it from a distance or flipped a switch. The phone's a dead brick now.

I hurl it against the far wall, the tinkling sound of it smashing into composite pieces and shards of plastic the tiniest of balms on my wounded soul. I pull out another burner from my etheric storage and dial Aicha. She picks up instantly.

'Where are you, *saabi*?' Straight to the point. Good. She's ready to get moving again, get on the hunt. Now I just have to steer her in the right direction — for her own sake.

'I'm in Purpan again. Home away from home.'

'Want me to come get you?'

I think about it for a moment. 'Honestly? Get Isaac home safely. He'll need a stiff drink and an empathetic ear. I think having had to stab me in the heart, it'll be better you than me. Considering he's Jewish, he does a remarkable impression of Catholic guilt.'

'Got it.'

We stand silently for a moment. I can imagine them there, surrounded by dead wolfmen. Thankfully, Aicha threw up a *don't look here* spell across the area, or we would have some serious explaining to do.

'I look forward,' Aicha begins slowly and deliberately, 'to pulling his lungs out of his nostrils, inflating them with an air-compressor, and then turning them into pin cushions.'

I blink. 'Oddly specific, but yeah, seconded. Do me a favour — clean up there, will you?'

Will, who owns L'Astronef, is a good guy. Cleaning up werewolf entrails isn't in his job description. She grunts affirmatively.

'Right, I'm going to jump on the tram and head home. Try to get some rest. We'll get our revenge on the shithead, don't doubt it.'

'You too. I'll be round at the crack of dawn.'

'What's Dawn going to say about you being round her crack?' I ask, searching for a bit of normality.

'Probably that you're a dickhead and thank fuck it's me, not you.'

'Touché, *laguna*, touché.'

'Nah, no touché — she doesn't want you to touché her, that's the whole point. Sensible Dawn, I reckon.'

'Thanks, Aich. Kick a man when he's down, why don't you?'

'With great pleasure. If you're not up when I get round tomorrow, I'll be more than happy to wake you with a few choice rib shots. Deal?'

'Deal. See you tomorrow.'

'Tomorrow, dickhead.'

The line goes dead. I feel marginally better, which is a lot better than I expected to feel when I woke back up here and realised whose body I was in. Staring at my hands —his hands— I wonder how he died. Who will miss him. His desk stands on the other side of the room. Selfishly, I'm glad that I'm on this side of it. I can see the backs of some photo frames. The Good God knows I don't want to see whose pictures are in them.

How much of this is my fault? It's a question I'd love to ignore, but it keeps coming back, buzzing around at the edges of my consciousness, demanding an answer. It's all very fucking weird. If he's got Jakob, why isn't he going after Isaac, chasing him, *calling* him? Sure, he made Isaac kill me, but messing with him was just a bonus. It was to talk to me in private, to threaten me. Somehow this all feels very personal, as though Phone Dick has a score to settle with me.

I wonder what I've done that's caused him to hate me so much. The problem is, over the centuries, I've given plenty of people plenty of reasons to despise me and want me dead. Since my very first life, each time I left a body, heading off to start anew without a backwards glance, I seem to have left a trail of destruction and misery in my wake, intentional or not.

It's a slow, painful walk up the steps from the morgue. Each one feels weighed down by every idiotic mistake I've made over the past eight hundred years.

CHAPTER SEVENTEEN

LAVAUR, 3 MAY, 1211

B lood and smoke. Who could have ever imagined how utterly intertwined those two could become in the mind? I can't remember how
one might smell without the other. Blood and smoke everywhere.

My robes are ruined, stained through with both grime and viscera, and
my face is streaked with mud and the precious cargo of so many veins that
lie open now, spilling their essence into a broken ruin. The ruin of this once
magnificent castle and of our dream of a purer, more noble Christianity.
Both lie shattered. My heart is too.

Time is limited, almost up. Not just for the poor, broken souls I tend to
as I rush around the walls, seeking to give them solace before they pass. No
— but for us all. This, here, is the ending. My heart knows it. True, there
are still Good People left, still other Perfects out there to carry on the faith.
But as we fall here, *when* we fall here, a large part of our faith will fall too.
Will die too.

I stumble over an arm half-outstretched, fingers rigidly grasping out
towards something in death. I know not what for. Rescue? Mercy? Beyond
my knowing. My feet struggle to regain their footing, slipping in the mess
that spreads outwards from the crumbled stonework lying on top of the

body, and I know I'm unable to check myself. Sheer exhaustion is pulling me downward. Before I can collapse though, an arm is under mine, around my shoulders, catching me.

'Easy now, Paul. You push too hard.' A voice, more familiar almost than my own now, breathes a little warmth back into my chest.

'Brother Ben. It looks like you're not done saving me from myself just yet, even if you wear the black robes now.' My best friend, now my peer. A proud if bitter moment the night before, when I performed the consolamentum, the ritual confirming him as a Perfect. Now our souls are inseparably linked. It would be a weight on my shoulders —that if I am to sin, then his Perfection will be undone— if I expected to live much beyond this day.

Perhaps something of my soul's despair is in my face, for Ben lifts me back to my feet, looks at me with a passion that speaks of pure faith and hope. I envy him that. My faith is not damaged, but I find myself entirely without hope.

'My brother...' And I know he means it in more of a sense than just a religious one. 'Don't despair. Nicetas has returned to us. Perhaps we stand a chance still.'

Papa Nicetas. Yes. There is a strange arriving. A Good Man all the way from Constantinople, who helped set the very tenets of our form of Christianity many years ago. That done, he disappeared without warning or explanation. Now, decades later, he's returned at our moment of despair. Here, in our stronghold, filled with four hundred Good People, many have seen it as a sign, an omen that we can yet prevail against the brutal Frankish forces and their terrible crusade brought down upon us for heresy. Franks that will see us burn, all of us Perfects. Despite that, my fellow Black Robes hold out hope because of this miraculous return.

And yet. And yet, I find myself unnerved by him. Despite the warnings of that peculiar Israelite rabbi when we passed to Foix, I have not since encountered man, woman, or creature with that same strange glow Isaac held. Not until I saw Nicetas. There's a reddish aura that I catch from the corner of my eye when he swoops from one group to another, urging them to stand fast in their faith, encouraging others to take the consolamentum and pick up the black robes, to join the ranks of the Perfect even though it will mean a death sentence for them when the army at the gate breaks through. I avoid him, uncertain, unnerved, but I know Ben has found motivation in his words. Certainly enough to have begged me to raise him up to Perfect last night against my own wishes.

For now, I'll take the comfort of Ben's companionship. He lends me more than just a steadying arm. Through it, he lends me strength. Together, the two of us hurry back and forth across the cracked terrain, seeking to bring aid to those we can and peace to those we can't. The pain and misery are a miasma, hanging over the keep thicker than any morning fog can, and it seeps deep into my soul. All we ever wanted was to live in peace, to do no harm to man or beast, only to worship the Good God in the way we believed fitting. Around me, crushed and dismembered carcasses, the wailing of friends and loved ones left behind, the weighted grief that drags at my heart — all mark the price paid for daring to carry such a dream. And the stench of blood and smoke.

As we slip and stumble towards the main gate, a cry rises in front of us. I thought the level of noise almost unbearable before, the sound of death and the keening of those standing witness. Now, though, it goes to another level. The clash of metal, the chaos of cries, shouts, demands, pain, and victorious roars is only accentuated by the rumble of collapsing stone. Ben's face whitens, and I know mine must do the same.

It can mean but one thing. The wall is breached. Lavaur is falling.

It's only a matter of time now. Until they round us up and dispatch us to the fire. I see the draw of Ben's lip, the realisation of our ending coming. He clings to my arm, and I feel his fear in his trembling. Still, I don't doubt he'll stand resolute, right to the bitter end. My sole wish is that he doesn't have to.

Then behind him, I spot something. A small side gate, a servant's entry, cracks open. As I watch, scullery maids and serving boys slip away quietly. Very wise. We Good People will die, burned as heretics. The nobles will be ransomed. But the poor others — the servants, the maids, those who've done nought but their duty to their lord? They're the ones who'll bear the worst excesses of a drunken, triumphant mob later on tonight.

I push at Ben's shoulder, stirring him to action, pointing at the doorway. 'Come, Ben. Let's away. Now.'

His face, already pale, loses even more colour until he's completely washed out, almost translucent with shock. 'Are you now a coward then, Paul? To flee our fellows and leave them to their doom?'

'Not a coward.' I stress every word, pleading, trying to make him understand. 'A staunch believer. I'll not see our faith falter here. Let us away where we can still spread the good word. To die a martyr here helps not our cause.'

I can see the doubt, the uncertainty rife on his features, but I don't have time to persuade him. Instead, I push him, shoving his shoulder, corralling him into action and towards freedom.

As we approach, I hear a sound. A weak cry, almost indistinguishable. Turning my head, casting about, searching for the cause, I see a young girl, decked in the scullery's outfit, her leg trapped by a fallen beam. A stable boy comes rushing past, sobbing, 'Sorry,' and I push Ben to him so that they tangle arms.

'Take care of him!' I yell and let each decide for themselves that I speak of the other. I linger a moment to make sure they're gone through the gate, then turn to the trapped young girl.

Lifting the beam is no simple task. It's wedged by a fallen lump of the stonework thick as my leg and made of sturdy, solid oak. I get my hands beneath it and heave, but nothing moves. This may be beyond me.

That my last righteous act might be frittered away, meaningless, is almost more than I can bear. Closing my eyes, I dig deep inside, crying out to the Good God to give me this, to aid me, to save this innocent girl. There, in my heart, in my guts, I feel something stirring, a force or energy that swirls and lifts. It floods out to my limbs, my legs and arms, and slowly, ever so slowly, the beam lifts upwards.

'Out!' I grunt through gritted teeth. 'Go!'

The girl realises her leg's freed, the trap released, and she scrambles up, gone through the gate. Not a moment too soon. As I release the beam, soldiers pour in through that side just as the main forces flood around the corner of the main hall.

Now it is I who am in the trap, caught. I close my eyes to offer a last prayer to the Good God to guide my soul homewards, but something hits me behind my right ear like a thunderbolt, and the next moment, I know nothing.

When I open my eyes again, I'm not alone, though the Good God knows I wish I was. All my fellow Good People, all the other Perfects of our faith who sheltered here in one of our last bastions are sat together or lying, in my case and that of a few others who've clearly been equally mistreated. There's more than a few bloodied rags being clutched to the backs of heads, more than a few bruises already visible, sprawling across faces, painting them in greens and blues. Considering not a one of these Good People would have lifted a hand either in aggression or defence, it speaks to the violent nature of the arriving Crusaders.

Four hundred. Perhaps a half of all the Good People left. A little less, I think, but still a good part of the whole collective of Perfects. We're inside the main hall, but the huge double doors, metal-barred oak-work, are thrown open. Even were they not, I'd have felt the heat. It's rippling through the hall, the waves pouring off, rolling, roiling from the pyre they've built.

There's no respite. While I'm staring at the fire, a jab comes to my side, the blunt end of a pike. It takes a second, sharper blow to get me up. The strike to my head must have been harder than I first believed for one moment, I'm feeling the billowing hot air and seeing the flickering hungry flames waiting to swallow us, and the next, they seem to thin, become ghostlike, and I imagine I see the plain wood below, stacked neat like a stage for a troubadour to sing upon. It all flickers with an otherworldly glow, burgundy like the blood that stains the courtyard floor on each flag I can see. Then the next moment, the fire's back, ready to swallow us down.

The second jab got me to feet, but it takes a third to make me move forward. It's strange. I know I'm going to my death, but it doesn't seem real. Perhaps it's this unnatural illusion that keeps coming and going from the bonfire, this result of my head injury. Perhaps it is a part of the human condition, a natural instinct to refute our ending right until the last moment. Whatever it is, my attention wanders, straying away everywhere, going along the tumbled chunks of stone and mortar, bigger than a cart and horse, that litter the open air. The smell of bodies, the buzz of flies. Blood and smoke.

I've a chance, just a moment, to be glad for one thing. That Benedict, my most loyal friend, student, and saviour, is not here to burn with me. While I know his faith is unbending, still it does my poor heart good that I could save him in the end. Maybe I'm about to escape this world —perhaps that is, after all, what we should aim for, to escape these physical bonds— but he might have a little while longer to enjoy the many wonders and pleasures this prison can hold.

And then a flash. Claret lightning from a tower up high on a parapet to the right. It seems to shine down for a split second on the pyre, connecting to it, illuminating it. The whole assemblage is swallowed in the bright red glow. Then it's gone, and the flames come again, and we're close. So damnably close that I can feel the hairs on my face singeing, my beard crisping from the proximity, and oh, by the Good God, what will this do to my skin? What will this feel like? Tears fall, but they're gone, evaporating, wisping off from the intense wall.

Then a last pike-blow strikes me in the back, and I stumble forward and into the flames' hungry maws. Except, as I fall screaming, it seems as though there's a wall of ruby-red light that I'm crossing over, and on the other side is nought but cool, damp wood and fresh evening air. Then I'm falling but not just physically. A deep heavy darkness sweeps me up, like sleep but powered up by draughts of potions beyond any an alchemist could mix, and my eyes close of their own accord. Then I'm gone, though whether to the flames or to something else, I cannot say.

Only that I am gone.

CHAPTER EIGHTEEN

TOULOUSE, 9 MARCH, PRESENT DAY

Absolutely delighted to be up before Dawn has even cracked. Fuck my life.

Aicha likes to compete against me for early morning readiness. The moment the sky lightens and colours appear pastel-like in the half-dawn, my doorbell rings with a determined aggressiveness. But she isn't the only one who can get competitive.

'I was wondering when you'd finally show up,' I throw out casually, incredibly grateful for the second alarm I set on my phone. The alarm clock on its own never stood a chance.

There's no way I'm going to let Aicha know I feel like a gnome crept in and spent the night sandpapering my eyeballs (which is just the sort of thing the sneaky buggers love to do) and that I'd love nothing more than to crawl back under the sheets. I smile my breeziest smile and hope my peepers aren't half as bloodshot as they feel.

She narrows her eyes, clearly unconvinced, and says, 'I'll drive.'

We walk down from my plain Toulousain terraced house. Well, Aicha walks; I stumble over my own feet, wincing in the harsh early morning light. She's parked by the Canal de Brienne, and to my surprise, she's still got the Alpine. Aicha's got a low boredom threshold for vehicles and a penchant for stealing them off arrogant over-privileged arseholes. Considering how many of those there are in the world, she switches out cars more often than most people change clothes. I'm not going to complain. A minor *don't look here* spell after keeps the police away, and everybody needs a hobby.

Her casually possessive pat on its hood is the equivalent of a kneeling declaration of undying love. I contemplate casting an illusory scratch down its side just to mess with her. But we don't have time for her to hunt that non-existent someone down to cause their painful and protracted death, so I resist the urge.

I slide into the passenger side. As she turns on the engine, the horns-heavy funk of El Michels Affair gives way to the neck-snapping break beat of a collaboration between super-producer I.N.C.H and local legend Droogz Brigade in the automated mix of early morning radio. Scratched-up service station sunglasses are an essential protection against the increasing early morning glare, and I put mine on as the low angle of the rising sun delivers rays like golden boxing jabs into my fatigued irises. I look at the fuel gauge.

'Think we've got enough fuel? We've got half a tank of gas,' I point out.

'Half a pack of cigarettes. It's getting less dark, and you're wearing sunglasses?' Aicha replies, turning the music up and pulling out. I'm going to take the Blues Brothers reference to mean "shut up and let me handle the car and our fuel planning, idiot", so I settle back to enjoy the music with so much rigorous attention that I feel the need to close my eyes to concentrate fully.

I do not actually doze off for a few minutes despite the cough-covered, 'Bullshit,' Aicha utters when I inform her of that fact as we approach the outskirts of Muret on the A64, heading southwest. The landscape's starting the blending process, passing from city to country, fields and farms dotted between towns still sufficiently populous and socially mixed to count as suburbs. Signs showing turn offs for the town fill me with the usual bitter sadness. A shiver of someone walking over my grave runs down my back, except it is me driving past it — the grave of a place where a brilliant dream of equality and moral perfection died to the fire and sword of a jealous world. The last grand stand of the forces supporting the Good People against the Albigensian Crusaders. After the Battle of Muret, it was only a matter of time before they put every single one to the fire or sword. Not that I was there. My first death had already come, wrapped up in sin and bloody magic.

I try not to take it as an ominous sign, but it's hard not to feel downcast. I do my best to shrug it off and get ready for what lies ahead.

As we pass the turnoff for Saint-Élix-le-Château and the Village Gaulois (a fascinating living Bronze Age Museum site, made even more interesting when you know that at least one guide is from the actual time period), the radio signal becomes increasingly choppy, the static making it not listenable. Aicha inserts a CD — a mix of Toulousain rap, mainly CMF Records but with some old members of the Kilotone Collective for good measure. It cheers me up immensely. What can I say? I'm a sucker for a banging beat and clever wordplay.

The first unreal impressions of mountains appear ghostlike and gauzed by the sky's greys. They are otherworldly giants pushing through into our reality, majestic and ethereal. When we stop off for coffee (at some insistence on my part) at the Aire De Comminges services, I take a moment to appreciate the beauty surrounding us. Green swathes the nearby hills, attentive trees standing in a pin cushion covering. From here, the first of the mountains are clearer, close enough that the icing sugar snow dusting over the foliage is distinct from the frosted grass.

For a moment, through passing clouds, the more distant mountains become fully present. Then swirling cloud-banks break their clean lines again.

Once inside the service station, I order a double espresso from the coffee machine, which I knock back in swift order while getting another one to go. My quick work with the first is because of my wanting to get past the acclimatisation required for machine-made coffee and nothing to do with being half-asleep at all. Honest, guvnor.

Aicha gets back into the car moments after I do and spills her haul across the centre dash. Two packs of Hollywood gum, one mint and one strawberry, protrude from underneath a brown grease paper bag of chouquettes, alongside a bag of chocolate madeleines and a bottle of cloudy apple juice. It all seems a little excessive for the hour and a half or so we have left of the trip.

'Got enough stuff there?' I inquire sarcastically. 'Sure there's enough sugar? Don't want a Pez dispenser just to top out the sucrose delivery system?'

Aicha doesn't reply, just leaps out of the car and slams the door shut. A couple of minutes later, after disappearing back into the service station, she swings back in the car, popping a tiny Pez brick from a Minion's head onto her stuck-out tongue.

'And you can't have any now either, you rude git, so nyeah,' she says, then starts up the motor. For a moment, the broken signal of Radio FMR reclaims the speakers before the CD spins back up. We're once more on our way to Hastingues.

'So you know Lou Carcoilh personally?' Aicha drums her fingers in time to the music on the steering wheel as she casually flips off the idiot who tried to speed up when she indicated to pull out, only to find himself out-matched by a freshly fuelled Alpine.

'Know him is a bit of a stretch, but I had an encounter of sorts. You know the general legend?'

Aicha waggles her hand back and forth. 'Bits and bobs. Not sure I know everything.'

'He's been in Hastingues a long time, at least as long as I've been alive. Back at the end of the thirteenth century, the local abbot gave the territory to Edward the First, King of England, for him to build a fortified town on. Probably intended it as a poisoned chalice. I reckon the abbot knew what lived underneath that particular hill. Luckily for the king, he had a magician in his service. This is a total guess on my part, but I always thought it may have been Merlin himself, back from an extended self-banishment, making a last dalliance with English royalty before fucking off out of the pages of history. Whether it was, he went below the hill, and though he didn't slay Lou, he seemed to either make a deal or weave a successful spell.

'Lou went into hibernation, waking occasionally, and the town prospered. Only the foolish wandered under the ground through the few openings that existed, and if they were locals, they even occasionally came back out. Strangers, particularly invading Spaniards, funnily enough, went missing; they were greedy treasure hunters, so no one particularly missed them or went looking for them. Plenty of pilgrims passed that way on the Compostela route through the Pyrenees, but aside from a very plausible risk of robbery by bandits manning the river crossings, there were no unusual disappearances, and I paid no real mind to the area or the monster presumably underneath when I was in the vicinity.'

Aicha pulls out to overtake the lorry in front despite the earnest efforts of the car behind to speed up hard the moment she indicates. They lean on their horn because they obviously feel the need to underline exactly how much of a prick they are. Luckily for them, we're in such a hurry.

Otherwise, Aicha would have taken great pleasure in demonstrating how it works by introducing their face to the steering wheel.

I carry on. 'That all changed around the start of the twentieth century. I heard rumours that children —local children!— were disappearing every few months. The residents were terrified, and all believed it was because of Lou Carcoilh waking and feeding again. I was down in Pau visiting an old friend when I caught wind of it. You can imagine my reaction at the idea of a child killer underneath anyone's feet, so I went to have a look for myself. The locals had long told their children to be good, or Lou Carcoilh would get them, and it seemed to have come true.'

The grief of a parent whose child has been taken from them is an emotion strong enough to almost break the world. I can still feel the wretched despair, the fury and hopelessness of those poor villagers. The Good God knows I sympathised with them, understood that raw pain. I didn't need much in the way of motivation, but that was enough. More than enough.

I arrived to find them armouring up with pitchforks and torches, ready to throw their lives away in the dark under the hill to seek a vengeance they were incapable of achieving. It took some doing to persuade them to let me go in their stead, but I managed it in the end.

'I went down into the grottos to find the monster and hopefully rescue any children he'd not yet consumed. I found him and realised I was going to need to dramatically adapt my strategy of attack. He was enormous, on a scale I hadn't imagined, and I knew I had a titanic battle on my hands. There were no children down there; I could find no traces at all, and the creature was asleep in an obvious hibernal state, so I retreated and went to get the metaphysical big guns.'

I can still see it in my mind's eye. That huge cavern empty apart from the beast itself. No trace of a child, no discarded jackets, no torn scraps of trousers. No blood patches. No one to rescue. Just a monster to slay. I went there, soaked in all the villagers' fury, ready to bring destruction on its head. Looking at Lou? I knew I needed a better plan than just white-hot rage.

'So what happened?'

Aicha's question makes me start in my seat, the belt pressing tight across my chest as I come back to the here and now.

I carry on. 'That same night, another child went missing. I ducked back into the tunnels as soon as I got word, and the beast hadn't stirred, hadn't moved an inch. This was either magic of a type I'd never encountered, like a sleepwalking form of feeding, or there was another explanation. The latter turned out to be true.

'I found a man, a well-respected burgher of the town, fat and jolly, a friendly shoulder to all and sundry. He circulated stories that had apparently come from other folk of how they'd seen a glimpse of the creature, retreating with the latest victim, keeping all the riled-up attention on this terrible curse claiming the children at random intervals. When I broke into his house, I found a locked cellar door reeking of the psychic imprint of misery and suffering. And the boy.'

That cellar. Good God, but that cellar. I don't have to see that in my head. It comes to my dreams often enough. Rank odours of piss and blood. Stains across all the equipment the bastard made or brought down there. Metal and cord. And the boy.

'He was like a beacon, shining bright amidst a scene that...' I break off. Look over at Aicha. She'll understand. 'If there were ever a moment when I nearly broke faith with humanity, nearly went down that route of "to hell with them all", that was it. Only the boy stopped that.'

I see her grip on the steering wheel, twisting on the rubber. She gives one single nod. An affirmation. She's been there. She gets it.

'What happened to the bastard?' Of course she wants to know that. She wants to know justice was served.

'He was there, of course. I think he tried to speak to me, to bribe me, to offer me all that his wealth and status could provide in exchange for my silence, but I didn't even really hear him. I just focused on that boy, getting him out. And making sure that the burgher couldn't leave. Not ever again.

'I took the boy back to his family and told them the truth, what had happened, who had done it. We gathered the parents of the missing children, and I gave them the one thing I could. A small gift — that whatever they did would burn with him when I wiped his house from existence and that I'd return at nightfall. When I came back, the cellar door had been locked again, and they were gone. I made a bonfire of that dwelling that they could see from all their windows. I shielded it from the outside world till the entire structure collapsed. Then I made the ground swallow it up, the soil roll over it, and the grass lay itself blanket-like over that accursed place. It was like it had never existed. I don't know whether it brought them any comfort or closure, but it was the closest to justice I could deliver for that most heinous of betrayals by a man they'd all trusted implicitly.'

I see from the set of Aicha's jaw that she wants to go back there, dig the bastard up, and burn him all over again. She dips her head in acknowledgement and says, 'I forget sometimes that you're not someone to piss off.'

'Thanks, I think?' I reply. We sit for a moment, quietly. I don't know what she's thinking about. All I'm trying to do is not think about it anymore. Of course, that never works, so I carry on with the tale.

'Anyhow, to answer your original question, I've seen Lou Carcoilh, but he's not seen me. There's no surety what his reaction will be, but I certainly wasn't going to take him to war for the crimes of a mortal. If negotiations fail though, it's going to be a hell of a battle. I can tell you that much.'

As we pass the exit for Capvern, the mountains suddenly spring present and prominent on our left, crystal distinct in contrast to their distant reaches that stay brushstrokes of grey on grey. Not long after, the city of Tarbes stretches before us, various ancient markers of lives past still present amongst the modernity.

The sign for Lourdes comes up on the right, casting a black cloud over my mood once more. Aicha surreptitiously falls back on old superstitions, her hands making the sign to ward off the evil eye as we drive past. It is no place for the likes of us, nor would I advise anyone I cared for to go on a visit either. The Church's PR team there operates as a forerunner to the advertising industry, making the news of miracles go viral, pulling in the destitute and desperate. What they don't say is there are often unforeseen prices to pay for the Lady's benevolence.

Between moments of banter and comfortable silences, it isn't long before the sign for Peyrehorade signals our turn off. We pay the exorbitant rate at the tollbooth, and I chuckle, remembering what I paid to various brigands while travelling these roads centuries back to cover distances we now do in less than a morning. Convenience comes with a price that often suddenly seems worth paying when compared to the past.

We pull into a world mixing idyll with industry. Modern construction intersperses the hedge-rowed farmland unchanged for decades — slaughterhouse factories and grain processing plants. Biomass rises high in a storage yard as we turn onto the narrow road signposted towards Hastingues.

Charming little houses dot the roadside, highlighted by cheery shutters of varying shades of reds, blues, and greens. Clearly loved and cared for, the monies present to maintain their upkeep are evident. They luxuriate in their spacing, neighbourly, but without being forced cheek-to-cheek with those nearby. So many other small towns in the south are rich with history and natural beauty but impoverished in terms of employment options, leaving them with ageing populations and lacking opportunities. This small town feels comfortable and well-to-do, shutters thrown open, new builds appearing where space allows. Cars even line the ancient streets of the bastide as we pass under what was once the south gate of the fortified town. Now a road runs straight through the isolated squared tower, modernity playing with wooden train tracks around its exasperated feet.

The terrain mounts rapidly as we head up past beautifully preserved houses, still looking much as they did when built hundreds of years ago and still lived in. Hastingues isn't just a museum exhibit you can walk around. It's a living village, wealthy, comfortable, revelling in, but more than just its history. I wonder how much of that has been shaped by the creature living in the hill below their feet. Lou Carcoilh is a hoarder of treasure. Perhaps the surface's prosperity results from having him slumbering, dreaming of riches, down under the village's foundations.

The road opens onto a central square dominated by a church. A castle flanks it, and its reincarnation as a nineteenth-century-style wedding venue is implausibly modern beside the church, which carries weighty age without bowing. While it isn't quite as weighed down as I, it feels close enough for camaraderie, and I can't help patting its walls as we enter.

It's a simple building compared to the grandiose standard that dominates churches throughout the land. A small plaque tells me it's nearly as old as me, although little remains of that first construction. The stained glass is beautiful without being gaudy, and there's more wood along the stone than gold trim.

A single flickering candle burns at the feet of a gracefully carved Virgin Mary by the entrance, but a second female figurine draws my eyes. It could be another Virgin Mary, so important within Catholicism, but I prefer to believe it to be that lady of the night, Mary Magdalene, who us Cathars believe to have walked the hills of Occitanie in the company of Lazarus. If we had a patron saint, it would be her. I slip her a bawdy wink. I feel sure the former courtesan would've appreciated the gesture.

Figures of local saints and symbols of noble families are present in crests and statuettes. The crucifixion, to my distaste, is depicted across multiple stained-glass windows. Still, I know all too well what happens if you suggest perhaps there might be a better way of doing things, such as focusing on the simple message of hope and love rather than being obsessed with Christ's dark and painful ending. Or choosing to live simply and correctly and looking after your fellow man instead of amassing wealth and status. I experienced the bonfires first-hand.

We dip off to the right into a vestibule and descend the chilly stone stairway into the church's basement.

When humanity encounters undeniable powers but hasn't the *talent* to understand it, it tries to either assimilate it, explain it, or contain it. The entrance leading into the darkness of the hill's barrow existed long before they covered it with sanctified ground, hoping holiness would restrain any inexplicable nightmares below. To our considerable relief, we find our way into the cellar without bumping into the priest. I pull aside a wine rack stacked with sacraments to reveal what looks like a solid earth wall to most. For us, it glows with the energy of the locks and chains I covered it in when I was last here. I pull them aside, opening the dark mouth of a tunnel. Musty odours of natural decay and clay-rich loam reach out to welcome us as we stride into the entrance of Lou's home.

CHAPTER NINETEEN

HASTINGUES, 9 MARCH, PRESENT DAY

Understanding perfectly well why Mole
prefers messing about on a river with
Ratty rather than pissing about in
underground tunnels.

The narrow earthen passageway is straight out of a claustrophobe's nightmare, slanting steadily downwards while slowly constricting so that we become ever more hunched. A conjured were-light, a glowing halo bouncing through the air like Tinkerbell lighting Peter's way, is our only light source. I finally bend double, feeling my way with my hands, my eyes fixed on the small lit globe to keep me moving. Just as I feel the need to change to a kneeling crawl, the tunnel opens out, and we can straighten back up.

Nourishment-hunting tubular roots weave out and back into the soil walls. As we advance, the tunnel continues expanding, beginning to feel cavernous. Then the path drops away a good thirty or forty metres, crumbs of dust skittering out into space in front of us, and we're standing on an edge looking down on a gigantesque, cathedral-sized space with worn smooth-packed earth forming a vaulted ceiling.

As I send out my ball of light, passages on either side of this main area are slowly revealed, standing at least fifteen metres high. Tunnels pit the whole dome, ranging in width from a tennis ball to wide enough for four or five people to walk comfortably side by side — if they were insane enough to take a casual stroll through a monster's lair. From about two-thirds of these, long rope-like strands protrude, falling to the soft ground below before grouping together and heading towards a tunnel on the right. More of them stretch from there across to the left.

Aicha points out a narrow one opposite where we're standing. 'Five feet high and three may walk abreast,' she murmurs softly in my ear.

She's right. This could very well be the Lonely Mountain from Tolkien's world, and I feel very much like a poorly trained burglar hobbit hovering above the lair of Smaug the Magnificent. Sadly, I lack a ring of invisibility. Having said that, I'm not looking for subtlety or overly concerned with a matching of wits. As Aicha speaks, a nearby hanging strand from a metre wide tunnel just above us twitches and lifts off the wall, leaving a silvery pattern behind. It shines in an unattractive manner in the reflective light, mucus dripping down its hair-lined surface.

I look at Aicha and grin. 'Time for some action, I reckon.'

'You're no Reggie Noble, *saabi.*' True. Redman's much cooler than I am. Still, let's do a mic check.

I whip my hand out and seize the flailing strand, heaving downwards with all my might. The fact that it has already semi-detached itself helps me massively... and catches me completely by surprise. It slips through my fingers and plunges rapidly towards the floor far below. As the end of the appendage, for an appendage it is, falls past me, I grab it again and holler into the central hollow, which is ringed by translucent sucker pads not unlike those you use to fasten sunshades to a car window. Though, those don't tend to be dripping with viscous slime.

'Oi, Lou, a word in your shell-like, if you please.'

I let it drop and throw up a defensive shield across the mouth of our tunnel. Just in time, as all the tentacles retract, unsticking themselves, and launch themselves at us like the Hundred Crack Fist of Kenshiro

— a flurrying blur of blows bouncing off the protective orb I cast. The tentacles all screech, sounding like a thousand demented bats expressing their rage as the grey tendril-ends, curled up like fists around the central hole, their sucker pads squashed together, hammer again and again against my protection. After a while, the realisation seems to seep in that they'll never reach us. They regroup in a centralised mass before sliding upwards and outwards to cover the chamber walls and ceiling, sticking in place but looming and present as the ground rumbles. The vibrations threaten to knock us off balance, and I have to replant my stance to keep my feet.

From the enormous ground-level tunnel on our right, Lou Carcoilh comes to find out what is going on. Swivelling furiously, five-metre eye-stalks emerge first from the darkness, the elliptical orbs fixing on us. Vellus hair slicks back from behind the orbs towards the emerging head, which looms over the ground at the height of a three-storey house. The maw arrives next, a yawning black hole, big as a motorway tunnel through a mountain. This is the origin of the ominous feelers coating the room — they're attached around his mouth, in the place of his lips, covering the lower part of his face like a wriggling lithe beard. The shaping of the distended jaw and the way the head joins the body is serpentine, but instead of scales, shaggy brown fur covers it, gleaming in the light of my glowing ball. As Lou slithers out, its shell comes into sight — a Fibonacci spiral on an immense scale. The stalagmite protrusions covering it, perfect for impaling the unwary, are the only things breaking the pattern. It looks like an implausible fossil, some prehistoric monstrosity preserved in a moment for future palaeontologists to marvel at. It certainly doesn't look like it should move, carried on the back of a monstrous snake-like gastropod.

The head rears upwards until the gigantic eyeballs, like rounded gondola lifts, peer into our tunnel.

It attempts to roar, 'Who dares lay hands on us?' but shaping words is difficult when you have hundreds of appendages attached to your mouth, so what comes out is more like, 'Who dareth lay handth on uth?'

Aicha snickers behind me, and I elbow her for silence. While speech impediments are never a reason for mockery, coming from a snail the size of a couple of apartment blocks, it knocks the edge off his intimidation.

'Hi, Lou — you don't mind if I call you Lou, do you?' I start, turning up the charisma to eleven with accompanying flashing pearly whites.

'Not if you don't mind me calling you The, ath in The Annoying Snack who Keepth Talking,' the gigantic creature bellows back, clearly not taken in by my charm. '"Lou" meanth "The" in your language, ath in "The Snail" — "Lou Carcoilh". Bloody ignorant food,' it continues in a grumbling voice. 'No rcspcct for ctymology. Call me bloody Lou indeed.'

I try starting over. 'Look, sorry, inauspicious start, Lou Carcoilh. The main thing is, we're here on a bit of a time-critical mission, and I was wondering if you might help us with some information.'

Two tendrils detach from the wall and make exploratory jabs at us, disappointed to find the shield still in place. 'Snackth coming and asking for bloody information. Do we look like a bloody oracle? Wasn't so long ago they'd have had the decenthy to run bloody screaming and now they want to have a chat. Whole specieth hath gone downhill in the lath couple of hundred yearth. No wonder they tathte so bloody horrible now. All thothe additiveth and prethervativeth, I should think...'

Aicha can't help herself. 'How do you know about additiveth, err additives and preservatives? I wouldn't have thought you got out very much?'

The gastropod's tone shifts into an even higher gear. 'Oh, now they mock me. Just becauthe I got a bit bigger than you'd think initially and can't get back outside, they think I'm an ignoramuth. Morselth used to do leth insulting, more digesting when I could get out, I can tell you. You'd get bloody agoraphobic too if you had humanth trying to stab you every time you left your bloody home to eat some of their livestock and borrow some of their treasure. No good telling them it'th just you obeying your bloody nature; don't want to bloody hear it, do they? All swordth and those irritating bloody arrowth prickling your eyeballth and "back to the pit, foul beath". Bloody rude if you athk me. Still' —he waves one of his appendages about— 'I get to hear what'th going on through thethe, as you seem to know' —the pitch and indignation in his voice ups considerably— 'considering you grabbed my bloody tentacle and screamed into it. When I'm not being given a splitting headache by inconsiderate snackth, I can send them outside. Do you know how engrossed humanth get with their television serieth? Far too much to notice a sucker stuck to the outside window so I can listen in, I can tell you! Do you know I heard a program all about the different typeth of snails? It wath fascinating, I can tell you, but they named an African specieth the Giant Snail. Do you know how bloody big it wath?'

The eyestalks seem to lean forward conspiratorially, sharing an unbelievable truth with us.

'Bloody twenty centimetreth. Call that big? It'th bloody tiny. Sir David Attenborough, all respect to him, would have a bloody heart attack if he saw me. Make hith bloody career it would, I reckon...'

There is a dreamy quality to his voice, which lets me know the reverie he is slipping into is one that he happily indulges. The conversation threatening to edge into the realms of the surreal, I feel the need to pull it back on track. 'Are you hunting the inhabitants of the town above?'

One eyestalk swivels up and regards me with what even I, who has limited experience of mollusc expressions, can recognise as incredulous contempt.

'Feeding on the inhabitantth? Do you know how many bloody people there are in Hastingueth? About five bloody hundred. Know how many of them I could eat before people started getting upset? Not bloody many, that'th for sure. Good way to have them heading down here with pitchforkth and some of those fancy new machine gunth.' The whole of the visible part of the creature ripples in what I realise after a moment is a shudder. 'No thankth, mister food. I don't need much to eat, long ath I have my treasure to nourith me. An odd boar once in a while ith a nice treat, pluth the ancient deal still standth — anyone foolith enough to walk into my lair is instantly considered food — like you two!' he says brightly, and an additional three tentacles lash out at the shimmering energy wall separating us from him.

I'm intrigued to know who he made that ancient deal with and whether it was Merlin, but a sudden shout from behind me distracts me. Looking over my shoulder, I see Aicha has caught a tendril that crept up the passageway behind us. She pins it to the wall with a dagger lodged deep into the rock, straight through the centre of the pad.

'*Owwwwwwww!*' the enormous invertebrate howls. '*That bloody hurtth, you know!* Really incredibly rude. Sinthe when did food get so uppity? Bloody walk in here, shouting in my ear-th and then goeth and pinth one to the bloody wall. Jutht plain unpleasant in my view, that ith.'

My patience for a tactful approach is diminishing at a rate approximately equivalent to my mounting headache. 'Look, Lou Carcoilh or Mr Snail or whatever you would like to be called, we came here for a specific item, a magic veil called the Vernicle. You'd have got it from a group of Spanish soldiers who came treasure hunting here in the 16th century.'

The snail nods his head eagerly in recognition. 'Oh yeth, I remember them very well. They were proper food, they were. Sure, they had swordth and all that, but came all the way in on their own! None of thith weaving magic or trying to talk to me. Jutht the usual — them trying to kill me, me eating them all instead. Ah, happy dayth.' It hums contentedly.

'And did they happen to be carrying a magic veil with them?' I am battling to contain my frustration in my voice.

'Oh yeth!' the creature says, much cheered up. 'That wath wonderful. Having that much magic close by hath kept me full up for centurieth. Absolutely warmth my heart it doeth — quite literally!'

I look around, wondering if he has a treasure trove piled up somewhere. Then my eyes latch onto his enormous shell — a massive potential store-house that he can always carry with him and the safest place he could keep anything. *Fuck.* That most likely is the location of our sought-after relic. A location that is also, undoubtedly, incredibly slimy, foul-smelling, and coated in secretions. On the inside, it is my turn to shudder at the thought of the potential deep dive, but I do my damnedest to turn it into a shrug. 'Is there any chance you'd give it to us?' I enquire hopefully.

The happy mood surrounding the gigantic being dissipates instantly, and his regard is far darker.

'Give you my treasure?' he asks incredulously. 'Do I look bloody stupid? That'th my bloody pride and joy that ith. No, of courthe I won't give it to you. Ruleth are ruleth. I'm afraid I'm going to have to eat you both up now, if you'd be so good ath to get rid of that bloody shield, please.'

Chapter Twenty
Lavaur, 3 May, 1211

It is a strange feeling to come back from a death so certain that you thought all over forever. For a moment I wonder if this is a new life beyond the walls of this world as grey blurs start to streak with colour. Then as my sight returns, as the grey assumes the form of stonework familiar to me, that of the Great Hall, and the colours into pennants and people, I know I live still. Although, maybe not for long.

It's hard to assess too much for I cannot move. Not my body nor my head. Even my eyes will not shift from gazing straight ahead. In front I see my fellow Perfects, Good Men and Women both kneeling. Though I can only see seven or eight familiar faces half-obscured by cowls, I must assume there are more. From the angle of how I look at them, I'm in a similar position. It's hard to be sure though because my attention is pulled to what is between us.

We're at least two rows deep, and the slight curve, plus being opposite my fellows, makes me suspect we must be in a circular arrangement. Between us stands an altar, plain and simple, naught more than a wooden table with a white cloth laid across it. But what makes it beyond all doubt an altar, what makes it holy, and what makes my heart sink deep down into the depths of my stomach is what sits upon it.

The Holy Grail. An object delivered to our order just after the death of Christ by Mary Magdalene herself, if the tales are true. Our most precious possession, indeed perhaps the most valuable in all of Christendom. And one I myself delivered to the safety of Foix. It looks like the Israelite rabbi was right to doubt the security of leaving it there. I curse myself for not having stayed to guard it, but my peoples' needs were great, and no one expected me to stand in perpetuity over it. All believed the vaults there impenetrable. As far as I know, Foix is not besieged, has not fallen. Apparently, their vaults are more permeable than we believed.

Initially, my attention is all on the holy item, unsurprising given my head seems to be tilted to look directly at it. Now, however, I become aware that there are people in the centre, as well as the Grail. And when I realise who, then my horror becomes complete.

Perhaps I should not be surprised to see the two leaders, physical and spiritual, of the Crusade here with us. One is bedecked in armour, a ruddy-cheeked, filled out face wrapped in a curly brown beard. If it broke into a warming smile, you could believe the man to be an innkeeper, a welcome sight for respite on a wearying road. His expression, though, is dour, frozen, and his eyes give the lie to that first impression. They're cold, grey, almost dead. The eyes of a killer, and one who does so without hesitation or doubt. If I don't miss my guess, it's none other than Simon De Montfort, the newly raised-up hero of the Albigensian Crusades. A man who's covered himself in such military glory in this conquest that he's gained more land now, here in the Languedoc, than the King of the Francs himself holds to the north.

The other man I've seen before, once long ago. He's no calmer now than he was then, when he railed from the pulpit against us, condemning us as heretics and sinners all. Now, as then, his eyes gleam with that same fanaticism that saw him put an entire city —seventeen thousand souls— to the sword to find a handful of Good People. 'Kill them all, God will know his own' were his words then, when he earned the title he now carries. The Butcher of Beziers. Archbishop Arnaud Almeric. His tonsured scalp glistens with sweat that sticks the scraggly mess of remaining red hair down to the sides of his head. His button nose might seem almost cherubic were it not for the wide-eyed madness of his wild eyes sitting just above. Each time he strays into my vision, I can see his lips working furiously, his expression and the flecks of spittle flying from them making it clear he's ranting in undoubtedly puritan fury. My hearing has not yet returned, the world utterly silent around me, but I don't need to hear to know he's spewing forth his poisonous form of faith on all and sundry.

But it's the third man that I can't quite believe is here. At least, not free, walking in liberty, in companionship with the mortal enemies of our order. A balded pate shining in the candlelight is my first clue, but it's the black robes he wears that bring to mind who he could be, as unbelievable as it seems. When he turns, when I see the eagle-like nose and the tightly drawn smooth skin that could mark him as a man of fifty or equally of seventy, ageless but undoubtedly senior, it's clear who he is.

Papa Nicetas. The mysterious Good Man of Constantinople. The man who helped us establish the tenets of our faith and returned to us in our hour of need. Now standing shoulder-to-shoulder with those sworn to destroy us.

And there is the other matter — the matter of the strange light that haloes him like a bastardised version of a saint. It surrounds him, a glow that seems to come from the inside outwards, pouring from his skin. And not just him. It connects, stretching out languorous burgundy tendrils to each of the Good People, encircling them. I can't move my eyes still, but I can see one reaching towards my midriff, and I don't doubt I'm similarly tethered. Perhaps it's why I can't move, why all my fellow Perfects are kneeling, their eyes open but vacant. I have no doubt they are all bespelled. We are all bespelled, but some of the effect is lessened on me somehow, allowing me to be aware. Perhaps because of the rabbi's gift. Right now, I'm far from sure it's a blessing.

Nicetas is not the only glow in the place. The Grail is luminant, puissant with a glaring light that makes me want to close my eyes. An impossibility, but one I'd resist even if it were not. I need to see what's going on, what's coming next.

There's a popping noise, such as when a cork is pulled from a bottle neck, and my hearing comes pouring back. It's a deafening rush for a moment, the sensation of being swarmed by all the background noise I cannot see, the murmurs and clashes from outside as people rush to and fro, the sound of stone being heaved from one spot to another. No doubt to allow corpses to be carried for burning afore the rats set to with aplomb on the feast laid out for them. It takes me a second before I can focus on the conversation. When I do, it's to hear the Pope's man, Arnaud Almeric, his high-pitched voice whining, demanding.

'... you think I cannot take it now, wizard? Do you believe yourself stronger than the Pope, heathen?'

So... it sounds as though all is not paradisiacal between these assembled enemies. Nicetas looks entirely unbothered by the bandied insults, but I see De Montfort's hand stray to his scabbard. So he's Nicetas' man more than the Pope's. It would be interesting and something to exploit were I able to move or in a position to exploit anything at all.

Nicetas' eyes flick to the soldier, and he gives a subtle shake. De Montfort relaxes, but his poise remains readied. A man of action through and through. The treacherous Black Robes turns his attention to Almeric, a reassuring smile across his stretched-skin features.

'Of course not, good priest. I am here to serve his Holiness in all things, though you may not approve of my methods. My magic is why I have been entrusted this mission by Innocent, and I must ask you to have faith in me a little longer. These satanic dogs have woven strange, poisonous spells around this most holy of vessels, and were you to carry this all the way to Rome as it stands, I cannot think of the damage it might wreak. Upon the world, upon the Holy See were you to reach it. Upon yourself, carrying it.'

'I fear no such witchcraft!' Almeric spits, a green globule that splats on the floor in front of the feet of the Good Man opposite me. 'The Lord is my shield and sword.'

'And I am his. The instruction is clear.' There's a bass rumble to De Montfort's voice that speaks of arriving thunder and impending doom for those not prepared to listen.

Almeric's eyes blaze. 'You are Phillip's and the Pope's before that. It is by his authority you lead this holy endeavour, not this accursed creature's.'

'And yet...' Nicetas' voice is calm, calming, seeking to soothe the enraged monk. 'And yet the Holy Father has faith enough in me to proceed with my plan to regain this holy relic and return it to its rightful place at the heart of Christendom. Would you question his wisdom as you question mine?'

The monk is practically spitting feathers, but he has no answer to that. Instead, he changes subject. 'And how will you lift these foul workings? When will it be ready?'

'Why, tis simple.' Nicetas' voice never changes, never lifts from that musical placid state. 'What better way to cleanse it than in the blood of the heretics? It won't take long, my friend. Simon, if you would be so kind?'

De Montfort leaves my field of vision, but a moment later he is back with one of the Good Men. Guillhaume of Plaisance Du Touch, a bastide near to Toulouse itself. The man's legs work as the knight pushes him forward into Nicetas' waiting arms, and the murk lifts from his eyes, awareness returning to him. The spell woven over him is unravelling.

Too late. As he reaches Nicetas' embrace, the thin Bogomil's arm whips up, and a razored athame kisses deep into poor Guillhaume's throat. A second later, his life blood gushes, pouring out, spattering across the simple wooden cup that somehow shines like a beacon, befouling it, defiling it as it sits on the altar. As the Perfect's life spark gutters, Nicetas lets him drop. But his hand is not empty. Contained within it is a strange lit ball, like from the stories one might hear that tell of marshland spirits, will-o'-the-wisps, floating in it. As he turns his back on the discarded corpse, as De Montfort seizes it and starts pulling it backwards, he casually drops the ball with a backhanded movement into the mouth of the cup itself.

It seems to me the Grail's light dims, darkens. Whether it's the blood or the strange ball of energy he deposited, I do not know. I'm already gripped by nausea, though still unable to move to retch or expel my sickened grief from my gut. And it's only just the start. A moment later, De Montfort returns with Elaine of Castelnaudary and hurls her, staggering, into the mad wizard's arms. The blade comes up and bites once more, and the same thing occurs. And on and on. Good Person after Good Person is sacrificed, blood spilled across the holy relic. But it's the energy that's worse. If I have not missed my guess, it's that which is more precious to each lost person, and I can't escape the horrified feeling that Nicetas holds their very soul in his grasp. Even more terrible, each time he drops one into the cup, the light changes, reddening. And the world around the cup is not as it once was. It seems as though reality itself is *thinning*. There's a pressure, a sucking weight surrounding it. As if the air is a membrane, stretching. And there is something on the other side. A presence gathers. I cannot see it, and for that I thank the Good God, but I can feel it. A malevolence full of poisonous hatred towards all and every living thing pours through the weakening of whatever separates us from it. It holds no good intent, no love, no offer of anything but domination and destruction. It is a perversion that will swallow us all whole to satisfy its own smallest whim. Terror like I have never known runs ice through my blood.

And I'm not alone in my unease. Almeric is sweating even more profusely than previously. His skin has taken on a chalk-like quality, and great rivulets run down his cheeks, down the nape of his neck. De Montfort is less affected but still clearly disturbed. He shifts from foot to foot, a gauntleted hand flexing, opening and closing as though around an invisible pommel. It's as though he knows something is coming that will require fighting, but he also realises he lacks the tools to do it. No easy sensation for a man of action, but I feel no sympathy for him. That is beyond me as I watch him deliver friend after friend to the mad bastard's blade.

The air is thick with menace, a sensation so poisonous it feels like it might sneak into my veins and corrupt my flesh, turn it gangrenous. I want to flick my eyes down, to see if I still possess my arms, my legs, my chest itself, or if it's all just a putrid mess, riddled with rot. Of course I can't move my eyes, cannot act, cannot even weep. All I can do is bear witness to what I feel more and more sure is the end of the world.

Suddenly, there's a disturbance, a timid but insistent knocking at a door just out of sight to my right hand. A tremulous voice cries out, 'My lords. Please! My lords.'

The voice is familiar, but I'm struggling to place it. De Montfort shoots a look across at Nicetas. The mad wizard snarls, his teeth bared, genuine emotion crossing his face for the first time, but he nods his acquiescence. De Montfort passes out of sight, though I can still hear his voice.

'What is it, boy?'

'Please, my lord. Troops approaching from the south. Raymond of Foix's men, riding, seeking vengeance.'

'What?'

Now De Montfort sounds motivated, excited even. This is his field of expertise, more so than his patron's strange workings. Almeric, too, is drawn by the clamour and comes across. Even Nicetas' attention gets pulled that way, and he steps over towards the entrance.

And for the first time, it is a good thing I'm restrained by whatever foul working Nicetas has put upon me. Because if not, I'd have jumped from my skin and screamed loud enough to wake the devil himself. For an arm wraps around mine and pulls at me.

'Come, man, let's be gone!' The familiarity brings me so many emotions. Joy. Love. Despair. My best friend, the man I love beyond all others. My brother in the black, Benedict.

Now I know from where I recognise the boy who knocked at the door. It's the stable boy who fled through the side door with Ben. This is all some scheme he's laid. Perhaps originally he planned to try some sort of rescue for all the Good People, but even he can see that lies beyond his capacities. But the Good God love him, and damn me for having put him in this situation, he will not leave without trying to save me at least.

Of course, his efforts are in vain. The arm he's furiously tugging on is weighted dead meat. He's not realised he needs to do everything, that I'm incapable of acting. His yanking becomes stronger, and for a moment I have hope. But suddenly they cease. And a second later he passes into my viewpoint, pulled forward against his will, hogtied in that same claret energy. Nicetas advances upon him, magic crackling along his sable hood, fury in his eyes.

My one relief is that Benedict doesn't wear the black robe, only simple peasant garments, doubtless aiming to pass in disguise through the streets.

Nicetas hopefully doesn't recognise him as a Perfect. He clearly recognises an enemy though.

'Who are you that dares to disturb this most sacred of moments?' Now the Bogomil's voice is furious whirling gales of words that aim to lacerate this bold intruder.

Ben can't move, can't reach for a weapon even if he could still use one without risking his own Perfection. But he stands resolute, endlessly brave, his head held high. And without hesitation, he spits clean in the face of the world-ending wizard to whom he is captive. He may not be able to lift a hand against the man — both due to the magic and the risk to his Perfected soul — but he can still show his righteous disdain.

'A pox on you, you treacherous whoreson.' His voice never wavers, never cracks. His courage is so strong, so true. I want to applaud, to weep, to pay tribute to his bravery. But of course I cannot.

Nicetas wipes the phlegm from his face delicately with the sleeve of his robe and looks at my dearest friend with contempt. 'It matters not,' he says, his voice once more calm and under control, looking directly at him. 'I know who you are.'

For a moment, my heart sinks, terrified he's recognised Ben as a Good Man, that he'll steal his soul too for his perverted Eucharist. Instead, the faintest smile flickers across Nicetas' face.

'You're a dead man.' And the athame whips out, razor sharp and true in aim, for his throat. There's a moment, a noise halfway between a gurgle and a cry. And my student, my best and truest friend, my would-be rescuer. The man I love as a brother, my strong right hand and shield...

Falls.

The only mercy is that Nicetas turns from him, doesn't take his soul, not recognising his Perfection. It's ashes in my mouth though, seeing him lying there. He thrashes a moment, then stills, and I could weep.

Then comes a shock, like a bucket of ice water thrown liberally to the face.

Because I *do* weep.

I feel the tear rolling down my face, and for a moment I think that my grief is so strong, it alone has broken the spell. And then, I realise I can move my eyes, that I can choose where to look. So I glance downwards and see that Ben's tugging was not in vain.

The toes of my right foot were knocked from their original position with the jostling and have crossed the chalk circle I did not even realise I knelt in.

And somehow, with that action, the working has been weakened. The spell is breaking.

CHAPTER TWENTY-ONE

HASTINGUES, 9 MARCH, PRESENT DAY

Wondering whether paracetamol, ibuprofen, or raining down screaming death would be the most effective against snail-induced headaches.

F our more tentacles make tentative attempts to slap past the barrier, but my magic easily repels them. Another peeks around the corner behind us, so Aicha taps a vacant spot next to the sucker pad already pin-boarded to the wall with another knife. It makes the wise decision to retreat. I think about how to manage this Mexican stand-off which we've found ourselves in.

'Do you know who I am?' I call down to the giga-gastropod, who looks as annoyed as I feel.

'Not a clue, sorry!' he calls back brightly.

'Does the name Paul Bonhomme mean anything to you?' I holler.

'Umm, doethn't ring any bellth, I'm afraid. You wouldn't happen to know what flavour you are comparatively, would you? Maybe if you let me take a tathte, it might jog my memory,' he attempts hopefully.

'Not going to happen, buddy. Even if you ate me, it wouldn't help you at all. I'd just reincarnate in the nearest body and come back for another go.'

'Ooh, that soundth wonderful! Like that take-away delivery servithe I keep hearing about,' he says, his eyes brightening at the thought.

'Yes, but at the moment, I'm using defensive magic and trying to talk this out. Eventually, I'm going to get fed up and start breaking out the big offensive guns.'

The eyestalks rear back in horror. 'Not bazookath?'

I nod positively. 'Exactly so — the magical equivalent of bazookas!'

Worry diminishes in the weaving protrusions, blinking relief. 'Oh, magic'th okay, Mr Snack. I'm imperviouth to magic being catht directly on me, unlike thith very frustrating barrier you insitht on using to delay the inevitable. Magic tathteth deliciouth. You'd be most welcome to catht some super strong spellth ath you go down my gullet; it'll act like seasoning! Ooh, I bet you're ever so flavoursome!'

I grind my fingers into the corners of my eyes, feeling a somewhat desperate need for a stiff drink — or six. 'Okay, look, eventually, if my spells don't work, I'm going to think about rounding up some firepower. I'll even let you have two or three bodies on the house 'cos I'm going to cart up a shit-tonne of white wine, butter, and a whole fucking field of parsley in a rucksack each time. Then I'm going to come in here and cook your miserable hide and have the world's largest fucking Escargots à la Bourguignonne, my friend. We'll be picking you out in serving pieces with pitchforks.'

'My shell'th imperviouth to fire,' he answers back smugly.

'Fucking hell.' My frustration is getting the better of me, and I am about to go medieval on his tail with my sword just to ease my desire to chop something into smaller somethings. I turn to Aicha. 'You try talking to him.'

Aicha looks at me, then at the dangling pod-like eyes. She pushes past me and glares straight at them. 'I am Aicha Kandicha the Undying, the Druze Queen, Protector of the Sacred Spring. I cannot be killed, even in your foul digestive juices, and if you do not stop this inane discussion and hand us the veil at once, I will climb inside your mouth and then I will cut my way out of your rectum with my dullest blade over a prolonged period. Do not try me!'

The waggling globes peer past her at me. 'Ooh I like her, she'th *fierthe*! Much more impressive a deliciouth morsel than you bloody were.'

'What's with every monster we meet falling for you?' I mutter under my breath to Aicha.

She shrugs dismissively. 'Real recognises real, *saabi*,' she replies.

The supersized snail seems to reflect on what she said; one appendage detaches from the ceiling to scratch the back of his optic orbs. After a few moments, he answers, 'No, sorry, really liked the whole pitch, very scary. Problem ith that I need the magic it hath to stay alive, so I have to either take a chanthe of managing to digetht you before you can kill me or I die anyway. Good try though, much bloody better than the other food wath. Top markth.'

Aicha waves me forward. 'Well, I tried. What now?'

It is my turn to reflect. 'You need the magic to stay alive?'

He nods his waggly storks eagerly. 'Oh yeah. It keepth me so young and beautiful. I can't go out and hunt, and few people thethe dayth are foolith enough to come wandering into my cave system, present company excluded of courthe. Pluth, even the animalth have gotten wise to "stay outside, stay alive" as a motto to live by. Luckily, I can draw sustenanthe from other magicth just as well as eating the liketh of you.'

'How long could you go without the nourishment it provides?' I ask.

'Hmm, well I suppothe I could manage a year or so before I got really hungry but only a very short period of time like that. Any more than a decade, and it'd be a huge problem, but that'th only jutht long enough for a decent bloody nap.'

I think I can see a resolution to our stalemate at last. 'Look, I don't actually want the veil. I only need it to catch a bad guy. Afterwards, I'd be happy to bring it back to you.'

The massive mollusc seems to consider the offer, then narrows his eye slits at me. 'Wait a minute. Onthe you leave, what'th to bring you back? And even if you would come back, what happenth if thith bad guy destroyth my veil?'

'Well, in terms of coming back, I'll make you a vow on my *talent* freely given to come back with the veil. If it gets destroyed, I'll find you a magical item or items of equivalent power or greater and bring them to you in exchange as swiftly as possible and certainly within a year. Honestly, I'm really impressed by how long you've kept this hidden. In fact, I would like to turn this into a long-term deal. If it keeps you fed and simultaneously avoids you having to eat people, then bringing you objects of power that need to be kept away from the sticky fingers of evil bastards seems like a win-win to me.'

Several of the tendrils sweep in curling motions backwards over the enormous shell, preening and polishing it while the head of Lou looks deep in thought. Eventually, he gives a firm nod. 'Okay, you've got yourselveth a deal. Could you pleathe unpin my pad now?'

Aicha yanks the knife out of the wall, and we watch warily for the possibility of a double-cross. The club-like limb seems to stretch and flex like fingers trying to work out kinks after a gruelling day in the office before rolling in on itself to form a curled ball like the world's biggest role of liquorice. It hovers, larger than my head, right in front of my face. Aicha tenses, ready to spring into attack mode, and I wonder if the limb itself is also impervious to magic and whether my *talent*-imbued blade will have any effect.

'Don't leave me hanging then, Snack,' Lou Carcoilh calls up from down below.

I wonder if he is asking for what I think he is asking for. Cautiously extending out my closed hand, I fist-bump the enormous appendage. It retreats down the twisting corridor out of sight, leaving my knuckles coated in its opaque viscous goo. As I try to shake the clinging gunk off my hand, Aicha leans forward and whispers, 'You've been Slimed.'

A tentacle ceases actively polishing the shell and slips inside to root around. After an, 'Ah hah!' from our new friend, the tentacle retracts, carrying a grey, slightly damp cloth that it proffers up to us. There's a sheen to it, from the thick gloop that it's coated in liberally and dripping off it from the snail-dragon's grip.

I drop the shield and pick up the item, which is utterly nondescript apart from the radiating power making it blaze like Goku going Super Saiyan in the *sight*. It's far too powerful to put into etheric storage —a sure-fire route to an explosive combination that will make these tunnels very toasty for all of us— so I carefully fold it to face-cloth size and put it in my jacket pocket before surreptitiously wiping my hands on my jeans. I would have worried about the dry-cleaning cost for said jacket if I seriously believed there was a chance of getting through the next few days with this body intact, let alone my current outfit.

'Lou Carcoilh, you have my word I'll return with the veil or an equivalent item or items of value,' I shout down to the cephalopod. The words echo off the walls of the palatial space it carved out for itself beneath this tiny town.

'Or die trying. Don't forget that third possibility,' he calls back cheerfully as he slowly turns himself around. 'Alwayth liked when they say that in filmth, soundth so dramatic,' he mutters to himself as he slips back away into the darkened tunnel behind him, leaving a luminescent slicked trail wider than a train-track on the tamped down soil.

I look over at Aicha, who is watching the gelatinous slime yoyoing up and down off her knife as she wiggles it with utter revulsion. 'I can't quite work out if that was incredibly easy or unbelievably difficult,' I say.

'Little from A, little from B, I reckon. Here, present for you.' She hands me the slime-coated knife before starting the slow upward trudge to the surface so very far above. That, at least, I can put in my etheric storage, so I stow it, intending to clean and return it at the first opportunity. Taking a last look back, Orpheus-like, I rub at my poor aching temples, then head back along the uphill slope as well.

CHAPTER TWENTY-TWO
HASTINGUES, 9 MARCH, PRESENT DAY

Knackered, splitting headache, in need of
a beer but feeling like we've finally made
a bit of progress. Waiting for Murphy to
come and piss on our parade.

As we crest the entrance, the sun is well into its steady western descent, and I am famished. I estimate it to be three or four in the afternoon, and I failed to bring provisions. Even a conversation with a slime-encrusted, hairy, giant snail wasn't enough to sufficiently diminish my hunger. Plus, holding up the shield was a drain.

As we clear the cavern entrance, my phone alerts me to a text from Isaac. He left around midday and arrived in Hastingues a few hours after, only to find it held exactly zero open eateries or watering holes, so is now across the river at a small café in Peyrehorade.

When we arrive, Isaac is sitting at a table, two small carafes on a red-and-white tablecloth so synonymous with the French bistro experience; one jug is clearly tap water, the other, the house red. He enjoyed a diluted afternoon snifter while waiting for us and now motions for us to sit with his empty glass. He pours a little of the water into a stubby wine glass and winks at me.

'Water into wine, Paul, my boy,' he says and tops it up to nearly full with the red in the other jug.

'More like wine into watered-down, less tasty, and less alcoholic wine,' I reply. It is a process I've always found semi-sacrilegious, and I rescue the remaining wine from his cruel machinations by pouring it into my own glass.

He is keen to get into how our trip played out and no doubt has information of his own to share, but I tap the menu forcefully, determined to order first. We are too far from a proper town to find much vegetarian options, and a goat's cheese salad just isn't going to cut the mustard today. Tempted as I am to order the snails out of spite, I suspect I'll regret it once it comes to eating them. I am hugely relieved to find a vegetarian burger, something only possible this far into the countryside in the last decade or two. I order mine with an extra helping of chips, and Aicha asks for a steak, medium done.

To the server's credit, he controls his expression, looking only mildly horrified. For most French people, there are only two correct options for serving red meat: literally still bleeding (rare) or practically still breathing (blue). Her request for a large apple juice instead of alcohol almost undoes him, and I suspect he'll need to drink a large Ricard to recover once he's relayed our order.

While waiting for the food, we fill Isaac in on our meeting with Lou Carcoilh. He is equal parts amused by the tale and impatient to see the cloth. Having no wish to push our server further to drink than I suspect we already have, I wait until after we've eaten our fill (and he has retired to weep quietly into his pastis in the corner) before unrolling it on the empty table beside us. I'm quietly grateful that the plastic cloth will be relatively easy to wipe clean.

Isaac examines it silently, almost trance-like for a short period, and I know he is *seeing* what there is to see. After a while, he looks up at me, appearing troubled in spirit.

'What do you *see* when you *look* at it, my boy?' he asks me.

I open myself up and *look*. It is radiant in terms of power. Massive amounts of initial energy combined with millennia of fervent belief have combined to create a wondrous article that shines like a beacon when seen by the Talented. If it wasn't hidden in a magic-nulling location like Lou's damp-infested shell, it would've attracted the attention of a shitload of magic users.

'No wonder Phone Dick needed help to find it,' I say. 'There's no way something so chocked full of magical power could stay hidden so long without being in the hands of someone with major *talent*. He obviously expected us to be going up against some form of seriously dangerous super Talented. Using us as his proxy kept him from getting his hands dirty.'

'Fair play. I'd say Lou is fairly dangerous to most people, Talented or otherwise,' Aicha adds.

'Yeah, I think where it was stashed was as lucky as we could have hoped for, really. It could have been the fucking Tarrasque who had it.' There are shivers all round. No one wants to have to go and talk to the fucking Tarrasque, grade A wanker that he is. Weird not-quite dragons seem to be a French speciality, but the Tarrasque is one of a kind. Thank fuck for that.

Isaac scratches at his chin, one side, then the other, his fingers restlessly massaging the skin. 'Let me put it another way. Remember that roleplaying game we got into for a while back in the eighties?'

'Dungeons and Dragons? That was totally radical!' It was hilarious playing missions with "fantastical" characters I'd drained a glass with more than once and who would have sprayed said drink in all directions if they'd realised how they were being portrayed.

'Okay, well, remember the alignments of good and evil, lawful and chaotic? Where would this item belong on that scale in the game?'

I *look* again, but it only reinforces my already formed opinion. 'Lawful Good, no doubt.'

'So there's no way that someone can easily use this to raise armies of undead. They could bring back a recently deceased saint to perform more benedictions, perhaps. Restore an innocent child to the arms of their grieving parents, undoubtedly. But launching a zombie apocalypse upon an unsuspecting populace? Not that I can conceive of. This is an item made for bringing blessings and healings to the needy and deserving. Did Phone... Person sound like that sort of individual to you?'

'He doesn't strike me as altruistic, no, what with the torture, murdering, kidnapping, and blackmailing since our first encounter. Oh, and forcing a load of werewolves to commit suicide-by-Aicha. Perhaps we just got off to a bad start?'

Isaac ignores my attempt at levity. 'So if he isn't going to use it for those sorts of things, what is he going to use it for? Does he believe himself powerful enough to wrest it from its natural purpose and bend it to his?'

'If he's forced Nanael to do his bidding, it might not just be a thing of "believing" himself to be that powerful,' I say solemnly.

Seeing Isaac wince, I bite my lip. Damn it, I hate making him feel like this, but we can't avoid it. Just as I'm about to try again, he sighs, slumping slightly. 'You're right, my lad. It still seems unimaginable. I've never met a Talented who can even come close to standing toe-to-toe with one of the Bene Elohim. I suppose if he's that blasted strong, perhaps he feels he really is strong enough to force it to perform evil acts.' He frowns again. 'Or perhaps he wishes to destroy it and has some other twisted aim of gaining something from removing such a, dare I say, holy item from existence?'

'You can dare to say it; doesn't make it true. Goodness doesn't come from a higher being. It comes from us alone. If anyone should know that, it's you. Nithael is good, but he isn't holy. He's just not from the here as we know it.'

Isaac smiles beatifically at me. 'You put your spin on it, lad; I'll put on mine. Just because we didn't get our understanding of it right in the various scriptures doesn't mean there isn't an element of the divine that connects us all.'

Aicha harrumphs. 'Theological discussions, boo. Actual planning to prevent piss poor performance and stop us from wearing our internal organs as earrings, yay.'

I glance at her. 'Okay, so we think he might aim to destroy or somehow deface the Vernicle for some ulterior motive, so taking it directly to him is a no-no. However, we've had no joy tracking down any information about him. I assume that's still the case, Isaac? No idea what's driving him or any theoretical associates?'

He shakes his head.

I sigh. 'Well, I can't see how we're going to gather anything without getting a better starting point, so we need to get a meeting with him. We're all tough-slash-theoretically-indestructible, but this? This doesn't bode well, honestly. He knows us too damn well.'

I don't bring up what Phone Dick said about being able to annul Aicha's immortality. Honestly, I'm not sure I believe him, but he knows enough to make it a credible threat. Last night, I told Aicha, of course. I couldn't have brought her along not knowing. She just shrugged and told me she'd shove his antidote where the sun didn't shine, and she wasn't talking about

Norway in the winter. Rehashing it now for Isaac won't help any, but I can't lie. I am fucking scared about meeting this shithead.

If magic and its ilk truly made us immortal, we'd see Neanderthals kicking back in Talented speakeasies alongside the gnomes and goblins. I never met a human much over fifteen hundred years old, though that doesn't mean they don't exist. Just our paths haven't crossed. Still, no matter the forces we harness, eventually, we reach a point where either fatigue or fallibility takes centre stage, and we retire willingly or not from the mortal coil. To consider ourselves unkillable just because nothing has managed it yet is like a normal human assuming they are immortal just because they haven't died yet. Eventually, Death makes fools of us all.

Still, Aicha made it clear she's in to the very end, and I learned quickly that it isn't my place to decide on her behalf. She's older than me, definitely wiser, and considerably scarier. I'm not about to tell her what she can and can't do.

'Isaac, you're not geared up for the offensive,' I say, turning to him. 'While I suspect Aicha has some pent-up tension she'd like to exorcise through some violence —'

'*Ultra-violence.*'

'Sorry, yes, ultra-violence. Me? I want to have a little natter with Phone Dick and find out where he's been getting his intel and whose arse I need to kick for grassing on me. So I suggest you take on the home defence,' I say slowly, thinking it through. There's every chance the discussion with Phone Dick isn't going to turn out well. If we don't make it back? Getting the Vernicle well away from his grubby little clutches is the priority. Hopefully, between the home turf advantage and Nithael, Isaac can keep both himself and the artefact safe.

'Get the veil back to yours and behind the heaviest protective wards you and your plus one can whip up. Also, that'll give you time to study it and work out what the hell he might want it for. Aicha and I will go for a more direct approach, mix in some misdirection, and see if we can't grift him into a meeting and ideally out of possession of your brother or Nanael — or both.'

'So basically, wing it and make it up as we go?' Aicha clarifies.

'Well, I mean, yes, if you want to strip it down to its bare bones, then fine. All the taste is in the meat though, so you're the one missing out.'

'Says the vegetarian,' she points out.

'Right, fine, it's a rubbish metaphor, and we're going to improvise *from the basis of all this intricately discussed planning* and go slap up Phone Dick. What do you reckon?'

'You son of a bitch. I'm in,' she says, sliding her sunglasses into place for dramatic effect.

CHAPTER TWENTY-THREE

PEYREHORADE, 9 MARCH, PRESENT DAY

Feeling less likely to gut the next person who glances in my direction after a sizeable meal. Note – less likely does not equal no chance at all.

We pay our bill, and include a decent tip for our traumatised server. This is mainly to salve my conscience for soon pinching the dishtowel draped over his apron strings, a quick sleight of hand as he bends to pick up the saucer containing the cash payment and bill. There's a possibility I might just need a dirty rag in the not-too-distant future.

Isaac sputters off in his rust bucket of a Citroen, the Vernicle stored in the boot within a heavily warded strong box he had the foresight to bring. I feel some relief that even if the engine blows up on his two-hundred-and-fifty-kilometre drive home, the box, and coincidentally Isaac, will both be safe because of the angelic magic surrounding them.

It's getting late by the time we start the journey back towards Toulouse in the Alpine. We stop at a nearby petrol station and top up the car to full as it drinks down petrol like a lapsed alcoholic offered a free bar. Inside the station, I purchase a watery, bitter, burnt-tasting concoction that they have somehow mistakenly mislabelled as coffee, but I still buy two of them to keep me moving.

As we are about to get back in the car, I feel a buzz in my pocket. The screen of my burner phone is dark, a lifeless lump in my hand. I fish in my pockets like a self-imposed stop-and-search until I find the offending item — the phone we took from the shit wizard's bathroom. Caller ID displays the same number that previously rang us. I look at Aicha. Her focus is on the phone, but she looks up as I turn my attention back to the mobile. Glancing back up at her, I see she has shifted her gaze once more to the screen in my hand.

Though of course she raises her head back again as I lower mine.

I puff my cheeks, clicking my tongue, then decide the whole thing is ridiculous. Time to get on with what needs to be done. I push accept and put the phone on speaker.

'PD, just the man! Would you believe we were just talking about you?' I know my mannerisms annoy the hell out of him, but he's had us on the back foot since the get-go. Anything that gets his back up might also knock him a little off balance. Had we not already found the veil, I might be concerned about irritating him enough to hurt innocents, but we are in the endgame now. It's worth trying to throw a spanner in the works. At least, that's the idea. His cold, dead-fish tone comes through, arthritic vocal cords not dispelling the deadly nature lingering behind them.

'I would have been incredibly surprised and almost disappointed had you not been, Mister Bonhomme. I have somewhat elevated expectations surrounding you and your partners, and I do so hate to be let down by those I work with, whether willingly or otherwise.'

'No need to worry on that account, P-Diddy. We are golden and down to fucking get the job done.'

'Crudity is an ignoramus' refuge, but it is neither distressing nor distracting. I didn't ring for a bit of banter, as you would put it, but for a status update. Where are you with the recovery of my item?'

Of course, I could act like we still don't have it. Stall for time. But, again, all that's likely to do is lead to dead civilians. There's no advantage to be had from buying a few more hours in blood. None that would outweigh the likely loss of life, anyway.

'We have secured the package. I repeat, we have secured the package.' I don't feel like I am making headway with my clowning, but it might annoy him into giving something away. It might also, at some point, cause him to underestimate me for the idiot I'm currently presenting myself as. I desperately hope I'm not exactly that idiot and can take advantage of said moment if it arrives.

'And despite my previous comment, you continue with your pointless attempts, Paul. Truly, you never change. I assume you are still near Hastingues?'

My mood plummets with the velocity of an elevator with a cut cord. I smash into the bottom at a rate of knots. 'If you know where we are, you presumably knew where the Vernicle was. Why didn't you tell us or recover it yourself?'

'The reason is the same as why I don't need to answer your impertinent questioning. My reasons are my own, and my commands are to be followed. Nothing else requires further clarification.'

'How do we know you actually have Jakob? Or even that he's still alive?'

'I do not believe you to be ignorant or asinine, any of you. Surely you have discussed possibilities as to how I might have control over Nanael's power. I am not inclined to reveal my whys and wherefores like some overblown theatrical villain. You will bring me the Vernicle. In exchange,

I will provide some of the information you try so desperately and unsuccessfully to worm out of me during our conversations.'

Aicha's expression reflects my own dour internal emotional landscape, but I don't think either of us sees any alternative. We have to continue playing along, at least for now.

'Where do you want to meet then, so we can make this tradeoff?'

'To the south of Hastingues is the castle of Gramont. Not much further south in the same direction, you'll find a road to the left called Carriere Dous Caperans with a signpost for the Pont de Gramont. The bridge isn't as old as either of us, but it's still a remnant of a forgotten time. It seems an appropriate rendezvous point. It should only take you about fifteen minutes. Do remember to bring the Vernicle along. I would much rather play nice than resort to metaphorical fisticuffs, ch?' The line goes dead, and I turn to my companion, my frustration levels beyond boiling point.

'Who the bejeezus is this fuckwit? How does he know so much, and how is he managing to keep us so spectacularly in the dark?'

'Either way, he's been staying a step ahead of us the whole way. Doesn't seem to be changing that himself any time soon. So how do we change it? Now's the time to break out that fantastically intricate and detailed plan you've been working on, Paul.'

I pull out the server's dishcloth I stole and wave it unconvincingly in her direction. 'Tell him this is the Veil of Veronica?'

'We're fucking doomed.' She shakes her head in disbelief, but the fire in her eyes only burns brighter. Aicha Kandicha always does like taking on impossible odds.

Chapter Twenty-Four

PEYREHORADE, 9 MARCH, PRESENT DAY

Meal's positive effects are completely wiped out. I'm pissed off and ready to bring the pain. Ideally to someone else other than myself for once.

I t's about a fifteen-minute drive through the town of Bidache to get to the turnoff Phone Dick described, nestled into the forest. The trees seem to mock me as we pull off onto a single lane road. Their branches are barren from the winter months, yet cloaked in the green of strangling ivy, a semblance of borrowed life. I wonder if they look at me and see the same thing.

We pass by a couple of houses, bright-faced and airy, before reaching the end of the line, the dirt track narrowing even further, the bridge's hump visible down the winding trail. Leaving the car with its hazard lights flashing, aware of the way locals speed on presumably abandoned roads, we head for the only visible edifice — an ancient mill house accompanying a stone bridge. It looms large, red-shuttered, and closed off. Someone clearly lives in it, but no one is currently home. It's dark, lifeless, locked up. There's no other car here but ours. For a moment, I wonder if I should head over, investigate. Perhaps this is Phone Dick's hideout? But I can't quite believe he'd give us his address, all neatly packaged and tied up in a bow. After all the hoops he's made us jump through, there's too much chance of us bringing some backup cavalry charging in. Not that we have anyone else. There's just us, but he's been far too damn cautious until now to risk that.

Unless it's a double bluff.

My eyes narrow on the house...

I shake my head.

Nahhhh.

That would be ridiculous.

Midges swarm over the water's surface, the mid-afternoon warmth enough to call them to their dance. Enough to bring the bastard mosquitoes out too. The couple of months of sweet winter relief from their endless bites ended a few weeks ago, and they're happy to sup on us like our blood's the ambrosia of the gods. Maybe it is for them. They certainly seem to enjoy biting me enough, the little shits.

The bridge is simple, local solid stones hewed from the landscape and stacked centuries back, still holding solid. A mud-slicked path climbs steeply through the trees on the other side, disappearing into the foliage.

Waiting is a bind. I want to spring into action, to do a Scooby Doo and unmask the villain, bringing everything to a satisfying conclusion so we can all head off for some celebratory cookies. Problem is, I'm nowhere nearer to an answer, and we're holding none of the cards. There's no option except to hope that by meeting Phone Dick in person, we can somehow gain the upper hand between our combined brainpower and my dish cloth imitation Vernicle. In the meantime, there's nothing to do but bide our time.

My eyes flicker back to the cottage.

There's no way it's his...

Shaking my head, I perch against the packed stone of the bridge as Aicha stares down at the mud-browned waters of the stream on its westward route. I pick at one of the many mossy growths in the joint. It seems almost prickly, resembling nothing more than tiny green hedgehogs.

Aicha speaks up, her voice strained. 'I'm petrified, Paul.'

Pride floods through me — she has the confidence to be honest, to open up, to tell me how she really feels. 'You hide it well, *laguna*, but I guess we all have those worries and fears. This one seems so out of our control that we're just constantly reacting instead of getting out ahead. It's normal to feel afraid. I'm glad you told me. I'm here for you, you know.'

'Paul, you dickhead, the only thing I'm scared of is that I am literally petrified, in the sense of being unable to move a fucking muscle.' As her words come out more strained, I realise her lips must be locked in place.

I try to turn to see what the matter is, only to find my leg muscles have quietly organised a unified overthrow of my dictatorial regime and are no longer obeying commands. The open mutiny has passed along the organisational chain, fed by my central nervous system, so my arms still reverse grip the stone of the bridge. Even my neck won't obey the simple directive to turn and look at what is going on with my paralysed friend. I remain locked into a meditative observation of the heavens. My relaxed posture is at complete odds with my internal composure, which is screaming at my muscles and skeletal structure to knock off their unified strike action and get back on the job. The reply appears to be chants of, 'We shall not be moved.'

I pull on my *talent*, intending to push it into my extremities to step outside whatever invisible fucking chalk line I stepped in, only to find it has also joined the picket line. It sits inactive, a useless lump in my spirit doing nothing but dragging me down into the depths of despair as I recognise what I've been hit with. It's not a chalk line. It is a tincture that, as far as I am aware, hasn't been brewed in near on eight hundred years. I thought only Isaac knew how to make it. Apparently, his brother's also aware of the recipe.

A steady *tap-shuffle-tap* sounds from the bridge's northern end, opposite from where we arrived. Straining my eyes sidewards, I gain my first view of our recent tormentor.

The slow morse code gait isn't solely for dramatic effect. The man is ancient, hunched over his stick so far that the handle is almost obscured within the mass of his long white beard. He puts me in mind of Dick Van Dyke's bank owner in *Mary Poppins* but with none of the jovial nature carried in the actor's twinkly eyes. His are ice blocks, grey-scale windows of darkness in the reflected moonlight, void of any redeeming human quality. They are pitiless and mirthless and entirely determined, holding that controlled craziness of one who's passed through madness and arrived on the other side at a rationality only belying their utter insanity.

The air shimmers as he steps onto the bridge, and I feel an enormously powerful *don't look here* spell snap into being, surrounding us from bank to bank. Even if we were visible from a nearby window or road, we could blow ourselves up in a mushroom cloud of magical warfare and nobody would even notice.

My head starts to follow my eye movements, and I feel a moment of hope. Even magicless, I'll stand more than a decent chance of defeating this lunatic if I can get my hands on him. Any potential guilty feelings about breaking the bones of a frail geriatric is easily assuaged by the focused psychosis so clear in his steely gaze. I pull on my *talent,* but disappointingly, it remains comatose.

Because of my glacially slow neck twisting, I am now looking both at him and Aicha as he gradually crests the bridge. Sadly, he also clocks my movement, and he gives a low whistle that unintentionally quavers across a couple of octaves.

'Already overcoming the poison, are we, Paul? Very impressive. No doubt your companion is equally capable. A second dose might be advisable.'

A small sting at my neck, and my movement grinds to a halt. A mosquito, obviously one of the swarms of biting beasties harassing us since we left the car, dances drunkenly into view from the area of the bite and flies to Aicha. She falls victim to the same delivery system.

'Ingenious, don't you think? Soon as the weather warms, who questions mosquitoes, especially around bridges and waterways? A minor magical enhancement and puppeteering, and I have the equivalent of an almost invisible blow dart. Even an expert can't notice it until it's too late. Luckily, one only needs such a teeny amount, eh, Paul?' The wizened old bastard is entirely too pleased with himself.

'You plagiarising git.' It is clearly a strain for Aicha to even talk. For some reason, the poison is affecting her worse than me.

Phone Dick, proving to be no less of an In Person Dick, looks genuinely confused. 'I beg your pardon? What did you say?'

'First, fuck your pardon. I'll give it to you when I can accompany it with my foot up your ass. Second, you're a plagiarising, thieving toerag, and I'm going to message Jeunet and Caro's lawyers so they can sue your descendants once I've ripped your wrinkly old bonce clean off your turkey-skin neck.'

He blinks twice. 'What are you talking about, woman?'

'Jeunet and Caro? *The City of Lost Children*? Man delivered poison with mosquitoes by fitting them with special metal needles, then playing them a tune? You've seen it, you thieving little shitbag.'

Here we are, rendered completely incapable of movement, at the mercy of this amoral genius who's played us for fools from the get-go, yet he's the one turning bright red, blood vessels tracing their way across his papyrus-like skin. 'I, I — I don't know what you're talking about.'

Aicha cackles in a way that were she able to move, would have had her bent double, gasping for breath. 'You did. You properly just lifted it from that film. "Oh, I'm an evil dickhead. Want to deliver poison. That's an excellent system. Going to monologue it as my own." How'd that work out for you, you inappropriate, appropriating bastard?'

I don't know if I've ever admired Aicha more than for her audacious verbal assault on a man who's holding us entirely under his power. She is fearless in her indignation at his fraudulent claims of originality, at his unwillingness to pay tribute to the film genius who inspired it. This is a culture nerd embracing her righteous outrage and genuine in her furious anger. Sadly, although left initially flat-footed, Phone Dick quickly regains his self-control, breathing out a calming breath and composing himself, although incensed regard remains in his reptilian eyes.

'Indeed, perhaps I may have drawn some inspiration from the aforementioned source, but then "nothing is original, steal everything", eh, my dear?'

He draws level and pats her cheek with a dark-spotted, palsied hand, and all humour leaves her far faster than it arrived. The temperature drops by several degrees, and the emotionless killer she is comes to the forefront most definitively, even with her being entirely paralysed.

She growls, 'I am going to choke you on your wrinkled, cured-sausage excuses for fingers, then I'm going to Heimlich you and do it all over again until your black little squeezebox of a ticker gives out, you son of a bitch.' Each word is spat as a promise.

'Oh, Ms Kandicha, you are a delightful prospect, so filled with vim and vigour. Your accompaniment of Paul has been most serviceably utile. Were I to expect our paths ever crossing again, I would be honestly terrified, but I don't intend to exist much longer, and you won't be going anywhere — for the near future, at least.'

Lines trace themselves like silver spiderwebs along the floor surrounding her, forming runes of holding. They create a half-metre square box surrounding her feet. As it completes, he pats her cheek once more, a kindly smile on his face that goes nowhere near his eyes. Then he pushes his heavyweight *talent* into a word.

'*Burn.*'

I watch impotent as the air inside the magical enclosure explodes into flames. Aicha howls — a guttural, hoarse, cracking cry coming and going as her vocal cords snap and reform. Over and over. Her skin blackens, splitting and flaking away. Parts of her drop off, carbonised charcoal, as replacements grow underneath, pink passing rapidly through grey and brown to blacken anew. The air thickens with cinder clouds as she cyclically pulverises into dust within a matter of seconds. She's at the centre of her own personal firestorm — reforming only to burn all over again. Each blink covers her boiling eyeballs with new skin that crisps and plummets, twirling like a wingnut in the breeze. Aicha's been through her own personal hell, long ago for most humans but little more than the blink of a gnat's eye for the likes of us. And now the bastard's taken her back there, boxed in with nothing but the endless pain, the trauma, and the flames.

I rescued her from the nightmare the Nazis wove for her once. This time, I'm impotent, unable to do anything but cry with horror, tears streaming down my immobile cheeks as the strongest person I've ever met breaks on an unending pyre. It's unbearable. Her hoarse choking screams. The rippling heatwaves hovering over every inch of her. The burnt barbecue smell that wafts up my nostrils. I can't stand it. All I want is to make it stop. I'll do anything to *make it stop.*

Of course, the bastard who's done this to her doesn't seem bothered in the slightest. Without a sound, without even acknowledging her, he turns his back, and she's dismissed from his mind, irrelevant. The decrepit madman plods in my direction, dragging his weaker foot by a force of will, suggesting it's not a new infirmity. Now it's my turn to be on the receiving end of his paradoxical regard.

'I'll be seeing you soon, Paul,' he says softly.

He pulls something from the back of his trousers, then draws it across my throat in a swift, precise slash. I don't need to move my eyes to know that the initial painless moment signals exactly how honed the blade is. Arterial spray blossoms in the air like an artist's sketch of the tree of life and then my nerves explode in the equivalent of white noise.

As he moves out of my vision, there is a moment where —though I can't place it— I feel I recognise something about him, something from long ago...

Chapter Twenty-Five
Lavaur, 3 May, 1211

I've not more than a moment to come to a new equilibrium between the hope that Ben has given me by breaking the circle and his loss, carving huge gashes into my soul. Because further disruption arrives unexpectedly.

Outside but close enough as to be clearly heard, comes the thunder of an explosion, such as when sappers get drunk and demonstrate their pyrotechnic skills in the barracks instead of under the walls they seek to bring down. Chaotic noise peaks, hubbub building in shrieks and shouts, and it's clear that panic reigns supreme outside the walls.

De Montfort, his hand readied to seize another Good Man to my right, pauses and looks at Nicetas for instruction once more. The Bogomil curses, words in a language I don't speak but don't need to for me to gather his infuriated meaning, and spits.

'Come, I'll find out what goes on myself. We'll put an end to this uprising and then return to what needs to be done.'

The three men hurry from the room, through the door where the stable boy called for their attention, and I'm left, if not alone, then the only man or woman aware in the Great Hall.

Movement has not come back, not fully. My head is moving slowly, but it's too little, and if I wait for it all to come back, I don't doubt it'll be too late. There's no way Foix rides to our aid. Raymond is no fool, and he knows a lost cause when he sees it. This is some additional distraction Benedict prepared to give us cover to escape. My time is limited, of that I have no doubt.

I concentrate on my toes outside the circle. These I can feel, can move. They wiggle on command. I attempt to dig them into the cold stone flagstones. It's no simple task, but inch by inch, I drag my foot to the side, pulling my knee, my leg in that direction. As they move, it changes my balance. Slowly, far too damnably slowly, my stance widens, destabilises. Finally, it is more than my body can maintain, and the spell can't counter-balance the change in position. I tumble, twisting to the right, following my foot's path.

And my torso clears the circle.

My hands come down instinctively, catching me. But they're enfeebled and do little to check my fall. My face plants onto the cool stone sharply, but I welcome the pain. I can feel. It means I'm alive. There's still a chance to stop this evil madness.

Tears stream down my face as I pull myself forward. Strength has come back to my arms, enough at least that combined with my willpower, I can cover ground, dragging myself towards my downed friend. I'm blessing him for giving me this chance and berating myself for his death even though I know it's not my fault. Determined to honour his sacrifice.

I reach his body; it's still warm. But I can't stop, can't hold him, embrace him, mourn him as I wish to. Instead, it's arms forward, up and over, as I pull myself across him, past him. Towards the Grail.

I'm close now, maybe a metre or two. My legs are regaining some feeling, though they're still trembling, putty-like. I press my hands to my right knee, forcing myself up to standing. Then I reach a hand forward to grab the Grail, to dash the energy from it, to destroy it if I must, to stop whatever Papa Nicetas is trying to make happen here...

My arm comes up. But I can't move forward.

For a moment, I think the magic has struck again, that I'm paralysed. And in a way it has, but it's not the same one. No, this a different magic. Looking down, I can see ropes of energy similar to those that hold the other Perfects captive looped around me.

But not quite the same. There's an orange quality to the red, like new rust on a well-used plough blade. It's spun around me like a spider's cocoon for a fly, and it wraps more and more, enveloping me.

'What do you think you're doing, you foolish heathen?' It's not those dark velvet tones of Nicetas, but a half-screech, half-demand, high and quite insane.

It isn't Nicetas that's enrobed me in magic. It's Arnaud Almeric. The Pope's envoy to the Crusade.

'What are you doing?' he demands again.

But this time I can talk, can present an argument. We may be on opposing sides, but this is still a man of God. Surely he can be made to see reason? 'You may call me heathen, heretic, Father,' I start, 'but the working that... *creature* is performing is a million times worse than anything I might perform. Can you not see the corruption he works upon the Grail? We must disrupt it now while he's gone, while we have a chance. In the name of all that's holy, can you not see what he's bringing through?'

There's a moment of silence. Then a giggle, a screeching sound like nails on slate, emanates from behind me. 'Do you think his Holiness the Pope a fool? Do you think *me* such? That we would trust a dark magician such as that accursed cat-buggerer? No, we knew what he is, what he wants. He seeks to bring the Dark Lord, the Evil One himself, through to our world. But I am the Pope's anointed one, blessed by our Holy Father with miraculous strength and power. We see it! We know! This is the moment long foretold! The ending battle between good and evil, and I will stand righteous and resolute and defeat that arriving demonic force!'

He speaks with tones sure and certain, and my heart sinks once more. There's no reasoning with him. Here is a true zealot, one convinced of his rightness, of his righteousness. He's lost to the mania of his twisted faith and so sure in his arrogance that he believes himself capable of taking on the monstrous thing that seeks to enter our world. The fool. What will arrive when this working is complete is beyond his power to defeat. Of that much, I feel sure. There is no reasoning with his form of madness though.

When the echo of approaching footsteps carries from the open doorway on the right, Almeric steps forward, releasing his magic and pressing a blade to my throat instead. It seems Nicetas is not aware of the monk's power, and that Almeric is in no hurry for him to find out. Perhaps I can turn that to my advantage somehow?

The black-robed mage strides in, De Montfort by his side, eagerness permeating his movements. Then he sees me, and his brow furrows. His countenance darkens till I think I can almost see sparks flying from his eyes. 'What is the meaning of this?' His voice is low, but the menace contained within it is not.

'This one got free. Perhaps your powers are not as great as you thought.' The sneering mockery from Almeric is clear. I'm surprised Nicetas hasn't killed him yet. I can only assume he still has some part to play in the Bogomil's plans.

Nicetas spits again, then looks back at me. 'No matter. He can be the next to feed the cleansing.'

And so this is it. We've lost. Almeric's knife is to my throat, and I cannot move towards the Grail without slicing my own windpipe. Nicetas draws his athame, ready to add my soul to this perversion he works. All to bring about this terrible freeing, this almost certain ending.

For a moment, time seems to slow. I think back to the girl trapped under that wooden beam, of the strange force I found swirling around in my belly that flooded my limbs and gave me strength beyond my own meagre measure. I dig down deep inside myself, searching for it. *There*. I can sense it. My thoughts go to the cords of magic Almeric has tied me in, to those Nicetas has attached to all the surrounding Perfects. My arm is still outstretched. There remains one last possible chance.

I close my eyes, reach deep inside myself, and *pull* that force up, channel it through my arm. I know what it is now. Magic. When I used it to save that girl, I did it without knowing, without thinking. This time it's deliberate, and I know what it means. I'm damning my soul. When I die, which I will and soon, I'll be nothing, my essence turned to dust. My thoughts stray to poor Benedict. I'm glad he's already dead. His soul should be freed from this world, my damnation not undoing his own salvation. It makes me sick to think it, but it's a relief he doesn't live, doesn't see what I do next.

Gathering the force up, I hurl it outwards at the Grail. My eyes snapping open, I see ropes of magic extending towards it, wrapping around the cup. But not red like the others I've seen. These are green, the colour of a jade as it catches a sunbeam. It'd be truly beautiful if it weren't a mortal sin. It's a price I'm prepared to pay though. The obliteration of my soul to save the world. That's a fair exchange.

Nicetas yells unintelligibly, but he reacts too, damnably fast. His own hand comes up, and his sticky red magic also wraps the Grail. He *pulls,* and I do too. A tug of war with the fate of the world in the middle.

For a minute, there's a stalemate, each of us straining against the other. Then everything happens all together, suddenly.

Nicetas shrieks, 'Kill him' and I can feel the *power* he puts into it. Almeric doesn't even make a choice. The knife sweeps across my throat in an instant.

But as it does, I give my whole soul to the magic. I give it permission to devour me, to swallow me whole if it will just lend me this last strength. And I *pull* all the harder as my life drips away to pool on the floor below me.

At first, I think it's in vain. Nothing happens, nothing changes. The stand-off remains, and I'm dying. Then suddenly light spreads like a spider web across the Holy Grail. It takes me a moment to realise it's cracking, that the cup itself is fissuring.

The magic starts pulling inwards, the ropes of energy being devoured by the cup. Almeric is gibbering in my ear, and he releases me, pushing me forward. Across the divide, I see De Montfort back away, his instincts telling him rightly that nothing good is about to happen. But Nicetas...

Nicetas is trapped. The look of sheer horror on his face makes my sacrifice worth it. He's trying to untangle his magical threads from the Grail, but he's failing. And the cup is sucking them in, drawing on his magic greedily as it breaks. Pulling him closer and closer towards it.

For a moment all is silent, the room almost like a painting, so as I can see the expression on each face. Terror. Despair. Failure. Not the worst thing to see on the faces of your enemies before your soul is lost. My lifeblood is gushing around my knees, pooling where I landed after being released. I look back at the Grail...

And then it explodes, a green light flooding outwards from it like a broken barrier cracking, no longer holding back the ravaging river. It strikes me as white heat roars around me, swirling, growing, expanding to fill the room with unbearable heat...

And then I die.

For the first time.

But I'm not gone. I thought non-existence was where I was headed, into oblivion and ending. Instead, my eyes come open once more, and I find myself on what resembles a beach, although only in the loosest of senses. The substance I'm on is sand or as like it as I can't tell the difference. Except it's grey, and there's not a division between sea and land but an endless monochromatic constant. For a moment, I wonder if it's not powdered bone, but I'm not about to plunge my fingers in, and even then, I doubt I'd be able to tell the difference.

I'm dead. That much I'm sure. This isn't like reawakening after the burning pyre. That razor cut across my throat by Almeric's hand was no illusion. This is nowhere in the world, nowhere inside of life itself. There's no doubt in my mind. Where it is? That I have no clue as to the answer.

Looking around is no help. The landscape is uniform in all directions, unchanging. If I head off, if I leave this spot, I've no sense of where I should go. As I debate a course of action, something else catches my eye.

At my feet, I see a line appear in the substance I decide to think of as sand for my own mental wellbeing. It's like when a child finds a stick at the beach and carves shapes with it. Only, there's no stick nor any visible wielder. Only the scratched marks themselves appearing. And they aren't making shapes. They're forming letters. Letters which say —

NOT YET

— and then the grey landscape fades, turning black, and I'm gone from this place, though where I'm going to, I've no more idea than where it is I'm leaving.

I come to with a gasping breath I immediately regret considering the smells I swallow down with it, so rancid as to be almost solid. It takes a moment, but I get my bearings, and to my surprise, I know where I am. I'm in a soiled, shit-stinking alley behind a local tavern that stands just outside Lavaur's castle walls. Glancing down, I see my clothes are the humble threads of a local peasant, and as I roll over, I glimpse a face in a puddle of a substance I'd rather not identify, a face that's not my own. I recognise him though. A local happy drunkard, oblivious to the lingering military threat thanks to the comfortable alcoholic haze he spends his days drifting around in. I've no idea if he's a victim of murderous banditry or a vengeful faction of the Crusaders, but it's the face of a dead man looking up at me, and his death was deliberate. They made the slash across the throat with a more blunted but no less deadly blade than the one that was used to kill me.

As I study the ragged wound, it closes up, sealing as though never having existed. Even more astonishingly, the man's features melt away, replaced by my own. It's incredible, unbelievable and yet after all I've so recently witnessed, I feel too numb to search for any sense of understanding, too stunned to appreciate the wonder of living once again.

I stagger to my feet, seeking both my balance and my composure. As my brain slowly sheds some of its befuddlement, I turn towards the castle, thinking to seek what has befallen my fellow Good Men and Women and whether any of them survived that terrible confrontation. I don't go many steps, however, before I catch sight of the wanton destruction.

The castle is ablaze, and more than one nearby building is damaged, sporting a section of the stonework that once formed the main hall's walls, flung ballista-like outwards from the explosion. Through the sapped wall section, I can see the hall itself is no longer existent — it's been razed to the ground, the metre-thick walls shredded as though they were parchment, carried outwards like said scraps fed to the wind. Guards rush aimlessly around, clearly lacking any sense of direction but aiming to look busy. The military quickly instils a fear of being spotted as an idler during a time of crisis.

I draw closer. Part of a curious but wary crowd of locals, well aware that they might suffer by quickly becoming targets for the disordered and panicked soldiers. Creeping closer, I overhear some conversation from the nearby guards aiming to hold back any overly nosey villagers.

'... body parts scattered like blasted cards, not a one that were recognisable I 'eard,' says one.

'Aye, seems impossible that anyone could have escaped, though I 'eard 'twas due to them being at the door when the whole thing exploded. No idea how such an infernal 'appening befell 'em.'

'Still, if you were to lay a bet 'pon one man to survive, De Montfort would 'a been my first pick, no question.'

'No doubt, though that manic priest would 'a been a whole lot further down the list. They say there was 'undreds of 'em in the 'all, and just those two made it out alive. Unbelievable.'

'Tho I've 'eard 'e's less cocksure from wotsoever 'e went through. Broken 'is ankle, and you'd think it's 'im who died rather than all the other poor buggers inside. All shaky and weepy, gabblin' 'bout devils and damnation 'e was. Think 'e might 'a lost some of 'is taste for war if I'm any judge.'

'Ne'ermind, there's plenty more who'll be 'appy to take up 'is place and push for'ad the cause. Plenty more killing and plundering for us, all with a tidy signed 'eavenly place tied up and promised at its bloody end.'

The two men chuckle as they lean on their halberds, their eyes weighing up the jostling locals. I guess they're looking for targets either to rob or take out some anger on. Making myself such a target would be foolish indeed. I slip back into the shadows before they can catch sight of me and identify me as one of those thought dead in the recent explosion.

So. All the Good People are dead. Destroyed in the magical fire. That Nicetas is also dead is at least a small mercy. His existence posed a present danger to all humanity by my oath. But hearing that Arnaud and Simon have survived?

It's enough to make my blood boil inside my skin. Rage roars through my system, pounding in my ears. I'm no longer Perfect. That ended when I embraced the magic and damned my soul. So be it. As I see it, I have two targets to achieve with this strange second life I've been given. The first is to have my vengeance upon the Butcher of Beziers and that northern bastard De Montfort. I'll see them both dead and buried. The second is to gain control over these mysterious abilities, this bizarre magic inside of me. I suspect I'll require it if I'm to achieve my first aim.

I've few allies left alive and fewer still who will understand what I've done, what I'm now capable of doing. My thoughts go to that Israelite rabbi who gave me his blessing, a blessing that seemed to have unlocked this strange *power* for the first time, and I can't help but wonder how much of what happened he saw lying ahead for me. There's no other option, no one else who can help me or provide me with any guidance. My mind made up, I set off to see what I can get my hands on, if I can beg or steal some supplies. I'll need them for the long and tiresome journey ahead of me, towards the Mediterranean and Montpellier's bustling goods-laden port.

Chapter Twenty-Six

BIDACHE, 9 MARCH, PRESENT DAY

Dead again. Told you there was no chance this body would survive the next few days.

I come to, heaving in a gasping lungful of air. The rest of my body doesn't move. I'm locked into position, my head clamped in place, the rest of me similarly restrained. I'm upright at least, which is a small mercy because it lets me see where I am. That mercy feels exceptionally tiny when I take stock of my situation.

I am in a workshop — not the filth-stained dirt pit of the shit wizard nor a homely ramshackle mess like Isaac's place. This is as cold and as surgically clean as Phone Dick's soul. The pristine, glistening white tiles covering the walls and floor reflect harsh halogen lighting strips. They bring no warmth to the proceedings, only illuminating the horror show into which I've crash landed.

Medical beds hang vertically on each wall, cradling freshly dead corpses strapped in by restraints and head clamps identical to the ones on me. I can *see* that each is covered in Enochian runes sufficient to trap any *talent* as effectively as the leather straps restrain the physical vessels. I don't even need to test my *talent* to know I'm similarly held. There are at least fifteen bodies arrayed around the chamber. The only break in this pattern is a large metal door like those used on industrial freezers.

Intricate glyphs and patterns mark the floor, making my head ache — they are technically Kabbalist but in the same way as calligraphy is technically a scratchy line. This is a level of mastery I have only ever seen worked by Isaac and only on occasions rare enough to count on one hand. In the middle of the room sits a metal folding chair next to what I suspect is the *pièce de résistance* of the certifiable interior designer who assembled this chamber — an intricately designed pedestal I hope is made of laser printed plastic.

I don't believe it is though.

Steam-bent bones have been woven together to form a support column like a bleached 3D representation of a DNA strand. On top of it sits a human skull. I open my *sight* to look at it, and the intensity of the *talent* coming off it feels like I've just driven spikes straight through my pupils and into the part of my brain dealing with pain stimuli. So I do the only sensible thing. I pass out.

When I come to, it is with the worst headache I've had since I made a drunken bet with Isaac about whether alcohol-poisoning was possible with my metabolism.

Spoiler — it was.

Although using my *sight* again in this room will most likely give me a brain aneurysm, dying won't get me anywhere any time soon given the array of corpses conveniently prepared and magically pre-wrapped around me. Plus, *looking* might only risk something like blowing a load of blood vessels and having a major stroke, neither of which will leave me fighting fit for the next showdown with Phone Dick and any plus ones he might bring to the party.

So I hang here, studiously avoiding *looking* too hard at either the etchings or the more than mildly terrifying skull upon the pedestal. Now that I'm getting the use of my wits back —what little I possessed in the first place— I can feel the *power* radiating from it, just from the corner of my vision. That's more than enough. I'm in no hurry to look directly at it again. I'm not sure I've ever seen anything more powerful. Certainly not since I died for the very first time.

And then I remember what happened before I died, and it's like a bucket of ice-cold water thrown in my face, shocking my brain back to full awareness. Aicha.

The memory of seeing her burning comes back so strongly that I'd rather look at the skull again than close my eyes. There's too much chance I might watch her cremate unendingly, over and over against the backdrop of my own eyelids. Just that thought, the most minor recollection of watching her cracking, and I can already see her skin parching like drought-hit mud plains breaking open over and over...

I retch, feeling the bile rising in my throat, but I clamp it down, stop any escaping. That motherfucker's going to turn up soon, I'm sure of it. There's no way I want to give him the satisfaction of seeing how badly he's affecting me. Aicha is burning *right now,* and if I don't get out of here, she may never stop. Somehow, I've got to out-think him, outsmart him, beat him. Get free. Go save her. Preferably with Phone Dick tucked under my arm, wrapped up in a bow as a present for her to take her revenge on. Slowly.

My only comfort is that the fire tornado doesn't seem anywhere near capable of killing her. Part of me suspects that is only because he prefers to keep her in a state of perpetual torture. If I can break *him,* the spell will also break. Even significantly distracting him or forcing him to spend a large percentage of his own abilities might be enough to put it out of action (and consequently put her back in the game to come looking for me). Honestly though, if she sits this one out once she gets out of that hellhole, I'd fully understand; regardless of what happens to me, I just want her nightmare over as quickly as possible.

After a stretch of minutes, the sigils blaze to life and so does the skull. Roaring blue soul-fire reaches out in elongating fingers, magical flames licking around the sockets. They ignite like miniature cerulean suns. The door clinks and swings slowly inward.

Just as I hear the click of the door, a terrifying thing happens. One of the two azure stars that burst to life in the skull's previously empty sockets extinguishes before rekindling back to brilliance.

The door slowly pushes open, revealing the utterly unwelcome sight of Phone Dick looking unruffled and at ease outside of his aged decrepitude. I marshal my face, trying not to look any less at ease than he does while also frantically trying to work out what just happened. Did the terrifyingly powerful Skull (it definitely requires a capital S) just wink at me?

Phone Dick limps across the room, demanding my attention, and the faintest, most irritating bells of familiarity ring in the base of my brain again. He lowers himself into the chair with a relieved sigh. He doesn't seem the slightest bit bothered by the Feng Shui of the lab, but given he was most likely responsible for the careful arrangement of the morbid wall hangings, I guess he isn't too concerned about dousing himself in negative yang energy. He watches me, his chin resting on the crook of his walking stick with his hands on either side, quietly observing.

I was never particularly good with pregnant pauses. 'I just want to clarify that if Murray over there' —I nod at the Skull— 'starts talking, then it is a no from me. I'm out.'

The pause extends so far in its pregnancy that I'm pretty sure the doctors would have ordered an emergency C-section. He blinks in that crocodilian manner (and I try not to let the image of Aicha's eyelids detaching over and over seep back into my mind's eye) and continues to stare.

'I do not know what you are talking about or when you decided buffoonery was a comforting guise, Paul.'

I stir uneasily at that tone of worn familiarity but try hard to mask it. 'Murray? Murray the Demonic Talking Skull? *Monkey Island*? I don't know whether to be aghast at your lack of knowledge of point-and-click adventure games or envious you'll get to play all of them for the first time. If I wasn't going to carve your face off with a rib I snap out of your chest with my fucking teeth when I get down from here, of course.'

He sighs wearily. 'Yes indeed, you will kill me, insert profanity here, mix with distracting pop culture, threaten, and bluff. I'm not some foolish fae-kin to be taken in by such bluster, and I am saddened to see what little remains of the holy man I once studied under and placed such great, great faith in.'

The bottom drops out of my world, kicked away by the click into place of that faint tingle of recognition. It leaves me flailing desperately in space like Wile E. Coyote for a moment before diving into the wake of realising who I am talking to and exactly how impossible it is.

I stutter, my tongue alien, feeling too large for my mouth. It seems to no longer remember how to shape words once so familiar. I wonder if I'm having that stroke I was concerned about giving myself and nearly start giggling, a desperate hysteria lurking at my mind's edge, ready to seize control if I let it. I have centuries of experience in doing five impossible things before breakfast but nothing ever on this scale. I force myself to quit the stunned fish impersonation and to force out the word, the name, to make it real even though it can't possibly be.

'Benedict?' I ask uncomprehendingly.

This hideous bastard who killed without qualm, who caged my best friend in her own personal Tartarus meets my gaze, and for a moment, those dead fisheyes warm, and my oldest confidant, a man I believed dead for over eight hundred years, peers back at me.

'Hello, Paul,' he replies gently, and for once, the smile on his face reaches his entire visage.

CHAPTER TWENTY-SEVEN

BIDACHE, 9 MARCH, PRESENT DAY

Is this real life? Wish it was fantasy. Feels like an aneurysm that's affecting my brain plasticity.

My mouth reverts to fishlike movements momentarily, then clamps shut. Although my thoughts are in a state of disarray akin to the bedroom of a sugar-fuelled, temper-tantrum toddler on a rampage, the key question is so blindingly obvious that I force it out... eventually.

'How?' I ask plaintively.

'When you crawled across me in the Great Hall of Lavaur, so righteous in your desire to undo Nicetas' evil, I was dying but not yet dead, though close to it. I watched you as you neared that chalice, and I cheered you on even as I slowly lost my grip to the agonising pain, about to pass on, saved and ready to escape the endless wheel of the physical world, thanks to you. I shuddered in horror as the magics of Almeric stopped you, locked up inches away from the cup overflowing with the souls of the other Perfects, so desperately close to ending their plans with your hand outstretched. Then I watched you *damn yourself* as I died.'

The undercurrent of anger in his tone mounts throughout his description of that fateful moment, swirling around a bitter sarcasm that colours his words. I look at him, unsure of the reason but confident in my actions of so long ago. 'I did what had to be done,' I reply.

'Did it have to be done, Paul? Did it really? Did you think for one second about the effect that would have on your eternal salvation? Did you think about the effect it would have on each of the souls you had saved during your time as Perfect by marring yourself? About what it would do to *me* given my new status of Perfect that you'd gifted me the night before with my consolamentum? Ruined, meaningless. You might have been happy to become nothingness, to dissolve into non-existence, but I was not. I knew it was because of your interactions with that accursed Jew, the heinous poison he'd dripped into your thoughts that led you to embracing dark sorcery in that last moment, but I didn't have time to dwell upon it. I could only experience the dreadfulness of watching you fall, taking me with you before I was gone from that life but not from this blasted prison we remain in every single day.'

I shake my head. 'Are you suggesting I should have just left them be? Let them steal the souls of all our fellow Cathars for whatever lunatic fucking purposes they were going to use them for? They snatched their bodies — that was bad enough, Ben. Would you have had me leave them to torment our friends? Possibly for eternity?'

'So to beat them, you became them,' he hisses. 'Since when did the end justify the means? Look at the sordid shell you are now of the man of the Good God that you once were. I see the judgement that you pass on me written in broad strokes across your face, but it is you who deserves judgement. Those hollow smiles and quick empty jokes carried as camouflage for the unrepentant killer you are now. Steeped in your comfortable skin and all the trappings of modern life, the very antithesis of what Catharism is about. And how many have you killed since then, eh, Paul? How many souls did you leave in torment or throw back onto the lower rungs of the cycle of reincarnation, taking away their chance to repent and become better? Who made you the Good God damned judge to act as a higher force on those you see as unworthy of a chance at salvation?'

My features harden, a mix of anger tinged with shame at the bandied insults. 'I gave up on the Good God a long time ago, after he gave up on us. You know I'm no Perfect these days — that's why I'm still here, after all; but I've done the best I can with the time given to me to try to do the right thing. I've never killed without justification or for any reason except to protect others. I'm not claiming that I always got every call correct, but I've kept true to the moral code I've developed over all this time. I like to believe that Paul the Perfect would have understood how I've arrived where I am, both materially and spiritually. What happened to the man I called brother and held as my shield? To commit the acts that I've encountered — killing on a whim, torturing, kidnapping, who knows what else? What would Benedict the Saved have said?'

Ben sneers at me, the crinkling of his leathery, wizened face submerging that momentary vision of my old friend. 'Says the man who lies down with monsters? Partnering with the likes of that abomination lurking in the Garonne? Not to mention your heathen mentor and your Arab lover.'

The forge shaping my anger explodes in engulfing heat. 'I don't even know where to start on the latter part. I'll take the blame regarding Franc. There's some justice there — one between me and my conscience that I have to live with. But how have you remained so lost in your fucking idiotic prejudices as to judge others for their origins or faith? Isaac is literally the best human being I've ever met, but you're still hung up over him being a Jew? And you level accusations of unjustified superiority at me? As for Aicha, well. It's true I love and admire that woman more than you might understand. She is amazing. In a world that bends on a whim for praise, she stands unbreaking by her truths. She doesn't crack or cave before pressures like normal people, immortal or otherwise, but always acts as she believes to be correct, always embraces the consequences without making excuses or pleading ignorance. You know who she reminded me of when I met her? You. Or rather, who I always thought you were.

'I spent decades —fucking decades!— mourning your death. When I met her, I finally regained the strong right arm those bastards severed when I thought they killed you. I gained a sister to replace the brother I mourned across lifetimes. It fixed a part of my heart, broken since the moment I watched them butcher you. That's why I love her, Ben. That's how I love her, and I don't understand how you don't get it. Instead, you slander it because you cannot believe in genuine friendship, the philia definition of love between a man and a woman. It's a sign of your failing as a human being, mate. Not ours.'

The vicious, bitter old man in front of me pauses and seems to droop, leaning more heavily onto his cane. 'I was always your friend. There's been many days and nights I've cursed your name, times I hated you so much that I hunted you down, made sure you died just to assuage that anger for a moment, even knowing it was only temporary and you'd pop back up like the tarnished bad penny you've become. Do you know how many of your 'accidental' deaths have been because of my interference?' His hand trembles on the top of his stick, and his eyes flicker up to mine, tracing the shape of my face before they drop back down. 'And still, I've missed you, Paul. More than I can possibly say.'

Under different circumstances, that might have tugged at my heart-strings. Not least thinking of all the nights I've lived with the guilt of Ben's death. But Aicha is burning, and I can feel that same fire in my chest.

'For all your monologuing, I don't exactly feel like I'm in the welcome embrace of an old friend right now.' I flick my eyes upwards to the head clamp, then down to my restraints.

Ben pushes on the head of his stick, straightening up, his expression blanking, closing down. 'I hardly thought you'd be open to listening to reason. Even if it's all for your own good,' he replies, a maniacal gleam in the freezer-depths of his glare. It chills my building anger —his complete control— the same as it chills my soul. The only sort of people who talk about doing things for others' own good are parents and psychopaths. Possibly both. Definitely the latter.

'What happened to you, Ben?' I whisper. The restraints chafe at my wrists, rubbing at the skin, pulling me back to the present moment, the reality of this macabre hellhole of a chamber he's trapped me in.

Chapter Twenty-Eight

BIDACHE, 9 MARCH, PRESENT DAY

Genuinely heart sick. This whole situation sucks massive donkey dick.

T he old man, this murderous ancient I find it impossible to think of as the man who I thought died to save me, eases himself into the chair. His wince at contact with the cold plastic is impossible to miss. Ageing is no friend to the body. Good. Fuck him.

'What happened to me?' His voice wheezes, the lungs working hard, as though the shrivelled skin acts as bands compressing them, limiting their effectiveness. 'Not what happened to you, Paul, that much is sure. There's so much to tell you, I've waited so long to have you here, to recount my side of the —'

'Hold on a second,' I interrupt. My left shoulder's starting to itch, so I try to scratch it against the restraints. After some twisting, I realise it's fruitless, and all I'm going to do by thinking about it is make it worse. Ignoring it is the only answer. Settling back down, I realise Ben is staring at me, waiting.

'What?' I ask him.

'You interrupted me. What did you want to say?'

'Oh, no, mainly it was this itch. Oh, hang on, no, that's right. You were saying about waiting forever, yada yada, right?'

He blinks at me slowly. 'That's correct.'

'So yeah, what I wanted to ask was, why do you think I'd give a flying fuck?' I turn a full-watt beam in his direction to highlight the point. 'You're not Ben. Not my Ben anyhow. That Ben was the best man I ever met. He wouldn't have used the wolves like that. Wouldn't have set my friend on fire just because she annoyed him. Nope. Fuck you. Fuck your story. Not interested.'

And still, he doesn't stop looking at me, staring right in my eyes till I start feeling a million times more uncomfortable than I did with the shoulder itch. You know that thing where you suddenly wonder if you've got food stuck between your teeth, and this whole time, while you've felt like you were being charming and the centre of the conversation, it's only been because everyone's staring at the scrap of salami as it flaps back and forth like a flag of parley right in the middle of your mouth? It's like that. Like there's something I'm missing. Doubtless that's true, but the intensity of his regard makes more than just my shoulder itch.

'Am I really not?' His voice is low, barely above a whisper. 'Aren't you a new man, Paul, so far from that Perfect you once were? But you still told me he'd know you, that ancient you. This is Ben, your Ben, the same Ben who stood by your side all those years ago. You're marked by your misadventures, perhaps. All you're seeing are the results of mine. But at my heart, am I so vastly changed?'

There's a deep vein of emotion that runs below his words, soaked in pain and regret, and for a moment I *do* see Ben in this dried up old husk of a human. The man who steadied my arm, who chided me to take care of myself, who made me laugh, who threw himself into Nicetas' path to save my life. All those decades of grief I carried, those nights where they were my only companion as I lay awake and mourned the death of my friend.

But there's one thing that keeps me from going too deep into those feelings, a life-saving rubber ring that keeps me afloat, from being submerged in all that guilt I've carried for so very, very long. It's anger, still white hot, and I clutch it to my chest, holding it tight.

'And Aicha? What you did to her?' Good. There's just the right amount of scorn in my voice. No way am I letting him know how much he hit home with those words. Perhaps he is still the same Ben. The young man so full of charm he could talk the birds down from the trees if he set his mind to it. Maybe that's all the good I saw in him was. Talk and charm.

Ben shrugs, and some of the coldness is back. Perhaps because I'm not impressed by his persuasions. Perhaps just talking about Aicha. 'The Druze? Take it as a compliment. Incapacitating her was never going to be a simple task. That was the solution I came up with, to remove a threatening piece from the board.'

Unbelievable. 'That's how you see this, is it? As a game? A thought exercise to see what you could come up with? *You left her in eternal flames.*'

I can't keep my temper. The words roar out of my throat, tinged with my fury. The old man shakes his head, almost amused, and in that moment any slight sympathy I might have felt evaporates before my anger.

'That's a very religious image for a man who gave up his faith.' He chuckles, and I'd like to tear his fucking tongue out. 'Also, overly dramatic. It won't be forever. She'll get free eventually. More than could be said for either of us.'

'What? What does that mean?' Perhaps not the wittiest of ripostes, but that's an ominous turn of phrase if ever I heard one.

'Well, we'll get to that, Paul. But I've waited all this time to explain myself. Perhaps you're right. Perhaps at the end of it, you'll still not understand, still hate me blindly. But until I get to the end, your little Aicha will be a human torch, trapped on that bridge. So may I continue, or do you want to tell me to "fuck off" some more, eh?'

'No — hold on, yes. Fuck off. Fuck you. Fuck off, you fucking fuckhead fucker. Fuck.' I spit, the saliva having built up with the words like I'm rabid. Aicha would've appreciated that. Makes it worth it.

He leans forward, stick splaying with him precariously. I can only dream it'll slip out from under him and he'll brain himself on the cold floor tiles. Of course, I'm not that lucky.

'We don't always have your chances, my old friend.'

I can't help myself. 'Oh, is this what you call lucky?' I don't have my hands free, but I roll my head loosely around, indicating my current predicament. 'Hanging like a slab of meat from the walls with a load of corpses, listening to shitty monologues? I mean, I get some people are into BDSM and stuff, but honestly, if that's your idea of a good time, Ben, you need to get help. This is *torture*.'

His eyes snap to me, and I see a fire blaze in them, but he tamps it down, bringing up his neutral mask again. With a tiny grunt, he pushes onto his feet, then tap-stamps his way to me with his cane, slowly crossing the distance. Once he's next to me, he leans closer, his hand pushing a strand of hair behind my ear

'Oh, this isn't torture, Paul.' His words tickle my ear, the breath riding the curves to go deeper inside. 'There can be. We've all learned things over the years, haven't we? Things we aren't proud of.' He runs a finger down the side of my face, tracing my jawline. 'Don't make me show them to you, in detail.'

The last word is a sibilant hiss that raises goosebumps on my bare arms. Fuck me. His intensity alone would be terrifying. Combined with what I've already seen him do? Ice water chills run up and down my back.

Of course I will not let that control me. As he makes his way back towards his chair, I raise my voice. 'Oh no, poor Ben. Had it so hard, he has to take out his misery on everyone around him. Waaah, boo hoo.'

He whirls, turning on his heels, the action of a far younger man, the fury in his expression giving strength to his limbs that age robbed them of. 'You ignorant fool! What do you know of my suffering? Did you think you were the only one who paid for what happened at Lavaur? There was hardly any payment made by you. Just "oops, I'm dead, pick myself back up in a brand-new body and carry on". There was no such luxury for me. Just heavy payments to be made for your blasted arrogance.'

I don't get it. 'What payments?'

'Oh, didn't you realise? The essence in the Grail splashed across me when it broke. I was still alive. I came back too. But not in a dead body fully grown, all ready for me to pick back up on some stupid adventure as you seem to do without a care in the world. No. When I came back, I couldn't move. Couldn't see. Couldn't even breathe. I came back fully aware but into a foetus, swimming around in the womb of some wretched woman.'

Ah. Damn. I never even considered the possibility of another form of reincarnation. Still, I can think of worse. 'Doesn't sound too terrible.'

Ben chuckles, a mirthless sound that is far more akin to pain than joy. 'Does it not? Easy for you to say. For me, it was terrifying. I'd no idea where I was when I first came back. Do you know I forced my unformed mouth open and twisted in such a way as to choke myself to death with the umbilical cord? Dying, wriggling, and writhing in a seamless void. I thought myself in Hell. Only more so when I came back a second time, to a near-as-dammit identical situation.'

Fuck. I'd not thought of that. And Ben's not finished.

'To be utterly helpless each time, immobilised, trapped with nothing but your thoughts and terrors for months on end. Only to be born bawling into a world even harsher and harder than that whore-carried prison. Unable to walk, to talk. A tiny little Lilliputian in the land of giants, servant to the whim of those who believe themselves your parent. I couldn't even eat! Suckled time and again till the very sight of a breast fully clothed is enough to make me retch. I died helpless that first time. And each time I died after, I had that same sensation, that same suffering replayed over and over again. To be emasculated, utterly reliant on others when all I wanted was to be free, independent.'

'There's many who would be happy at a chance at childhood again.' The argument sounds weak even to my own ears considering there's a huge difference between being cared for with all bills paid to being an adult stuck in a baby's body, but I have to say something. There's no way I'm going to go along with anything he has to say. No way I'm going to feel sympathy for him. Not after what he's done. But Good God dammit, there's a part of me, the empathetic part, that wants to.

He spits and settles himself back into his chair with a groan. 'Do you really believe that? You know what life was like then. Not the pampered lives children live these days. No, it was suffering, struggling. Hunger and misery over and over. Do you know how many times I died before I even made it to adulthood in a life after that first death?' He leans further forward. 'Five. Five times. Over three decades of infirmity, utter reliance on people who expected fealty and love I was incapable of giving before I could even be my own man again. And all the time, knowing what was waiting for me next time I died.'

He raises his head, and for a moment there's something other than rheumy waters around his eyes. Again, he stares at me, like a child caught by a broken heirloom, willing the parent to believe their story. 'There's something even worse. I didn't just come into those bodies the moment they were conceived. I already had stubby little arms and legs when I arrived. And, once I knew what was happening, unlike that first time of sheer blind panic, as I came back to awareness inside another accursed fleshy prison for months, with nothing but time to think...'

There. The flash in his eyes, there. I can see my oldest, dearest friend for a moment, and the hurt he's carrying is engulfing him. 'What happened to those children's souls, Paul?' The words are barely a whisper, obscured by the tremulous nature of his voice. But the pain still carries through. 'Months sat bound and immobile in that dark hellish place, wondering if I displaced them? Killed them?' He pauses and his gaze is so intense, I want to look away, to close my eyes. I don't though. Whatever he's done, some part of that rests on my shoulders. 'Did I *consume them*, Paul?'

Now he closes his eyes, breaks the contact, and it's all I can do not to sigh with relief. When he opens them again, he keeps his gaze downcast. 'Misery. Suffering. A terrible fragile existence that faltered and failed time after time and always back to the terrible restraints of drowning in amniotic fluid, with nothing but my darkest thoughts to keep me company. I don't know how I survived it. To be honest, I'm not entirely sure that I did. Not all of me. Not intact.'

Okay. So Ben definitely drew the short straw in the reincarnating draw. 'That sounds shit. I'll give you that. Doesn't quite justify the whole "now I need to be an evil dick" thing, does it?'

He shakes his head disbelievingly. 'Still the little jibes carry on. No, you're right, I wasn't an "evil dick" at first. No, I thought maybe if I could live correctly, achieve Perfection again, I'd escape all this.' He waves his hand in the air as if to encompass everything. 'The misery of existence. I even tracked down the last of the Good People, Guilhaume Belibast in Spain. Got him to perform the consolamentum for me once more.'

Now his attention snaps back to me, and his upper lip draws back, pulling his face into a sneer. 'Didn't work. Couldn't make it stick, could he? No, not once I'd already been made Perfect before. Not when that Perfection, that chance for me to escape the physical realm, this sordid, shabby reality once and for all got stolen away from me by a man I loved more than my own life.'

'Is this love, Ben?' I can feel the pain I've carried in my heart all these years, the times I've mourned him. I'm mourning him afresh, seeing the man he's become.

'I loved you more than my own life.' There's an insistence to his words, an intensity to his gaze, daring me to disagree. 'But that was one life. This? This endless, miserable, torturous parade of life after life I can't escape? Oh, that changed my love. Transformed it into hate.'

'And that's my fault?' Don't get me wrong. I can see why he thinks it. The Good God knows I've held myself responsible often enough. But nothing justifies what he's done. I'm not letting him get away with thinking it does.

He's on his feet again without even needing the help of his cane that he waves at me. 'You kept me here! Your actions! Doomed me.'

He breathes heavily, his chest heaving visibly, shaking with emotion. His face reddens, and for a moment I think he's going to have an apoplexy and drop dead right there, on the spot. But he closes his eyes, gets the rhythm of his breaths back under control, and when he opens them again, they're calm once more, his icy mask snapped back into place.

'So, you see, Paul.' His voice is rigid as a frozen corpse again. 'It's all your fault. Everything that's happened, everyone who's died. They're all dead because of you.'

The bile rises in my throat again, but I clamp it down. No. I'm not accepting that. 'You can't put this one on me, Ben. I'm sorry for your suffering, in a way, although seeing how you've acted, you deserve a fuck-load worse, but you take responsibility for your own actions. Many people would consider what you've got as a gift.'

'Then let them come take it!' The mask cracks for a moment, but he pulls it back into place. 'No, they might say that, but if they lived what I've lived? They'd just want to die too.'

Ahh. 'Is that what all this is about? Trying to die?'

He smiles wearily. 'Of course. What else did you think it was for? I'm going to die. And so, my old friend, are you.'

CHAPTER TWENTY-NINE

BIDACHE, 9 MARCH, PRESENT DAY

Torn between sympathetic horror and righteous indignation. Sympahorrightation? Something like that, anyway.

Panic rises in my chest, terror at what he's got planned. Because there are many things, detailed in horrible description, that you can say about Ben. But not that he's ill prepared. Not then, and certainly not now.

'What are you talking about, Ben?' Sweat runs down the back of my neck, soaking the skin pressed against the cold leather of the restraining table.

'All of this' —he waves his hand as though at the entirety of existence, though I suspect he means "all the miserable shit I've just put you through" this time— 'was to serve a single purpose.'

A thought that's been lingering at the back of my mind, not fully formed, crystallises in this moment. 'How did you manage all this? Where has all your *talent* come from? Was it from the essence of the Grail?'

He chuckles, although the dry rasping sound is more akin to a wheezed cough. 'Oh no. The Grail just gave me this wretched existence-after-existence. I already had this' —he spits— '*talent* in my first life. From my childhood, I saw strange things — auras, faces below faces, evidence of demonic influence in my brain. It was that which pushed me to seek the Good People, to look to become a Perfect in the hope it might cure me of what I saw then as a curse. It was only after my new lives started that I learned what magic really is.'

It's like a glass of water thrown in my face. 'So the whole situation... even when we met Isaac the first time? The werewolf?' I take a sharp breath. 'Nicetas! You could see he had magic.'

Ben's lip curls, distaste clear, though whether at the name, the memory, or me, I can't tell. 'Yes. The bastard seemed perfect to me, no pun intended. He held a magnetic pull, an attraction so strange, so unique. A man, strong, dynamic, swirling with confidence and *power* but who didn't give in to the magic's dark urges. Or so I thought before we found out the truth about him. Before he slit my throat.'

The lip relaxes, and he shakes his head, tutting. 'Do you know, I really saw myself learning at his knee, becoming a better man? There's no one who impressed me more. Present company excluded. And no one who let me down worse — with the same caveat applied.'

Considering the antipathy, the distaste I feel towards the man, I'm surprised by how much that jibe stings. Perhaps because it's the same thing my inner voice's whispered in my mind for centuries, in the quiet of the lonely dark. 'I did what had to be done!' Even I can hear the plaintive touch to my tone. 'Would you have let that bastard win? Bring through whatever monstrosity he was summoning?'

Ben looks up again, looks me straight in the eye, and it is Ben who's there, the man I spent years with, day in, day out. 'For you, Paul? Absolutely. For you, I'd have let the world burn.'

Wow. For a moment, I'm speechless, my mouth hanging open. All those touches he used to give me. The long, lingering looks. Good God I was naïve. And he never said anything about how he felt...

I have to keep thinking about Aicha, about how she's suffering right now. Somehow, I've got to get this over with, break free, get away and save her. I only hope that somehow, somewhere in all of this, I'll find a weak point I can use, something to either bring back my lost friend or else break free and defeat this evil bastard he's become.

I find my voice again. 'And is that what you're planning to do now then? Burn the world, a petulant gesture because life is so unfair?' *Keep the tone mocking, disrespectful, Paul. Don't let him see how he's affected you.*

He taps at the floor with his stick, shifting in his seat as he does so. I'm not sure if he's trying to get comfortable, but apparently it's not possible because with a grimace, he leans hard on it and regains his feet.

'No, I'm not looking to stamp my feet and throw my toys out of the pram. I'm looking to *escape*. That's all I've ever wanted. For all of this to end. To get away from this unending, miserable cycle. If the world happens to burn while I do it? Well —' He shrugs, careless, casual. 'I honestly don't care. There's no love lost for it on my part.'

And like that, all the sympathy he regained washes away, and with it, that desperate illusion I might somehow persuade him back, away from this dark path he's been walking for so long. There's no coming back. The man I knew is lost. No. I need to concentrate on saving myself, on saving Aicha.

Perhaps by stroking his ego rather than direct confrontation. 'I don't understand how you never came across the Talented world before your death. To be able to overpower an angel...'

The words are out of my mouth before I've really thought about them, and now I realise I've been avoiding that thought too. All this time, I've been constantly reassuring myself that I'll find a way out, that I'll win somehow. But the truth is, if he's that Talented, that powerful, my chances aren't just slim. They're nonexistent.

Ben smiles — a strangely gentle expression that doesn't reach his eyes. 'Oh, my sweet Paul. Do you really believe I bested Nanael by using *talent*? Honestly, very flattering that you think so highly of me, but no. I'm Talented, definitely, but I doubt I'm even your equal on a one-on-one throwdown. Dear me, no. There's only one way to beat a Bene Elohim. When the odds are stacked against you, what can you possibly do?'

Ah. My mind goes back to an almost identical conversation I had with Isaac not long ago. 'You cheat.' My voice comes out quiet, almost inaudible.

He hears me though, still wearing that strange, patently false, kindly smile. 'Exactly. Just as I've done with you. Just as I'll do to get the death I deserve, the death I've earned with these endless miserable lives. I'll cheat my way out. I've spent lifetimes doing the same. Studying under master magicians, tricking them into giving me their secrets. Seeking for ways to undo this damnable curse. Charming them, learning everything they were prepared to teach me. Then often using pain and torture to learn everything they weren't prepared to include in my education. Each time I died —through sickness or a knife in the back or a curse striking me down in the dark— I had to go through the misery of pregnancy, birth, and childhood all over again. Do you know that's how I found out about you?'

He hobbles closer and lays a hand on my shoulder, his fingers gently stroking my skin. 'I was a skinny, half-starved boy, foraging in the back alleys for something, anything to keep me alive, to keep my so-called "father" from beating me to death as he threatened to any time I came back empty-handed. And I saw you, Paul. Saw you strolling past the alley-mouth, an arm thrown round the shoulders of that wretched Jew we met going to Foix. All careless smiles and fine clothes, well fed, prosperous. Untouched by the misery I suffered day after day, year after year, life after life. I realised then, of course, you must have been touched by the magic of the Grail much as I had been. And I realised too how much my love for you had soured, tainted. How much I hated you. And that bastard rabbi too.'

The stroking stops, and his fingers dig into my flesh hard enough to bruise. 'I kept my eye on you then as I learned the knowledge necessary to allow me to use my power effectively. Each life did slowly get easier.' He laughs once, a dry bark that's utterly humourless. 'Once I could use my *talent* to control the stupid sows who gave birth to me and their idiotic husbands, obsessed with their rutting, it made my childhoods much more manageable.'

If I felt sickened by what he's told me so far, now the nausea threatens to overwhelm me. Using mind magic on the Talentless, forcing them to do his bidding, that's a filthy working, the grubbiest usage of power almost imaginable.

Ben doesn't seem to notice my discomfort. Or perhaps he does. Perhaps he's enjoying it. 'Of course I made sure our paths wouldn't cross. Not always an easy task in the small circles the Talented world comprises. Do you know, one of the first teachers I had after seeing you was actually a monk? They had a monastery near Castelnaudary that was a place of refuge for Talented, both human and otherwise. The poor fool became besotted with me, declared his undying love. My only interest was what I could get from him knowledge-wise. He went from passing his time on the road, using his minor *talent* to heal the sick and help the poor to spending all his days searching for esoteric tomes to bring to me in exchange for a coquettish flutter of my eyes and perhaps a chaste kiss. Except, one day he came back and told me he'd arranged mentorship for us under a

Talented Jew in Toulouse. I knew who that was. While he prepared for our departure, I went and told my tale in floods of tears, of monstrous creatures and devil worshippers bedecked in holy garbs, to the local Inquisition. All of them put to the flame. A hundred Talented. Just to make sure no word of me got back to your ever-inquisitive ears. More souls to add to your account, eh?'

I can't even feel the fingers pressing into my skin anymore. All I feel is numb. I wonder how many died that day just to let Ben get away without even the risk of me hearing about him. Was he ever really the man I thought he was? Or had this always been the dark truth of his soul? Whether I was blind or he was broken later, the end result —and that endless bitter tally of deaths— remains the same.

Ben bends closer so that the smell of his breath —aged garlic and cloves— tickles my nostrils as he murmurs in my ear, 'Haven't you wondered how I managed all this? All of this dirty Kabbalah magic here, the same magic I gifted to that pathetic shit wizard to allow him to hold you captive? Haven't you asked yourself where your dear friends Jakob and Nanael could be?'

He hobbles over to the pillar next to his chair. My eyes are drawn to the thing they've been avoiding this whole time to protect my sanity. The terrifyingly powerful skull sitting on the pedestal.

'Don't you recognise it, Paul?' His voice is calm but insistent. And deadly cold. 'This skull that you cheapened earlier with your mockery? Can you layer it with flesh, fill out its features to picture the face it once wore?'

My blood runs as cold as his tone. It can't be. He couldn't. 'Tell me it's not Jakob!' I blurt out the words, unable to hold them back, my horror clear.

Ben looks genuinely confused. 'What?' Then it appears he parses my meaning because his expression clears. 'Oh. Oh!' He starts to chuckle. It builds and builds until he's leaning all his weight on the pedestal, wheezing, tears running down his face. 'Oh, no, Paul! Did you think I just chopped off his head? Somehow decapitated him without the angel realising? No, although both Jakob and his heavenly companion know it ever so well now. Look at it again. Add a little red hair clinging to the sides of the face, away from the shaven top. Make sure to include a certain amount of religious mania into the eyes as you add them too. You should know him, Paul. You killed him. The first life you took. The first of many after giving up even any illusion of being a decent man.'

And now I understand. Now I know exactly whose skull it is. A man I hunted, who I negotiated a century of apprenticeship with Isaac in order to gain the ability to bring him down. A man whose magic kept me from reaching the Grail and destroying it. Who I killed to get vengeance for the man now stroking the bastard's somehow *talent*-packed skull centuries later. The first life I took deliberately in cold blood.

It's the skull of the Butcher of Beziers. Arnaud Almeric himself.

But as shocked as I am, I'm also totally confused. 'I don't understand? You said it was to do with where Jakob and Nanael are!'

'Well, quite.' That terrible, placid smile remains stuck in place, and it sends shivers crawling down my spine. 'I needed somewhere to keep them. Somewhere where once they were suitably restrained, I could use their *talent* for my own, giving me power beyond measure.' His expression darkens. 'Not enough to break out of this world, to demolish the walls of this reality and give me escape. Nearly but not quite. But a suitable talisman that could also function as a prison so effective as to keep even an angel locked up.'

Realisation hits me. 'They're in there. You've locked them in the skull.' No wonder it's so damn powerful I hardly dare look at it. It contains the spirit or essence of both a master magician and a Bene Elohim. Incredible. And utterly terrifying. 'But how? How did you manage it?'

'Oh, I didn't, Paul. I could never come up with such a working. No. It was Jakob who designed the trap, not me.'

Chapter Thirty

BIDACHE, 9 MARCH, PRESENT DAY

Apparently, Jakob trapped himself. That sounds more like something I would do. And have done. More than once.

Well, I didn't see that coming. Actually, I'm not entirely sure I understand what he said to me. 'Sorry, did you say *Jakob* designed the trap?'

The old bastard nods, still chuckling slightly, the wheeziness lingering in his breathing. 'That's right.'

'What? How? Why would he?'

'Why do you think? Because I tricked him, of course. And it all started when I got my hands on this.' He rubs the top of the skull lovingly. 'When I heard about it, at first I wanted to get my hands on it just to piss in the bastard's eye sockets. But when I saw it, saw it aglow with so much *talent*, well, I was delighted. Thought I'd found the key to let me unlock the doors of reality and escape this pitiful existence. But *powerful* though it is, it's not enough.

'So what did you do?' I don't really care. A thought's coming to my mind, and I need to give it space to come together fully, let it become complete. In the meantime, I just want to keep him talking. Stalling, basically.

'Well, I knew about Jakob, obviously. I was keeping careful tabs on you and your heathen mentor. More than one of the men I studied under talked in hushed tones about their pet angels. They all thought of them as possessions rather than separate souls tangled in with their bearers, but then they were mostly short-sighted fools who sought power through force. Amazing how many magicians are vainglorious idiots, pursuing short-term plans, never able to see much beyond the end of their noses.' He sighs and walks away from the skull, painfully bending and taking his seat again.

'So you tricked Jakob in the same manner?' I can taste the idea... almost. It's on the tip of my tongue...

'Oh no.' Ben clucks his tongue. 'Jakob was never vainglorious, never short-sighted. Never a fool, except perhaps regarding the world and certainly to love. Isn't it funny how someone so incredibly smart, a genius about so many things, can also be so *naïve* about others?'

That certainly matches my memories of Jakob. Kind, gentle, brilliant. And far too good for this world. Somehow, despite all he saw, he always maintained this innocent hope, this belief in humanity that most of us have blunted by too much contact over too much time with too many people.

Now I get it. The thought that's been bothering me.

The skull winked at me.

The skull winked at me when Ben first came in. And if Jakob's in the skull, that means it was *Jakob* who winked at me.

Plus, Ben said all the Enochian runes, all of this angel-level magic isn't his doing, that he had to use the duo trapped in the skull, somehow wielding it to force them to do his bidding.

But if he can wink at me....

Perhaps he's not so totally under Ben's control as he thinks.

I'm less than half-listening to what he's saying now. Ben's rambling on, dishing out backhanded compliments about how wonderfully good Jakob is on the one hand and what a major weakness that is on the other or some such general blather. Considering how taciturn he was the whole time he ran us ragged looking for the Vernicle, he's got plenty to say for himself now. Guess he's been storing it all up for eight hundred years.

My eyes are fixed on the skull. I'm not *looking* at it —I don't need to explode my frontal cortex and turn myself into a vegetable— but I am trying to study it, to understand if the flaming eyes mean it can see me.

Whether the holes in the sides mean Jakob can hear the entire conversation. Can hear me.

I've got to do something. This is all taking too long, and all this time, Aicha is suffering. If I can just get out of here, go get her and Isaac, with what we know now, Benedict won't stand a chance. We can ride in, clear him out, and rescue Jakob and Nanael. No problem.

All it needs is for me to escape.

So I look at the skull, staring at it. Thinking through that "tip of my tongue" idea. I can't think of any other way to be sure except to try it.

Here we go.

I take some deep breaths, psyching myself up for what's to come. I yell, 'Jakob, Nan! Let me out!'

Then I clamp my jaw down, hard and fast, locking the clenched muscles tight.

But not before I poke my tongue out.

I've angled my head back so that as soon as I feel it sever, I can open my mouth back up, catch the severed appendage, and swallow hard. My mouth fills with blood. My cry startled Ben, pulling him back from his reverie, so he turns in my direction. Blood pours down the back of my throat, filling my larynx.

A larynx blocked by the severed remnant of my tongue.

Ben hurries over. It's obvious I'm choking, and he tries to push his fingers in, to work them through my pressed lips, to find out what's happening. But he's old, frail. I want to bite his fingers off, but I'm worried I won't get through the bone and that'll give him leverage to pry my teeth open. So even as my body's automatic systems press their equivalents of the panic button, even as my oxygen intake cuts off to zero, I'm strong enough, both physically and will-wise, to keep the prying fingers out.

And through it all, over the tilt of my chin half-obscuring my view, over the rising physical panic as my vision greys and spots red around the edges, I keep my eyes fixed on the skull, hoping Jakob can hear me in there. Hoping he can let me go.

And with that thought, darkness takes me, and my breathing stops completely, and I'm gone...

... I'm back. My tongue's here too, so Ben's failed. That body's dead. I snap my eyes open...

I'm in the same room. A new body, runc-covered, in the sterile white chamber. Ben's back is to me as he fusses with my last form, no doubt trying to see if I'm still alive. When it disintegrates, atomising, that gives him the answer. He turns, his eyes searching till they lock on mine.

Dammit. It didn't work.

He chuckles, wags his finger as he stumps over towards me. 'Now, now, Paul. That won't work. A lovely idea, appealing to Jakob for help but doomed to fail for two reasons. Thanks to his own designs, he's helpless in there to do anything but follow my instructions. And second, because of the skull itself.'

He pauses, takes a breath wincingly. Apparently, all this walking and talking is hard on him. As I just choked to death on my own blood and tongue, I don't feel particularly sorry for him.

'Something about it calls to our reincarnating. There's a link there, somehow. I experimented, of course. Do you know when you committed hari-kari to escape the shit wizard, there was a whole family of dead bodies just next door? I know. I killed them all myself. But thanks to my hiding the skull in Purpan Morgue — pop! There you were. Not this skull, but... well, we'll get to that later. Anyway, off you went, skipping past all those convenient corpses to come to where I wanted you. Made it much easier to put you in that poor morgue attendant's body after the fight with the wolf pack too.'

My heart is buried down in my guts. He's thought of everything. I've shown my hand, made my play, and it's not worked. Here I am back in another of these blasted wall-deco corpses he's strung up all around, and she's still burning. Somewhere out there, Aicha's still fucking burning. I've got to get out. Got to.

There's only one option. Talking's getting us nowhere. Appealing to Jakob's a wash-out. That means I can only do one other thing to get out of here.

Ben sees it, the moment when I make the decision. His eyes widen, and he starts to pole his way towards me, hurrying as fast as his crooked aged legs will carry him.

Not fast enough. Head tilt, tongue out. Bite. Ride out the pain, catch the severed piece. Swallow. Choke.

Die.

My eyes snap open. Ben's swinging his head around wildly, looking for me, trying to see where I'll pop up next. He's about two metres away from me. His gaze skips past me, then whirls back.

'Wait, Paul!' He stretches a hand out, pleading towards me. 'Don't make me do this!'

No time to listen. I've done enough of that. *Burning*. So tilt, bite, catch, swallow, choke, die.

My eyes fly wide. Ben's nowhere near me. He's on the opposite side of the circle from me. Except now he's not looking for me. No, he's *pulled* a metal box to him from the cabinet he's flung open with his mind. I've no idea what he's got planned, but whatever it is, it can't be good. Looks like I need to hurry up. Tilt the head back and tongue out…

Eyes open. His back's to me, and he's working away furiously like a man possessed, doing something to that particular corpse. *Worry about that later, Paul. She's on fire, out there. Tilt that head back…*

Eyes. Whatever he was doing is finished. He's back to looking around, trying to spot me, but there's less panic there now. Damn. I'm not sure what he's done but either whatever it is has settled his nerves, or he's a hell of a poker player.

'Paul, you don't want to do this. Stop now.' The certainty in his voice is unnerving, but I've got no other options. I've got to see this through. Tilt…

My eyes spring open, and I gag, retching at the bitter taste of metal. Then the pain comes. It's so close to the agony I've been inflicting on myself each time I've bitten my tongue off, it takes me a minute to recognise it as not self-inflicted.

There's a metal cage around my head like I've been inserted face-first into a bear-trap. A wedge fills my mouth. And attached to it is an iron spike driven through my tongue, nailing it to my pallet.

'I was afraid of something like this.' Ben pauses. Stops. 'No, let's be honest. I was afraid you'd bother me incessantly with inane interruptions and stupid braggadocio. I intended this to silence you if it became unbearable. Luckily, it works just as well for ending this petulant attempt to escape as well. A nag's bridle. So perfectly employed a few centuries back to silence those incessant women incapable of guarding their tongue in place and keeping their peace. It works just as well for keeping your tongue in place, doesn't it?'

The Good God dammit. Everything. The bastard seems to have thought of everything.

'Now where was I before you so rudely interrupted me?' He scratches his chin, relaxed. He knows he's got me. Just like he knows exactly what he was talking about. All of this is just posturing, rubbing in that he's caught me again, the fucking arsehole.

'Ah yes, we were talking about Jakob and the skull. I realised that the skull on its own wasn't powerful enough to break through reality itself and let me escape, so I needed to augment it somehow. There were... experiments. Attempts to combine various magical creatures with it or place their spirits inside. None of it worked. The skull's magic just burnt them away. So I knew I needed to think bigger, more Talented. And what's more Talented than an angel, eh?'

Man, I wish my hands were free so I could slap that shit-eating grin off his face. Ben looks entirely too pleased with himself.

'Of course, I couldn't go waltzing up like this to a Bene Elohim. Nanael would have smelt my sins, necessary though they were, a mile away. Luckily, I had an answer to that. Do you know the Jotunn? Oh, sorry.' He waves a hand in my direction. 'I forgot you can't answer that. Still, I'm sure a man as well travelled as you does. They have a technique for placing the soul in an egg and storing it away from the body. Well, I did something much the same, putting most of my soul —and all of my sins— outside myself, leaving them far away so Nanael couldn't feel them. Not without tearing my mind to pieces, and they do so hate to hurt us pitiful little human ants, don't they?'

He walks over and forces a finger inside my mouth, testing the restraint. He pushes it down gently, but it's still enough to make the pain explode, radiating up my jaw till my eyes ache with the agony. He tightens a screw, then brings his hand out, drying his finger by wiping it delicately on my cheek.

'So I went to meet this great magician, this angel-bearer, and what did I find? A simpering nancy, nothing more. Oh, yes, a charming man with the looks to match his wit and manners, but effete and clearly attracted to me. And that was when I hatched my plan, when I worked out how I was going to capture an angel.'

He leans on me, keeping his hand on my shoulder but not like before, not gripping to hurt me. More to keep his balance, to help him stay upright or as if he is drawing energy or comfort from the contact. It makes me want to spit — a hard task when every dribble of drool just slips uncomfortably down my throat, my swallowing reflex interfered with by the metal bit blocking my mouth.

'So I seduced him. Studied under him and studied him from under him as well.' His lip twists, an almost grimace but trembles too. 'He was kind and patient, and I took all I could from him regarding Kabbalah. All the time, I pushed him to be better, to do greater things. Told him that if he bore an angel, he carried the responsibility of all the Israelites on his shoulders. That he had to find ways to help them, to protect them from a world so keen to blame them for everything and to punish them with ghettoes and pogroms. Nanael wouldn't get involved directly, always the problem he came back to, so I tried to set his incredible mind to solving that problem, finding a way to bypass that natural angelic resistance. To find a solution that would suit them both. Then when time's ravages started to be obvious, when I knew my body's ageing would betray me, I died. But oh!' His eyes enlarge, a smile creasing his endless wrinkles, multiplying them so there's not an inch of skin on his face that's not crinkled. 'Oh, how I died!'

He lets go of my shoulder to rub my arm, an almost affectionate gesture, then steps away. I can see the excitement of the story has taken him now. I wish it would take him. Ideally straight to Hell.

'He told me the stories of what had happened to those who had tried to copy him and his brother's rituals that bound them to the angels. So I staged my suicide as an accident. I carved sufficient Enochian runes into my body to summon but not to hold, a higher being. Not enough to risk it working, of course. Just enough to summon a touch of the higher dimensions into a simple mortal frame. I believe my head exploded. What a mess it must have made. Brains and skull shards embedded in the walls. Of course, I left a note. In it, I confessed my eternal love and my desire to be equal to him and to live as well for eternity. I wanted the guilt of my passing to be the first worm I placed inside the apple orchard of his heart.'

The agony in my tongue multiplies because I'm shaking, that shivering reaction as shock sets in. But it's not just the physical pain. It hurts my soul to hear what he did. I knew Jakob, spent so many years with the gentle, kindly soul who looked for the good in everyone. To hear how his trust was turned to love and his love turned to this utter betrayal? It sickens me to the very core of my being.

And of course Ben's not even got to the worst part.

'Fast forward a few decades after I regained an adult body, and some careful enquiries told me that Jakob had withdrawn from the world. As I'd hoped, he'd turned to selfless acts, no doubt seeking to make amends for the guilt he'd ascribed to himself for my last death. When I heard about the project he'd done with Rabbi Leow building the golem to protect the Jews, I was almost beside myself with glee. It couldn't be more what I'd wanted. His reactions? Everything I'd dreamed of.'

He's pacing now, the aches and pains of his aged body apparently forgotten as he's swept up in the memory's excitement. 'It was simple to seduce him again. I was the only man he'd ever loved, the only physical companionship ever shared. What a distinct feeling it must have been compared to the cold, emotionless intertwining of his soul with Nanael.

Thanks to the Jotunn's magic, neither Jakob nor Nanael could recognise my essence, and it caused me no difficulty to worm my way into his heart once more.

'Except this time. This time, I presented a different character. A fellow Jew tormented by guilt over my unnatural preferences. After enough years to be certain of the impact, my suicide this time was not in the least magical — a knife to the wrists in the metal soaking tub was less dramatic than the dripping ichor off the walls I had left before, but the note was more impactful than even that had been. I spoke of my disgust, both with myself and him, to have committed such abhorrent and unclean acts, my certitude of damnation for us both because of our actions, and I laid all the responsibility with carefully constructed sentences at his door. It was his fault for having indulged in his desires and the damned temptations of the physical world. I made my death his burden to bear, and I made sure that the first worm spread to every single apple that could ever be born from the trees of his soul. I brought rot to his Eden, blighting his material paradise for all time.

'He went mad with grief and retreated from all engagements, a hermit that kept away from everyone else he knew, especially his beloved brother, to avoid marring them as he had the men he'd loved. My deaths tainted the physical world for him, and he fasted to extremes, living in poverty and squalor. He wanted to escape from the chains of his mortal frame, but more than that, he wanted to protect his scattered tribe as his first love had suggested he do. I would provide him with the key to both.'

By all that's holy. The salty taste to my saliva tells me just how close I am to throwing up. Maybe if I do, I can choke on that? Die once more, start getting away again? But no, there's enough bodies left, he could get the nag's bridle on one long before I could exhaust the total supply. Fucking hell.

There's no man there, nothing left in the wizened body in front of me that could be called human. No *human* could do this to another, especially one so pure and innocent as Jakob. This is work that Satan, if he exists, would describe as abominable. I don't doubt Ben pulled it off, convinced Jakob of everything he wanted, so he can't ever have been the man I believed him to be. Everything about him is a lie. All of it must have been an act. I can't bear the only other possibility.

That this terrible monstrosity all stems from one simple act by me, an act I believed to be selfless, trying to save the world.

When I embraced magic to destroy the Grail, I accepted the price was my soul. I didn't realise the price would be Ben's too.

CHAPTER THIRTY-ONE

BIDACHE, 9 MARCH, PRESENT DAY

It's funny how giving up our own soul
can seem like a simple choice. To find out
it ruined the soul of someone we loved?
Makes it suddenly unbearable.

T he thing that might once have been my best friend looks at me with pride engraved into every wrinkle of his face. He's so delighted by his own cunning. It turns my stomach.

'So I returned once more.' He's not done. I don't want to hear anymore, but it's not going to stop him from telling me. 'Not as a lover this time but as a wandering pilgrim with minor magical knowledge who had sought his wisdom for many years. I showed him the skull of Arnaud, claiming familial stewardship, and all those careful nudges and subliminal suggestions I'd given him previously in my last two lives crystallised into a "eureka" moment he thought he'd arrived at entirely independently. In his excitement, he set to work at once to incorporate it into his plans. I was happy to bequeath it to him, claiming to be enamoured by his plan to help the poor, defenceless Jewry and happy to gain knowledge under his tutelage as he worked towards that aim.

'And so for the third and final time, I became his disciple. Having gifted him the key to a conundrum that had consumed him for more than a century, his faith in me was entire and unquestioning. His initial plan was simple — put Nanael into the empty cranium. The angel would become a diffuse presence, a guiding energy protecting the Jewish diaspora. Nanael was willing, but they found themselves too tightly intertwined on a spiritual level for such a separation. Instead, they contrived a new method that corresponded perfectly with what I wanted.'

The glee on his face fills me with primal rage. I can't control it. I'm gurgling, raging, thrashing against the restraints. Each time I move just drives the spike harder into the bottom of my mouth, but it's nothing. Just pain. I know pain. Pain's an actual friend, one who's been with me through all of these different lifetimes. This bastard in front of me? He can't have ever been my friend. No one I could love could do this. Perhaps somewhere deep inside, there's a scrap, a shred of that ancient Ben buried away. I'll see if I find it when I tear him into tiny fucking pieces. Which is what I'm going to do... just as soon as I can get free.

The spike bites hard. The bonds don't budge. Not an inch. And Ben only watches, his eyes alight with amusement.

'Do let me know when you've finished, Paul. I'd hate for you to miss any of this.'

I sag, exhausted, defeated. I'm still furious —the anger I'm feeling isn't about to leave, not anytime soon, not ever— but I'm getting nowhere, just wearing myself out. This is the sort of reaction he wants. I need to be more clever, think my way out of here. Brute force and ignorance isn't going to work.

'May I continue?' Ben doesn't even wait for my response, just carries on. 'In his warded cave, Jakob created a magically charged plinth decorated with all his knowledge of Kabbalah and all his love for humanity and his

Hebraic brethren. Twenty years he spent carving and imbuing it with his essence, and it was truly one of the greatest works of magical artistry this world has ever known. And it only took one sacrifice to make it happen. Well, two, of sorts. Jakob and Nanael. They worked out how to put themselves into the skull. Once they did so, they'd be useless, trapped, unable to interact with the outside world in any way or form unless instructed. Until the skull was placed on the plinth anyway. That's where I came in. Once the skull was on the plinth, they'd be able to act, becoming this wondrous shield to shelter the Jews across the world from the misery forever snapping at their heels. Until then? Utterly vulnerable, powerless to act or move. Thank goodness they had a loyal, trustworthy acolyte who could aid them for that final essential step!'

The sarcasm drips from his voice. Oh, he's so delighted in his *cleverness*, so proud of himself for tricking a man who loved and trusted him three times, each time with an open heart despite the wounds he received prior. Jakob always was the best of us. And Ben used that to make his suffering the worst imaginable.

'Jakob did it all to himself, you know? He took the skull, and he merged it into his own, holy golden fire blazing from him, a blinding aurora that encircled and consumed him. When it finally dimmed, only the skull remained, replete with the combined energies of Jakob and Nanael.'

He walks over to the skull once more, gently caressing it. There's a covetous aspect to it, a greedy delight, like a dragon flicking his tongue over his treasure trove.

'And there it was. The single greatest magical artefact ever created. Two Talented souls —a powerful magician and an actual angel— bound in servitude inside of the skull. And they were completely helpless, tied to my will. I smashed the plinth, destroyed it entirely, turned the skull to make them watch as I turned their dreams, the culmination of their life's work into nothing but splinters and dust. Then I set to work to use their power. To finally escape from existence.'

The humour drains from his face, changing to a glower. He gnaws on his lip as he paces again. 'Despite that, it wasn't enough! Still, I couldn't get through, break out of this pitiful dimension, find a way to either escape to the higher planes or else cease to exist one way or the other! I was close. I could feel the walls bending, bowing before the combined might of the skull and its two new denizens, but no matter what I did, it wouldn't break.'

Well, excuse me if I don't cry you a fucking river, you shitbag. Breaking the walls of reality to escape it sounds about as sensible as smashing out one of the main walls of a house because you want to pop to the shops. And as someone still living in that house called reality, I don't want to see it collapsing, killing all of us left inside. I can't tell him all that as much as I'd love to. Looking at the manic gleam in his eyes though, I don't think he'll give a damn what I say. There are no words left that could sway him from his path.

The smile breaks through again though, which doesn't improve my mood. If Ben is smiling, it can only be bad news for the rest of us.

'Do you know who it was who brought me the answer to my problem, who answered my prayers?' He shakes his head as if even he can't believe the response he's going to give. 'Your dear friend, the shit wizard.'

He raises a hand and *pulls* the door open, then uses his *talent* to bring in an operating table covered with Enochian workings so powerful they're visibly carved across reality. And my heart, already fissuring under the pressure from thinking of Aicha's suffering, surely cracks clean in two. Because there, strapped to it, his eyes closed, is Isaac.

Now I can't help it. I throw myself against the restraints, straining, ripping the skin off my biceps as I try to move enough to get them free. The noise coming from my mouth is halfway to a groan, halfway to a grieving widow's wail, and neither does justice to the pain in my soul.

Of course Ben's done his job too well. Nothing helps. All I'm doing is hurting myself.

As I calm down, exhaustion creeping into muscles that are still struggling to remember they aren't dead, I take in the scene more clearly. Isaac is naked, his skin aglow with the looping curves of Kabbalist symbols light-years beyond my capacity. If I had to hazard a guess, they're the equivalent of an IV drip for Nithael, keeping him unconscious and subdued, Isaac along with him. Above his head, hovering, tied on with Enochian lettering loops to lock it into place, like a fixed orbit point over Isaac's head, is something else I didn't expect to see. Mainly because I can't believe there's more than one in the whole of existence.

It is another skull glowing in the *sight*, absolutely radiant with *talent*.

For a moment, I think I feel my poor, battered, already-broken heart freeze. Feel my eyes stretch, the horror pulling at the skin, tightening it as they widen at seeing my comatose angel-bearer friend with a powerful skull right above his head.

'Oh, so you've worked it out!' Ben stamps his stick on the ground with glee, like Rumpelstiltskin delighting in wrong guesses at his name. 'You're quite right. The plan is to pop Isaac and his feathered friend into this other skull. With the power of two angels at my command, making my escape from this miserable existence will be child's play. Nothing can stand against that sort of power.'

He stumps towards the table he *pulled* in, now neatly sat beside the skull containing Jakob and Nanael. As he passes, he wags a finger at it like a naughty schoolboy.

'Oh, Jak, you foolish dreamer.' He tuts as he passes. 'All of this magic, this genius-level work with the Enochian script so far beyond my capacity to create, I bet you never dreamt when you created all the workings to allow the transfer of your essence into that skull, it'd one day be the downfall of your beloved brother too.' He turns his attention towards Isaac, but his lip rises at the sight of my mentor. 'The pair of you. So quick to investigate forces beyond your knowledge. See where your meddling has got you.'

The bastard's gloating, and I can't blame him. He's won. All my hopes were on somehow getting free from here, saving Aicha, then pulling in the celestial big guns by bringing Nithael to rescue his brother. Instead, thanks to Jakob's research that Ben guided him into all those centuries ago, they're powerless. Ben's trickery has won out against powers well beyond his own.

The bastard waves a hand towards the door, simultaneously closing and sealing it, the runic locks glowing for a second before fading.

Delicately, he runs his fingers along the skull's jawline. 'I'd about given up hope, you know. Thought I would never escape. How could I possibly find power beyond this one skull? Then that idiotic shit wizard sought me out, looking for training. And in exchange, he offered me this.'

He turns back towards me, checking my face, making sure I'm paying attention. I am. I'm desperately hoping some fatal flaw is going to show itself, something I can exploit to get us out of here. Plus, I hardly have a lot of choice thanks to the restraints and the nag's bridle.

'They say this is the skull of Torquemada, the most feared and blood-thirsty of the Inquisition, a man who delighted in torturing and burning any he perceived to be heretical or impure. And somehow, it's also radiant with that same strange *talent* as the other skull is, as you and I are. This is how I tested your reincarnation capabilities, pulling you to that corpse in Purpan. Somehow, we are all interlinked. You, me, Almeric. This Torquemada. I don't know how, and I don't much care. What I care about is that, thanks to all that incredible theory Jakob created and we used to entrap him and Nanael in Almeric's skull, this will make a perfect new home for your bastard mentor and his own angel.'

He reaches behind the table and pulls out another object, one, which in a normal situation, would draw every Talented's attention like moths to a flame because of its radiant power. In here, though, it's dull, a candle in the middle of bright daylight. Or held up next to some industrial scale floodlights even. There's so much raw power in this room between the two skulls and the Enochian workings that the veil hardly even seems to be glowing in comparison.

'So now, I guess you're wondering what this is all about, aren't you?' He waves the Vernicle like a loved one bidding adieu as the train pulls away from the station. 'Well, it served two purposes. Firstly, it kept you busy and brought you here. Once you got the Veil, you all relaxed, especially the rabbi, who I really needed. Off he trotted with the Vernicle for safe keeping, straight into my waiting arms. But secondly...'

He breaks off, takes a step in my direction. He stops and looks at me, gazing at my face. He looks down and away, closes his eyes, then hobbles slowly over to me.

'This,' he says as he trudges, his voice husky, almost a whisper. 'Well, this is both a present and a payment. For you. My first master. The only man I ever loved. The person I've hated more than any other and missed just as much. The noble idiot who trapped me here and made me pay the price for his grand gesture while he traipsed off to adventures and happiness, forgetting all about me.'

He reaches me, folds the Vernicle, and dabs at my tears like a mother at a school kid's dirty face, gently wiping them away. 'You always were a confusion for me.' His hand trembles as he rests it against my cheek. 'From the very start. So many strange feelings. Wrong, perhaps, and yet they always seemed so pure. And no matter how badly you've hurt me, the terrible payments I've had to make because of what you did, there's still that seed of love that stays buried inside my raging thirst for vengeance. A confusion indeed, Paul Bonhomme.'

He lifts his hand, his fingers stroking my cheekbone, then pats my face gently. 'So I'll answer both at once. I shall punish you by saving you. The Vernicle performs the role of absolution at a papal level with no confession needed. *Forgiveness of any and all* sins. No wonder it was so popular among the corrupt priests of the Holy See. So you see, there's no need for confession. We don't have to sit through you telling me all your many trespasses. Let's lighten the load on your soul. Let's make you Perfect once again.'

My pulse spikes as I realise what he means, what he's trying to do. If he kills me when I'm Perfect. I'm not coming back. And Aicha and Isaac... they will be left on their own with no one to save them.

He holds out the gauzy cloth and gently lowers it as it shimmers, mirroring his hand tremors, over my face, some bizarro world version of a beau's first view of his ravishing bride. As it covers me, reducing my world to hazy grey shades of broken light sources, he whispers in my ear, 'I forgive you, Paul'.

A razor's edge kisses my throat, then bites deep.

CHAPTER THIRTY-TWO

BIDACHE, 9 MARCH, PRESENT DAY

A mere few seconds to come up with a solution and save the world before I die for good. No pressure.

Peace. Peace comes pouring out of the rag still sodden with Lou's excretions, its power flooding outwards. Peace driving through my system. Deleting my wrongdoings. Forgiving all my trespasses. Terrible, horrible, unwanted peace.

My pulse jackhammers, and each thump that bangs in my chest, in my ears sends spray gushing out my throat. How much time left? No time to do the maths. In a moment, I'm going to die, my soul cleansed, and that's it. Perfect again. Game over.

Ben turns his back on me, heading over to fuss with the skull and Isaac. He's dismissed me, a dead man already. Now that he's had his revenge or given his forgiveness or whatever exactly the fuck all that was in terms of him unburdening himself, I'm forgotten about. He's already onto the next stage of his plan to demolish reality just so he can die.

Time's slipping by too fast. I scrunch my face up in despair and agony... and the veil moves. It's still coated in the slime that comes as an unwanted extra on everything Lou Carcoilh touches. Means it's slippery. One chance.

I start gurning, pulling stupid faces, twisting and contorting my face muscles beneath the iron cage, between its "bars", trying to make them into a conveyor belt to carry the Vernicle away. It slides clear of my face, aided by the blood liberally coating my neck, catching on the spray.

My vision's greying, tunnelling in, the ceiling narrowing from arrays of spots to a single one, and it's like that damnable light they're always talking about, there to guide the soul away from this world. Tongue still spiked. Can't speak. Can't scream blasphemies. One chance. One second left. Good God dammit, but the official doctrine better be right about sin. *Thought*, word and deed. As even that one light fades, I'm screaming in my head the most horrible abusive things against every single religious icon. Particular mention goes to bloody Saint Veronica for her fucking veil. No idea if it's enough. My soul's not been this clean for centuries. No idea if it's going to be enough.

We're about to find out. Life fades to black.

I wake up where endless colourless, washed-out sands stretch incomprehensible distances, a nothingness so heavy it could crush the most strong-willed like leaves underfoot. Next to where I'm standing (though my presence makes no impression on the sandy flooring) are words from so very long ago, still fresh as ever —

NOT YET

I came here once before, lifetimes back, on that first death, caught in the Grail's demise, disrupting whatever fuckery Nicetas was trying to pull off, to get this scratchy sand message delivered to me. For a moment, I wonder if some desert wind is going to whip up and obliterate the "NOT" written in the grains. Is this it? Even now, eight hundred years after this first happened, centuries of me wondering exactly what or who gave me this little heads up, whether they are the same force that gifted or cursed me with my reincarnation, I've still got no idea where I am or why I ended up here after dying from a razor's embrace by Almeric's hand. Now here I am, my throat slit once more, back in this unsettling place outside of the lands of the living. Is it Purgatory? Or the nothingness I was promised for breaking my consolamentum? Maybe the sand granules underfoot are the particles of sinners' souls, and after my brief reprieve, I'm going to break apart and add to the endless dunes.

And just as I'm passing through despair into grief-filled acceptance over failing Aicha, Isaac, Jakob, the whole damned world...

More words appear next to those first ones, exactly as the first did all those centuries ago, lines engraving into the endless grey; scribbled, scratchy stick-carvings that say —

OPEN THE DOOR

— My eyes fly open. I'm back in a new body, and I clamp down on a desperate, natural desire to heave a breath into my revived lungs. There's hope in my heart even as the eyes of this body start to focus, and if I'm where I hope I am, if that message meant what I think it means, any noise will betray me, take away this last desperate chance. As my vision returns —the whiteout reassembling itself into lights, a ceiling, and walls— the brightness of the pool of blood next to me is a shocking slash of colour through it. It's a slap to the senses. Good. I need them fully operational. I still need to find a way out of here.

Because I'm back. Back in Ben's laboratory, in the dead body wall-hung next to where I just died, judging by the empty table and the widespread blood pool. I remain strapped in, covered in runes but with my mouth free of that bastard contraption he used to secure my wagging tongue. Ben still has his back turned, uninterested in my demise and, thankfully, equally ignorant of my reincarnation. Remembering the sand engraved message, my eyes shoot to the door, and I risk *looking* at it, hoping the locking spells have crumbled. It's not a shock to find that isn't the case — the arsehole wove them well.

Shit.

I consider my options. The glyphs are keeping me effectively restrained, incapable of any action, physical or magical. I wait until I'm sure Ben's attention is entirely elsewhere, watching as he imbues his power into another glyph on the skull. It's even more radiant, and it looks ready for whatever fucked-up working he's going to use to lock away Isaac and Nithael for good. I need to move. Now.

Looking down, I trace the sigils' paths, searching hopelessly for an exploitable weakness even though I know their potency surpasses my best psychic force. As I follow the flowing, glowing calligraphy down my arms and to my hands, my eyes widen. A tiny crossbar etched into the lettering blinks out, rendering one word meaningless.

With a mental effort, agency returns to the middle finger of my right hand. I've no idea what external force has intervened —god, angel, demon— but apparently they've got a juvenile sense of humour as well as a penchant for writing in sand unless I've missed my guess. Whoever they are, I like them even more for that. Focusing my energy through the extended digit, I silently unpick the door enchantment, my eyes locked on Ben and his preparations.

He's so near to completion. He lifts the skull off the table with Isaac, taking it over to the pedestal where Jakob's prison sits. He removed the other skull at some point, and it now sits on the floor, next to where it was. Clearly he's going to use Nanael's magic to seal the circle and power the ritual. Seating the empty skull of Torquemada on the woven-bone display stand, he steps backwards and kneels, powering up a circle around them.

Fuck. Unless I've missed my guess, all he has to do now is wheel Isaac over that surrounding line, and bam! Isaac and Nithael will be locked up in there for eternity.

Rivulets of sweat run down my cheeks by the time I approach the final intricate knot forming the sealing glyph. It's all I can do not to keep scanning over to Ben to see how close he is to making it back to the table holding Isaac. The stomping clonk of his cane taps across the room, imitated by my heart beating so hard in my chest I'm surprised it's not cracking my rib cage. I don't know if I can do this. Not in time. Got to concentrate. Unpick. *Pull. Unravel the fucking spell, Paul.*

I don't know how I keep my sigh of relief inaudible instead of screaming in delight when I finally unravel his working without raising his attention. I offer a desperate plea for a last turn of luck to whoever is helping me, push the last of my reserves out of my finger, and fling the door wide open.

On the other side stands a flaming avenging angel, an ifrit of righteous vengeance. A cloud of dust composed of her own particles billows around her, looking like a swarm of furious flies, the crackling of her flesh as it releases flakes to join the dancing swirl forming their enraged buzz. She pushes against the air with boned hands, flesh dissolving under the combination of heat and pressure, and forces the restraining circle (still replete with *don't look here* working) imprisoning her inside the fiery tornado to move via her sheer weight of uncontainable will. Aicha drives her smouldering, atomising form forward one step at a time, her path down the corridor marked by charred footprints.

Ben turns, agog at the sight of this warrior ablaze, who refuses to accept his imposed limitations. He stumbles over his words, and now it is his turn to blink, unbelieving at the sight of what confronts him. Greyed flesh pales further as he casts his *talent* at her in a mixture of glottal syllables and intricate gestures, only for the deadly casting to be undone on contact with his own constructed barrier. What's keeping her trapped inside with the fire is also keeping out all destructive magic. He looks wildly around, no doubt searching for Almeric's skull, to grab it, to use its power to defend himself against her. Except he's forgotten in his panic that it's powering the ritual. And is sealed inside the circle.

The old wizard fumbles in a pocket, pulls out a stoppered vial, pops the top off.

'Come a step closer, and it'll be the last one you ever take!' His breaths are wheezes, words obscured by the constriction terror places on his chest. 'This... this is the antidote to your cursed Aab Al Hayaat, woman!'

My heart plummets, sweat pouring down the back of my neck, as I start trying to angle my finger around to point at him, at the vial, to do something. The fucking antidote, the one he threatened to use on her, on the phone. The one I warned her about.

Aicha doesn't even slow down. It's not easy to talk when your vocal cords are crackling, snapping like worn guitar strings every few seconds, but she pushes the words out. 'Fine... take... you... with...me...'

Ben curses, backing up further, the glass beaker slipping from his fingers, as he lets it drop, discarded, useless. And I can suddenly breathe again.

It was a bluff. All another fucking bluff.

And Aicha called it. She continues her ineffable, defiant march towards him.

He dispels the binding he surrounded her with, the one sealing her inside with the fire but keeping his magic out, trying to call up his *talent*, to hit her with another working, but she's too close. Her hands shoot out and form a red-hot collar around his throat. He coughs and gags, the acrid odour of her long-charring flesh mixing with the tantalisingly fresh roasting smell of his own. She holds him, silent and pleading, then shoves him backwards into the sigil circle, the working he was creating to hold Isaac and Nithael.

As the old mad wizard stumbles into it, his arms flailing as she releases him, the markings flare in time with the eye sockets of the Skull containing Jakob and Nanael. The room lights with the eerie beauty of angelic otherness, and I garble out my fear and awe, unable and unwilling to tear myself away from watching his fate. All that radiance pools inwards, condensing into the frame of a man I once called my brother. Ben glows with a brilliance I would've once thought matched his soul, now as strong as my previous despair. It builds and brightens until unbearably pure, mind shatteringly perfect, and then it is gone, imploding back into nothingness. The light shoots back into the previously empty skull...

Taking Ben with it.

CHAPTER THIRTY-THREE

BIDACHE, 9 MARCH, PRESENT DAY

Thoroughly fed up with hanging from chains and restraints from the wall. I normally keep that as a treat for every alternate Tuesday.

The flames cocooning Aicha's frame extinguish as Ben's disappearance into the skull dispels the constraining magic. Her charred flesh rejuvenates, replacing itself, and she stands once more whole and proud, unabashed in her nudity as she snaps the restraints keeping me in place. We're family; she isn't embarrassed being around me in her birthday suit, and I value my kneecaps far too much to even think about ogling her, ever. Once I fall forward, freed from the wall-mounted table, I pull out another of her outfits, as well as one of my own from my etheric storage space. I dress quickly, then turn my attention to freeing Isaac while she finishes getting ready. As I erase the sigil markings covering both him and myself, I see the absent cloud-greyness depart from his gaze, and my friend comes slowly back to us.

A sudden explosion of light knocks me flying across the room, restraining me against the wall as effectively as the torture table setup. For a moment, I panic. It's a trap. Fucking Ben. He's booby-trapped the workings. One last "fuck you" spat in our eye to add to all the misery he's heaped on us. I can't move, held paralysed, a prisoner all over again.

Then the light dims slightly, and I can see the neon outline of crackling, impossible electric carving through the air, marking the shape of an angel's arm pinning me in place. Looks like Nithael woke up before Isaac did.

'It's me, Nith!' I croak the words out despite the pressure on my diaphragm. 'He's gone. We saved you.'

The light fades, along with the restraining force, and as I blink the last remnants of the angelic equivalent of a flashbang grenade from my poor abused eyes, I get something that makes up for it. I get to see Isaac open his.

I rush over to him, checking him over, making sure he's really still there. Once I'm sure he's okay, I start to fill him in on what's been going on while he's been unconscious, subdued by the workings painted onto him. As I do so, Aicha goes out into the corridor and comes back in with his clothes and satchel; I make a mental note to mock him about that as a man-bag later on. Then we reach the point in the story where I found out about Jakob and Nanael's fate.

My words faltering, I glance at the Skull. Then slowly, gently, I tell him about them. The look of sheer joy, true and complete, that spreads over his face at the news of his brother is a memory I'll treasure for the rest of my existence however long or short that may be.

He rushes over to Jakob and Nithael's Skull. Standing, his hand resting on the shined dome, he closes his eyes in what I assume is an internal communion between the two brothers.

I'm not done though. I tell him about the second skull, the workings that were laid, the fate Ben had planned for him, how he intended to use their power. Sheer dread swallows up that joy. Isaac knows exactly how close he came to not only being imprisoned but bringing about the end of the world. There's no way to sugarcoat something like that.

'It didn't happen though, 'Zac. We won. Despite it all, my man, we won. And we got Jak and Nan back as well. Take the victory for now. Worry about the might-have-beens later on.'

Fucking hell, I sound almost wise here. Guess maybe even I've learned something from this whole experience. Admittedly, only as much as you could learn from breaking open a fortune cookie from your local Chinese restaurant, but anything's a step forward for me.

Isaac takes my advice, closes his eyes, and rests his hand on the skull containing his long-lost brother. After a period of time, which I use to finish scrubbing the last of the restraining magics off myself, he opens his eyes. They shine with both fresh tears and quiet joy. As he reverently picks up the skull and places it carefully inside his satchel, he murmurs, 'I can feel him, Paul. Feel them both in there.' He smiles, a brilliant genuine smile, and gives me a nod of thanks.

Moving over to Torquemada's skull, the one Ben vanished into, he passes his hand over the top of it with a grimace before nodding assent. He takes this one too, though less kindly.

'The mad bastard is in here all right.' He shoves it roughly into the other part of the bag. 'I'll take him into my safekeeping for the meantime. Mustn't let any other evil sod get their hands on this artefact with him inside it. We can worry about that later though. My priority is Jak and Nan's prison. That scumbag can rot in the other for eternity for all I care.'

I nod sadly. I can't argue with him. Part of me is glad the evil shithead who burnt Aicha, killed the wolves, Pascal, the Good God knows how many others, is locked away forever, away from the world he would have destroyed in his insanity. And part of me needs to grieve for my friend I spent decades mourning all over again even if he was lost since my very first death.

We make to leave the cold, clinical laboratory, and I look at the dead meat puppets adorning the walls with a significant amount of unease. I doubt they were vacant corpses when Ben got his hands on them, and I suspect their deaths were neither peaceful nor easy. Either way, they are also dead because of me, potential vessels during my 'saving'. Intentionally or not, they are on me, and it's something I am going to have to live with.

Aicha's been silent, her head down, inspecting everything, no doubt using that keen analytical method to distract her from thinking about what happened. She's so accustomed to trauma. It breaks my heart; though telling her so will do her no good at all. All I can do is lighten the mood until she's ready to talk. 'This whole place needs eradicating. MMC?'

She blinks owlishly, then sighs. 'No idea what you talkin' 'bout, Willis.' Good, she's cracking wise too. We all have our survival mechanisms. I'm happy to play the role of the class clown to help. There's comfort in familiar roles, and I suspect some normality —or this utterly insane cluster-fuck of an existence that's as close to normality as we ever get— will help her more than anything else I can do right now.

'Your firebomb specialty. I was trying out a catchphrase. MMC? Magical Molotov Cocktail? No? How about Magictov Cocktail? Molotov Cast-tail? Magictov Casttail?'

'It sounds like an annoying magical talking bunny rabbit, which, inci-dentally, if we ever meet one, I will instantly incinerate it with a *spell*. Like this.'

She tosses her hand casually over her shoulder as if throwing a crumpled piece of paper at a wastepaper bin, and the room erupts into a firestorm she doesn't even look at. Reaching back with her other hand, she slams the heavy metal door, trapping the whole evil space inside a cleansing inferno.

We are in an earthen tunnel not dissimilar from the sort we passed through to talk to Lou Carcoilh. That sudden memory makes me pat myself down frantically. I completely forgot about it before asking her to burn the place down.

As I turn back for the door, Aicha pulls the Vernicle from her inside jacket pocket, an eyebrow cocked in challenge.

Sigh. 'You're the best, Aicha.'

'Damn right, *saabi*. Never forget it.'

I never could, Aicha. I never could.

The passageway slopes upward until we emerge into the arriving dawn, the crisp freshness in the air still reminiscent of the end of winter. Radiant warmth is already present in the arriving rays, and the scent of morning blossoms under the dew bears the promise of warmer days ahead. We stand on a slanted hillside, the crumbling remnants of Gramont Castle directly in front of us behind a cheery little cottage on the opposite side of the lane below the slope. To our side lies a two-metre-high weighty slab of stone, heavy duty *don't look here* spells dissolving off it at the sun's touch. It is a normal reaction to the spell-caster having been rendered mostly dead, at least physically. His essence being trapped in the skull has the same effect. His magic isn't his own to command anymore. Surrounding us are many other worn and faded rectangular blocks in neat rows with faded letterings in old French and Hebraic.

Isaac smiles sadly. 'It's an Israelite graveyard. Jewish families fleeing Spanish repression in the sixteenth and seventeenth centuries were welcomed into the communities here in the south of France. This area has always held affection for the different and the desperate, a bastion of tolerance in an intolerant world more times than not. Jakob's name is carved on this headstone. Whether it was that mad sod's little joke or intended as a form of tribute, I have no idea. For now, I think I'll replace and seal this stone and let those left here rest without being disturbed by thoughtless neighbours.'

He waves his hand, and the slab lifts back into place, sealing the dark tunnel physically with the telltale bluish glow of Isaac's Kabbalah. The *don't look here* spell might be gone, but nobody's going to move that stone any time soon.

We trudge wearily up the road to get back to the car, still parked by the Pont de Gramont. I marvel at the thought of how long this gentle twenty-minute walk must have taken Aicha, burning and bound, moving her prison inch by inch.

'How did you find me?' I ask as we walk down the quiet road.

'Simple. Appropriate considering it's you. Got fed up with always having to wait around for a phone call telling me where to come find you after you get yourself killed in some utterly ludicrous manner or other. So I worked out a solution. When I gave you the clothes after your shit wizard shenanigans, I put a tiny working on them. A fragment of my essence.'

'Okay.' So far, so clear. I've done something similar with inanimate objects before, letting me know where someone or something is as long as they're carrying it. 'I still don't follow how that helped you after those clothes disintegrated along with the dead body?'

'That's because I'm a genius, and you are a certified fuckwit.' Fair, can't argue with that. 'Altered the spell, didn't I? When you died, it hitched a lift, hooked itself onto your spirit. Wherever you popped back up, so did it.'

'Wow. You're right. You are a genius.' I never even thought of that. Bloody useful when you think how often I die.

'And also that you're a certified fuckwit. I know. Don't need you to tell me.'

We lapse back into silence until another thought strikes me. 'How did you move the circle Ben trapped you in?'

A shadow flits across her face for a moment. That trauma's still going to need to be dealt with. 'He bound it around me. Thought the firestorm would hold me. Didn't occur to him it could be moved if *pushed* hard enough.'

Damn. To draw up the wherewithal not only to activate a tracking spell and then *push* a heavy-duty binding circle by sheer power and force of will *while continuously burning alive*?

There's no one more badass than Aicha Kandicha. Never has been. Never will be.

We reach the car, still hugging the side of the road near the bridge. 'Can we give you a lift to your car?' I ask Isaac.

His face drops, his cheeks drooping. 'You can give me a lift all the way to Toulouse, lad. The bastard killed my car.'

I grind to a halt. Shit, he's not going to be happy about that. Another thought hits me. 'How did he get his hands on you?'

Isaac ruffles his hair, scratching his scalp as he does so. 'He boo-by-trapped the road. Stuck a log across it, then as we slowed down, BOOM — massive magical explosion. Nithael wrapped me in his wings to protect me from physical damage, but you remember that potion I created that nullifies magic and paralyses the body?'

I nod grimly. 'Vividly. The bastard used it on Aicha and me to get hold of us at the bridge over there. Mosquito bite delivery system.'

'Intriguing.' I can see the analytical part of Isaac's brain whirring into action.

'Nope. Plagiarism. Stick to your story.' Ah, Aicha. Never one to let us get distracted by a side quest.

'Well, anyway, the explosion pumped a huge amount of that up into the air to take me out of operation instantly. At the same time, a variation on the containing sigils Jakob created flared up around us and then poor old Nith was out of the game too. Bloody ingenious, your friend was.'

I shake my head. 'My friend died a long time ago. There was nothing left of him by the end.'

Isaac looks at me long and hard. 'Are you sure about that, lad? Jakob's less convinced.'

I start. 'You can hear him?'

'Bits.' He shrugs. 'Not words exactly, but I'm picking up feelings, emotions, reactions to what we're saying. I think the connection between the angels is making it possible.'

'So he heard everything? Saw everything?' I have to fight to repress a shudder. The wink made me pretty sure Jakob was conscious in the skull, but this confirms it. For his sake, considering all the evil shit Ben must have used them for over the years, I kind of wish he wasn't.

Isaac smiles sadly. 'Yes, he did. But that's a conversation for another time. If I must have lost the old 2CV, then getting him back makes it a worthy exchange.' He pauses, looks at me again. 'Also, shotgun.'

He speaks in the same kindly tone, so it takes me a minute to work out what he said. The sneaky bastard.

'Don't even think about asking to drive, dickhead.' Aicha nudges me with her shoulder as she passes, pulling open the car door. Isaac gives me a half-apologetic, half-fuck-you wave and gets in the other side.

I take a moment before I get in, thinking of a man I once held closer to my heart than any other and who nearly cost me more than I could ever bear to pay. Of those who carried the cost of his pain. The wolves, Pascal. Jakob and Nanael, suffering for centuries. Even the poor little shit wizard, played like a puppet, with promises of power he could never hold. So many caught up in the maelstrom of another's hate.

Over the top of the hill on the other side of the bridge, the heavy monochromatic clouds, all shades of grey, break for a moment, and there's a touch of that brilliant clear blue through the gap. A moment of peace in the middle of the gathering darkness.

Sometimes, that's the most precious thing of all. A single moment's peace. Take it and hold on to it tight.

It might just see you safely through the coming storms.

TOULOUSE, 14 MARCH, PRESENT DAY

Somewhat recovered from the previous week's madness. A long way from totally over it.

I double rap on the doorframe as I push open the door to Isaac's house. It's the first time I've been over since we got back from Hastingues. He sits calmly in the kitchen, perched on a stool, his right foot resting on his left knee, and browsing a dog-eared nineteenth century encyclopaedia of faeries. He smiles and nods at me. Closing the book, he gets up to envelop me in a hug. He pushes back and looks into my eyes closely, giving me a careful, thorough inspection.

'You look tired, my boy,' he says after a moment, giving me a hearty shoulder clap before turning to put the kettle on unbidden, recognising that caffeination is probably required.

'I've not been sleeping brilliantly,' I admit, giving my right eye a rub with the back of my hand.

He nods again. 'Bad dreams?' His inquiry is casual, but the loaded weight of worry is still audible.

I sigh. 'Not on my part. I think Aicha has been struggling more.' She's moved back in with me temporarily by mutual unspoken agreement. Her nighttime cries often wake me. In her dreams, she's helpless again, and it carries through in her slumbering groans. I have no idea if I'm really helping at all, if my presence nearby makes any difference, but I'm ready to be there for as long as it takes for her to find her footing again. We've not talked about it yet. She'll tell me when she's ready.

Isaac tuts as he lifts a couple of crumb-covered plates from what looks like an irreplaceable treatise on druidic ritual spell workings from before the Christian Era, captured on paper in the Middle Ages by curious and open-minded monks. He frowns at what might be an ancient, engrained blood stain on the cover but seems more likely to be strawberry jam. He mumbles something under his breath. The latter part is a material cleaning spell, but the first part, I'm certain, is an abject apology to the object in question, as though he has offended it personally. He heads through his study towards his lab, depositing the book on a partially empty desk as he passes.

I follow in his wake, slightly concerned by the descent from organised clutter to absolute mess that seems clear in such irreverent treatment of treasured items. He looks back and smiles apologetically. 'It's been a busy moment with little sleep here too, my boy. Come, I'll show you what's been going on, and I'm sure you'll understand. I'll be back on an even keel again soon, I'm sure.'

We enter the jumbled order of his workshop, the stacked shelves incomprehensible in their organisation to anyone but him. The large central desk stands out in strong relief to this chaotic organisation in its sparsity, empty apart from the two glowering Skulls propped on each side of the centre, a metre apart, looking straight at us.

'*Look* at them, Paul.' Isaac nudges me gently with a patched elbow, his intent clear.

I open my *sight* and gasp. Although they are both clearly and categorically magical, they are also vacant. Power still comes off them in waves, but it is from their own internal force, not that of any inhabitants.

Isaac pushes back his hair half-consciously and grins bashfully. 'I know you'd have preferred I consulted with you before acting, but I had to get Jak and Nan out of there. It was unbearable, them being locked up. You'd have done the same if it was Aicha or I, I'm sure.'

'But where have you put them, man?' I look around wildly, half expecting to see a clay-formed golem waving at me from a corner underneath the clutter, but I see no animated figures.

Isaac smiles apologetically as he taps his own temple. 'I'm used to sharing my mental space with another individual; adding my brother and his best friend into the mix isn't a problem. I've offered him a time-share in effect, allowing him to take control of our body when he wishes. For the moment, though, he's still recuperating and enjoying the sensation of liberated movement as a passenger. We're talking and indulging in long-missed intellectual sparring opportunities. It gives him and Nanael time to heal from their imprisonment and their embarrassment. No, not embarrassment. Pain. Sheer horror at the evil they were used to do.'

The soft joviality leaves Isaac's expression, and it is clear he's suffering along with them.

I feel it too. Saying Jakob was ever the best of us is no exaggeration. Kind, simple, with a heart full of love. A heart that got used against him. It's a weight on mine, knowing it was only because of their association with me, because of my actions in the past that Jakob and Nanael have paid such a heavy price for so damn long. And the healing process for them is going to be long too and almost as difficult as what they've already been through. The sleepless nights I've spent in the company of my own chittering demons stand testament to that.

Suddenly, a thought strikes me. 'What about the other skull? I can't imagine you've made the same offer of residency to the bastard who did that to your brother?'

Isaac laughs, looking almost proud. Once he lifts the Vernicle from a half-closed drawer just below the second skull, understanding floods through me, along with a torrent of warring emotions. The first is anger, white-hot. I've just been thinking about all that endless suffering Jakob went through, and every time I close my eyes, I can see Aicha ignite over and over. Ben deserved to pay for his sins. Instead, it seems he had them all forgiven thanks to a *talent*-given shortcut by the Veil of Veronica. There's a large part of me that wants him to have suffered.

But there are other emotions in the mix. Not least is awe. Awe at who was behind this if I've not missed my guess. 'It was Jakob who said to do it, wasn't it?'

Isaac nods, half-wrapping an arm around himself unconsciously, as though hugging his new spirit roommates.

Then he leans forward, an ironic grin on his face as he whispers, 'It delights me that my loving brother is still there, uncorrupted by his suffering. And, honestly, I think perhaps there are still some untainted memories of the Bens he loved in the mix. He hopes the Vernicle brought him the peace denied to him for centuries.'

I wasn't exaggerating with the whole "best of us" spiel about Jakob. Had I been held captive by an evil psychopath who seduced me and broke my heart twice, I'd have dedicated the same amount of time I'd spent locked up in coming up with crueller and more unusual punishments for them than any human had ever previously imagined. Jakob? Jakob looked for the man he fell in love with, the one underneath all that confused hate and rage. And forgave him despite everything he'd done.

So, yeah. There's definitely awe, fighting it out with all that unchecked anger.

And there's one last emotion. A little tiny one that's just forming at the corner of my spirit, manifesting in a dampness around my eyes. I'm not entirely sure what it is. Relief, maybe. Gratitude. A weight lifted off my soul.

'Thanks, Jakob.' I look straight into Isaac's eyes, letting his brother riding shotgun see I'm genuine. I am. He's done what I wouldn't have been able to do. Whether Ben finally got to escape this reality or whether his soul disintegrated with his imperfection, lost into the sands outside of life, I've no idea. What I do know is he's gone. He's never coming back. That's enough to bring peace to my conflicting emotions, allowing them to draw up a ceasefire and allowing me to finally, for the first time in weeks, properly relax.

I take a moment to luxuriate in the feeling that, however briefly, all is right in the world, that good people remain even when faced by unfathomable torments and the biting bitterness of the maws of life that maul our spirits, lessening us so easily.

Isaac indicates the two skulls. 'Even emptied, these two are mightily powerful magical artefacts, strong enough that I think it won't be long before they advertise their presence even through my warding. We need to find somewhere to keep them safe, at least until we need to study them further.'

I sweep the Vernicle out of his hand and use it to package up the two still terrifyingly powerful skulls together, tying it like an oversized handkerchief travelling bundle. 'I have to take the Veil back to a certain person, and I think he might make a reasonable guardian with little persuasion, masking their siren lure for the shitheads who might want to nick them.'

Isaac nods in agreement, and we head back to the snug next to the kitchen, Isaac pouring me a glass of whisky from a globular decanter on the sideboard. 'Penderyn sherry wood,' he tells me as he hands it across.

I take a sniff from the snifter, then offer him a half toast before sipping. It's fruity and elegant in its structure but carries a dragon's breath of warmth. The heat eases some of the last tightness in my chest, but there are still worries sitting heavy on my mind. One in particular. I try to relax back into my chair, but there are knots embedded in my shoulder muscles that aren't about to be dispersed quite so easily. Isaac raises an eyebrow at me.

'So you told me you weren't sleeping well but not because of bad dreams. What's been weighing on you so?'

I sit there, cradling the glass, rolling the amber liquid around and watching the patterned swirling of its movements before I raise my eyes to his. 'Do you remember when I first agreed to an apprenticeship with you? What you gave me to extract my promise to come and learn magic with you for a minimum span of a hundred years?'

Now it is his face's turn to go cloudy and troubled, linking it to recent events. 'Of course. I found it bloody hard to say no to you back then, to not concoct that damnable tincture that inhibits *talent* and muscle. Having been on the receiving end of it recently thanks to Benedict, I don't feel any better about having created it.'

He coughs, momentarily choking on a swig of his whisky that ran down the wrong path, clearing it by a thump to the breastbone. 'You were so lost though, so full of power and potential, I feared deeply where you might turn if I didn't bring you under my wing. I made the decision that it was worth the price but swore I'd never make it again.'

I don't reply, lost in the memories of my actions after I wheedled the small vial from the man who would help me learn how to live ihe new life I found myself in.

I hang obscured in the branches of the umbrella-like pine, the spring growth shrouding me from the view of the road winding through the craggy terrain. In the near distance, the light-sand coloured stonework of a recently constructed marvel, the Abbey of Fontfroide, stands proud and dominant, a representation of the wealth and extent of the reach of the Catholic Church, newly rooted in what was Cathar lands until recently.

At the other end of the visible segment of the road, a horse and rider resplendent in brightly coloured caparison, accompanied by a small group of footmen soldiers, drive up a minor dust cloud as they make their way towards the abbey. As the gap between us closes, I can make out the proud, belligerent features of Arnaud Almeric riding straight-backed on the bedecked beast.

I wait until they pass my hiding place, close enough I can make out the patterned motif edging the fabric of the Fleur de Lys and the accursed cross that Catholics insisted on using to represent their faith. Typical that they fixate on suffering and death rather than salvation and self-progression. When they are all clear of being able to spot my movements even from the corner of their eyes, I put Isaac's small hollow tube to my lips and blow, shooting the thorn directly at the robed butcher-monk riding aloof towards his gifted domain. A sudden jerk of his hand to the rear of his neck goes directly to the point I aimed for, knocking the tiny dart away, telling me I hit my mark. I covered the tip in a mixture of two tinctures — one being supplied by the Jew who has offered me apprenticeship as payment for it, assuring me it will inhibit any magical powers the bastard holds. The other, well...

The horse continues its casual canter, but I fix my eyes on the physical changes to its rider. He loses some of the rigidity in his posture, a slow stooping *manifesting in his shoulders. A few seconds later, he pulls his ride to a halt. The accompanying men look askance at him before springing into action with raised alarums as he slumps sideways, crashing to the dusty ground.*

I nod grimly. The secondary application was from an apothecary. He assured me it will compel a painful death but with symptoms consistent with any of the feverish maladies found in these balmy climes. I wait as the grouping hustle their fallen abbot towards the perceived safety of the nearby walls, then sling myself back to earth once the doors slam shut behind them. Walking away from killing a man for the very first time, assured of my damnation in my imPerfection, I feel not a jot of sorrow. In my mind, I see the dead Perfects, the befouled Grail. Ben's dead body, blood pooling on the floor in front of him. No, I feel no guilt for what I've done, only a sense of satisfaction as I set off, whistling a tune heard from an ale-sodden troubadour the night previous, the weight on my soul lightening my heart.

Rising from my reverie, I look bleakly at Isaac, having relived a murder I never once regretted. Now, though, I wonder if it really worked, whether the death stuck. 'The potion we were all recently exposed to would have no effect on hindering my reincarnation, would it?'

Isaac shakes his head, his eyes widening as he follows the path of my reasoning.

I clench my jaw at the ominous implications. 'A splash of the distillation in the Grail of the Cathar essence was enough to keep Ben tied to life, albeit under harder conditions than my own. The rest of the liquid in it coated the room, splashed over me, and just behind me....'

I leap to my feet, pacing back and forth, nervous energy pouring through me at the logical conclusion to that thought. I stop and look plaintively at my oldest living friend.

'That bastard Almeric was just behind me. And his skull is full of *talent* that calls to my reincarnating. I'm right, aren't I?' I ask him directly. He hesitates but can't deny the likelihood presented by the facts we've encountered. He nods his dour assent.

'You're right, Paul,' he says darkly, his tone matching my mood at the possibility. 'There's every chance that Arnaud Almeric is still alive.'

THE END

Afterword

So here we are, at the end of the first book but only at the very beginning of the adventure! The story continues in *imPerfect Curse*, the second book – and you can read the first chapter of it just after this bit of rambling from me. You can also read the prequel *An imPerfect Trap* for free by signing up for my newsletter, which involves a Nain Rouge, a deadly escape game, and a very pissed off Aicha. There's a link on the next page! If you've enjoyed this book, then please consider leaving a review. It makes all the diffence to independent authors, and actually helps me with a get-out clause on the Faustian bargain I signed at the Crossroads to get the magic pen that allowed me to write this book. If you don't want me to be dragged off screaming to the Inferno – and, if nothing else, pity all the poor souls forced to spend eternity with me if I am – then hit those star buttons, and if you can manage it type a few words of review. Even 'should go straight to Hell' would be brill.

But I want to take a minute to tell you about the world itself. I've done the best I can to keep things as accurate, historically and geographically speaking, as possible, with only minor tweaks where the story required. For example, the siege of Lavaur is absolutely true, as is the burning of the four hundred Perfects. The subsequent explosion of the Great Hall? Less so but necessary for my part of the story. And I've not seen any documents saying it *didn't* explode or explode magically, so who knows? Perhaps people just forgot to say. Simple thing to forget.

I'm no historian, so mistakes may exist. Please don't hesitate to drop me an email at chris@cnrowan.com to let me know if there are any clangers. I'm aware there's now some debate in the academic circles about whether the Good People really existed or if it was simply a term for the form of Christianity that existed prior to the formalisation of Pope Innocent, whether his paranoia about Cathari was why they ended up with the label. There's plenty of arguments both ways, and this version worked best for the story I wanted to tell. For those who want a well told, well researched, and not too heavy-going introduction to the Cathars and the Albigensian Crusade, I recommend *A Perfect Heresy* by Stephen O'Shea. It's a fabulous laying out of a truly peculiar story from history.

As for the characters in the book? Aicha Kandicha's story or legend is true to a point. She is the bogeywoman of Moroccan culture, and there is evidence she really existed as a noblewoman in Al Jadida, just south of Casablanca, who used her feminine wiles to seduce Portuguese raiders into a trap. The rest is my addition, although the Druze are a true religious sect and still exist in Lebanon and Syria today.

Isaac the Blind is also a real historical figure and creator of Kabbalah. Again, that really was happening just up the road from Toulouse at the same time as the Cathars and the Crusade, in Montpellier. Jakob, his brother, is my creation. Nithael and Nanael are two of the named Bene Elohim of Judaism.

Arnaud Almeric (or Amalric or Amaury – they were free and loose with last name spelling back then) , the Butcher of Beziers, is a real character and was a real bastard by all accounts. The story of Beziers, while perhaps apocryphal, is certainly attributed to him. Simon De Montfort is also a real person who rose to prominence from the middling ranks of the French nobility to incomprehensible glory during the Crusade. Perhaps he had someone magical helping him out?

Speaking of, Papa Nicetas is also a genuine character and a genuine mystery. He didn't reappear for the siege of Lavaur, but he did arrive from Constantinople at the time when the Good People were formalising their beliefs. He persuaded them towards a firmly dualistic belief (which arguably set them on a collision course with the religious authorities) and got them all to take a new consolamentum to become Perfect again because of doubts over the veracity of the original one. Then suddenly, he disappeared under a cloud of intrigue and the rumour of dalliances with married women, meaning everyone had to go through the whole consolamentum for a third time! He never popped up in known history again, and what happened after he left the Languedoc is just another of the strange unknowns about this peculiar character. Perhaps I did him an injustice by making him the villain of the piece, but there remain many unanswered questions about him. I just added a few more.

Historians will note I left out a whole array of colourful characters from the Albigensian Crusades, not least Dominic Guzman, the austere priest who later founded the Dominicans, an order that would go on to create the Inquisition. He was in mind to be the original religious villain of my story, but research showed him to be a considerably nicer character than Almeric despite what happened later in his name. Also, the original drafts of the historical flashbacks were packed full of endless real people from the siege of Lavaur, Guzman included, but were confusing and overly weighty because of it. Things needed to be trimmed to keep the story moving along, and Dominic became one of them. Soz, Dom.

Lou Carcoilh –The Snail– is a "real" mythological creature, and the town of Hastingues genuinely sits on top of the hill that he's believed to live beneath. The Pont De Gramont is real too and so is the Israelite cemetery. I stumbled across it, driving back from Gramont to Hastingues. When I saw the sign, I had to follow it. Finding these peculiar slabs stuck into the hillside, with houses just across the way, bearing Jewish family names from hundreds of years ago, and the ruins of the castle of Bidache on the horizon is a moment that will linger with me for a very long time, and I thought it a fitting place for the showdown to conclude.

Franc isn't real or based on anything but my twisted imagination. Thank goodness.

Everywhere else in the story is a genuine place. L'Astronef really exists and really is as cool and wonderful an establishment as I described it. Hell, I probably didn't do it justice. The only creation is the café in Peyrehorade. I couldn't find anywhere suitable when I visited, and I really wanted it to embody that typical French café, particularly like the ones I used to come across in the Buttes Aux Cailles in Paris. The café and the waiter are definitely very Parisian and very familiar to me.

Now it comes to a part that fills my soul with utter dread and terror – my thanks, because there are so many deserving people and I'm terrified I'll forget someone. My wife and family get first mention for putting up with my trips and endless tapping on the keyboard and for their tremendous support. My parents, for always believing in me even when it terrified them to do so. My editor Miranda, for taking a bloated monstrosity and helping me turn it into the thing in your hand that I'm immensely proud of. My beta readers Becca, Becky, and Lauretta, not least because Becca and Becky actually read the whole thing *twice,* which is above and beyond the call of duty; their advice has been invaluable in producing this book. Athena for her amazing proofing of the audio book. Catherine Webb, who was kind enough to read one of the first drafts of this when it was nothing more than a mess and still came back to me with endless constructive criticism that helped me to rethink and learn the craft. Heather G Harris for her constant support and mentoring, always on hand to give me advice. All the authors in the Clean Fantasy chat who've been incredibly open-handed in their words at all times. My extended family and the Semper Eadem crew. Craig Verbs for his unending belief and friendship. The imPerfect Gang. ASB, The Ill Smith Estate, Killa Tapes, L'Affaire, K7, and all my Toulouse hip-hop crew and worldwide beyond. Everyone who's encouraged and supported me all the way through, and all the incredibly deserving people I know I've forgotten and whose names will spring to my mind in the middle of the night the day after this is published, waking me up in a cold sweat. Know even if I haven't mentioned you here, you mean the world to me.

Remember, if you want to stay in touch with me, I'd love to hear from you. Drop me an email or a message on social media. I'm on Instagram but most active on Facebook and will always respond to DMs. You can also join C.N. Rowan's imPerfect Gang, my Facebook readers' group, which is incredibly active and full of hilarious and lovable loonies. Aka my kind of people.

That's it. My justification, or mea culpa, whichever way is more appropriate to view it. Now turn the page for a sneak peek at how things are going to go next for Paul and the gang.

Spoiler – badly.

The answer is badly.

Let's hope they find a way out of the trouble they get themselves into...

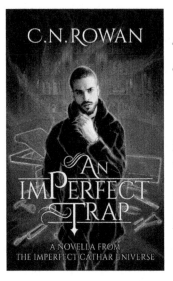

C.N. ROWAN

AN IMPERFECT TRAP

A NOVELLA FROM
THE IMPERFECT CATHAR UNIVERSE

Reincarnating every time I get killed doesn't help when the trap won't let me die.

Getting trapped in a psychotic fae's twisted game isn't my idea of a fun Friday afternoon. When one of them shows up in my territory of Toulouse uninvited, I was never going to just let it slide.

Now I'm stuck, in a locked room mystery in another dimension.

What does the faeling want? And what price am I going to pay to find my way home again? There's never a pair of red, ruby slippers around when you need them.

GO HERE TO GET THE FREE PREQUEL TODAY BY SIGNING UP TO MY NEWSLETTER!

https://freebook.cnrowan.com/imtrap

THE GABIA'S JUSTICE

C.N. ROWAN

'There's an irony about how often the elements are used to kill those supposedly capable of controlling them. Water. Fire. Air. Earth.

Drowning. Burning. Hanging. Burying them alive.

Those so keen to use such tools to instil terror and keep the population silent best hope they never capture a true Tal ented...'

In 16th Century Toulouse, when a local businessman is using the cruel threats of the inquisition to have his way with a hapless population, particularly its women-folk, the imPerfect Cathar himself is more than happy to teach him a lesson.

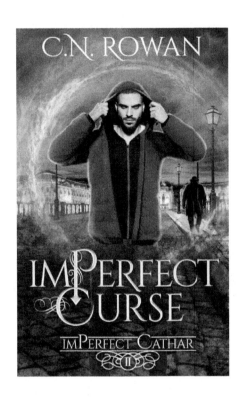

TURN THE PAGE FOR THE FIRST CHAPTER OF THE IMPER-
FECT CATHAR BOOK 2

'IMPERFECT CURSE'

CHAPTER THIRTY-SIX

CHAPTER 1 - TOULOUSE, 8 APRIL, PRESENT DAY

Approaching burnout at a rate of knots. Painfully aware that the odds of me slowing down before crashing into that particular iceberg are minimal.

There's nothing like coming home to find a kid bleeding out on your doorstep.

I'm worn out. Exhausted. Done in. Ready to slump in front of some mind-numbing eye-candy of a TV series with my own bodyweight of sugary goodness for company due to recent escapades involving torture, betrayal, dying (three times), and more twists and turns than a waterslide designed by M C Escher.

So you can picture my ecstatic joy when, on parking outside my humble terraced house in central Toulouse, just up from the Canal De Brienne, I see one of Franc's people sitting on my doorstep. Nobody knows what Franc is, but we can all agree on one thing. He's *powerful*, absolutely radiant with destructive *talent* and magic; even stranger than that, he uses it to connect him to his "lovely lads and lasses" — the homeless and desperate who swear allegiance for a magical blessing that keeps them alive, although not protected from misery and suffering. In exchange, Franc feeds off said emotional distress and uses them as a network of spies, encasing a tiny tendril of his putrid essence in their brains. We made an accord when I got back to Toulouse in the nineteenth century and found him, a monster, living in my beloved river, polluting it with his presence. I wanted to kill him on the spot. Problem was, I wasn't sure the city would be left standing if I tried.

He met me under a flag of parlay –a dirty rag stained with unnamed bodily fluids, but a "flag" nonetheless– and I was too broken, too worn down by misery to think clearly.

So we have an agreement, one sealed with oaths on our power. It's served me well many times, and I've regretted it bitterly even more often. It's pretty straightforward really. Franc reports any Talented who manage to sneak past my borders surrounding Toulouse –hard but not impossible– and I don't try to kill him.

But if this kid's pitiable state is Franc's fault, if he did this deliberately? That renders our agreement null and void, and I'll be more than happy to skip some much needed sleep to get to murdering him.

Well, to try, at least.

The kid is so young, it hurts to imagine they know anything of the unfair vitriol of life, let alone that they've lived the harshest it has to offer. Lank yellow hair curtains the kid's closed expression, layer upon layer providing a hiding place. A hood pulled up corrals the strands to cover as much as possible. Grease and dirt obscures all but the striking cut of cheekbones. That and the blood I can see. Their hands, crossed over their body, unconsciously push up the sleeves of their T-shirt, scratching at scabbed sores that speak of dingy squats and dirty needles. Their loose sleeveless hoodie and their lack of three square meals make their form androgynous, so as I can't tell if they identify as male or female, if either. When they raise their head, it doesn't matter. I'm looking Franc straight in his white eggshell eyes.

Normally, he's happy enough just to ride along in the backseat, voyeuristically watching from behind their conscious mind. But when he needs to, he can grab the wheel and hijack their physical form. It's all part of his deal with them. All part of what I despise about the deal I made with him.

'I calls upon our treaty-teasings and all promise forms, little lordling,' he says, but there is none of the usual bantering menace, the good-natured promise of waiting death for all and sundry – me, him, the whole damn world. The words wheeze out as crimson tears spill down the wretched shell's cheeks. Then they vomit blood.

ABOUT THE AUTHOR

It's been a strange, unbelievable journey to arrive at the point where these books are going to be released into the wild, like rare, near-extinct animals being returned to their natural habitat, already wondering where they're going to nick cigarettes from on the plains of Africa, the way they used to from the zookeeper's overalls. C.N. Rowan ("Call me C.N., Mr. Rowan was my father") came originally from Leicester, England. Somehow escaping its terrible, terrible clutches (only joking, he's a proud Midlander really), he has wound up living in the South-West of France for his sins. Only, not for his sins. Otherwise, he'd have ended up living somewhere really dreadful. Like Leicester. (Again – joking, he really does love Leicester. He knows Leicester can take a joke. Unlike some of those other cities. Looking at you, Slough.) With multiple weird strings to his bow, all of which are made of tooth-floss and liable to snap if you tried to use them to do anything as adventurous as shooting an arrow, he's done all sorts of odd things, from running a hiphop record label (including featuring himself as rapper) to hustling disability living aids on the mean streets of Syston. He's particularly proud of the work he's done managing and recording several French hiphop acts, and is currently awaiting confirmation of wild rumours he might get a Gold Disc for a song he recorded and mixed.

He'd always love to hear from you so please drop him an email here - chris@cnrowan.com

f   facebook.com/cnrowan

a   amazon.com/author/cnrowan

g   goodreads.com/author/show/23093361.C_N_Rowan

ⓞ   instagram.com/cnrowanauthor

Also By

The imPerfect Cathar Series

imPerfect Magic

imPerfect Curse
imPerfect Fae
imPerfect Bones
imPerfect Hunt
(release September 23)
imPerfect Gods
(release October 23)

An imPerfect Trap (prequel novella to imPerfect Magic)

Printed in Great Britain
by Amazon

38562065R00169